BARN 8

BARN

A NOVEL

DEB OLIN UNFERTH

SHEFFIELD – LONDON – NEW YORK

First UK edition published in 2020 by And Other Stories
Sheffield – London – New York
www.andotherstories.org

9 8 7 6 5 4 3 2 1

ISBN: 978-1-911508-88-5
eBook ISBN: 978-1-911508-89-2

Cover design and illustration: Kimberly Glyder

Offset by Tetragon, London. Printed and bound on Munken Premium by CPI Limited,
Croydon, UK.

And Other Stories gratefully acknowledges that its work is supported using public funding
by Arts Council England.

Supported using public funding by
**ARTS COUNCIL
ENGLAND**

MIX
Paper from
responsible sources
FSC
www.fsc.org   FSC® C020471

For Matt

BARN 8

A NEST. Built of 14-gauge galvanized wire mesh, twenty-five thousand water nipples, a moss of dander and feed. Six miles of feed trough runs down rows, up columns. Staggered tiers rise ten feet high into the shape of the letter A, the universal symbol for mountain. Wooden rafters, plywood walkways. Darkness. Sudden light. Three hundred thousand prehistoric eyes blinking. The entire apparatus ticking and whirring and clanking like a doomsday machine. Above it the purr, coo, and song of a hundred and fifty thousand birds at dawn.

1

THE MOMENT JANEY stepped off the bus she suspected her error.

Until then (through the long hours of the ride, pulling through town after town, the day dimming, the door sighing open and shut, the darkening, then the darkness, her head lobbing back and forth in a half sleep, stepping down to change buses in Chicago, waiting on the cement with her duffel, pulling out again into the dark, then the sunrise, the plaid day flipping by, her reflection laid against the window over the highway signs and strip malls) she'd felt she was at the start of a great journey. She'd peeled off from her former self, left the old Janey behind.

She could almost see the old Janey ghosting along her usual track, back in the city, headed to school. They were like conjoined twins torn apart: one would live, the other would die, and the doctors weren't sure which was which, so the world watched, waited. She trembled with anticipation (the states widening, the land flattening, the fields turning into fields, not tangles of brush and trees, the God signs whipping by along the roadside). She, the new Janey, had stepped out of the line of her classmates and walked away, and who knew what would happen now. She could almost glance back across the country and see the line move forward without her, the old Janey inch up, follow those in front of her like a cow.

But now, a day and a half later, she got off the bus, climbed down on gummy legs, and the station instilled her first doubt. The clean plastic seats, the antiseptic smell, the collection of very badly dressed people, their suitcases wrapped in cellophane and piled on the floor like the components of a giant packed lunch.

Mostly, her father: not there. She didn't know what her father looked like, but no man stood by the door with the expectancy and nervousness fitted to the occasion. No one shifted from foot to foot, turned a cap in his hands, glanced up at each person coming in from the bus. Or, a different version: no one waited in the middle of the room with a proprietary shine, arms folded across his chest, a batch of supermarket flowers wrapped in plastic in one hand, pointing toward the floor. No one around was the least bit interested in Janey's great journey. No one was having a great journey themselves.

She hadn't counted on him being at the station. He hadn't said he would be. He had said nothing at all, since he hadn't answered when she texted (the stupidity of a text in this circumstance) or called ("Uh, hi, this is Janey, your . . . daughter"). Janey lowered her duffel bag to the gleaming floor and checked her phone (another message from her mother, which she ignored). But she *had* counted on him being there.

Back at the other end of the long ribbon of the bus ride, on the other side of the country, the old Janey would be walking home from the train right now, school out at four, debate till six, a canopy of trees listing overhead. Janey could almost see her passing brownstones, swinging her backpack, tripping up the steps to the apartment, calling out, "Ma, you home?"

No, wait. The old Janey was an hour ahead of this one. She'd be eating dinner, settled into a chair, squatting with one foot on the seat, her fork in the air in a gesture of "holding forth," her mother leaning against the stove, laughing. Meanwhile, the new Janey, the one who now paused in front of a line of concession machines, had lost her appetite, though she hadn't eaten much on the slow, uncomfortable bus (she now conceded the discomfort, but while in transit she had posted photos of barns, hay, houses, population signs, along with cartoon faces expressing glee, humor, surprise, revelation, and other emotions she did or did not feel), concession machines of flat sandwiches locked in plastic compartments, cigarettes released by a coil. Jesus. She lifted her duffel and walked out into the cool spring evening.

Janey was fifteen years and five days old and she had found out five days earlier just where the hell her father had been all these years. Her mother had always plowed her with the old sperm bank story, and Janey had believed her, though really how could she have believed such horseshit? By the time Janey was old enough to count she should have figured out she hadn't come out of a vial. What woman gives up and goes baster at eighteen, the pinnacle year of love and abortion? But Janey had believed her and longed for a father all her life. Then on Janey's fifteenth birthday her mother had sat her down and said that Janey was old enough to know: her father was alive and well and back where Janey's mother had left him when she'd run away pregnant to New York to give her coming daughter a better life, left him back in southern Iowa, a gray land of truck stops, crowded prisons, and monocrop farming. Janey was lucky to have never laid eyes on the place. Her mother explained that Janey must not now develop debilitating parental issues that could bleed into the rest of her life. She was old enough to make a mature decision about meeting him and seeing the town of her conception. Her mother would take Janey herself when school let out.

In other words her mother (*the bitch!*) had *lied*.

School wasn't out for a month and no one should keep a daughter that long from her father. Let alone fifteen years and counting.

Janey walked through the town, down a Main Street of imitation antique lampposts and shut shops, though it was only seven o'clock. She shouldered her duffel like a bandit, followed her phone's glowing map. She found the address beyond the houses and platters of lawn, on one of two identical apartment buildings made of sad tan bricks. No buzzer, she just walked up the stairs to 209 and knocked. "Heyo," she called. She put on her clowning-around voice to cover the quaver. "Anybody got a beer in there?" She was not the sort of person to make stupid remarks but there you go. She did a quick thing with her hair.

The old Janey (the ribbon of road connecting them like a string and two cans, or like a game of telephone, the messages between them garbling, on the verge of losing meaning, dissolving) would be back in Brooklyn right now saying it wasn't her turn to do the dishes. The old Janey's mother would be at the computer saying it was always her turn to do the dishes. The new Janey's mother was calling. Janey could hear the vibration in her bag. She saw the doorknob to 209 turning. The lock clacked, and in the second between that clack and when her father was revealed, the new Janey felt a surge of hope and longing, so familiar and compressed, as if from the innermost parts of her being, an old-Janey ache.

She was startled to see a frightened grimace. She quickly corrected it into a smile.

"Surprise!" she said, lifted her arms. "It's a girl."

He was Fred Flintstone white, had the arms and stance of a bully.

She heard him (her father?) speak: "You're early."

She mock-pouted. "Was I supposed to wait till I was thirty?"

The new Janey, grinning with the bravado of the old Janey (the old Janey, who'd had the courage to send the new Janey off, pack her bag while her mother was at work, wave goodbye from the apartment window), stepped into the apartment.

Janey sat at one end of a sofa. Her father sat at the other. She felt comically female, even in her tomboy garb, like an invasion of femininity bleeding into this dead-fast male apartment. They were having a conversation that went like this:

Him: [not meeting her eyes] I thought your bus got in at eight.

Her: It's fine. I like to walk.

Him: I was going to come get you.

Her: [nodding manically and looking around] It's cool. So this is where you live?

Him: It's a temporary situation, a stopgap.

Her: Yeah? Where are you going?

Him: [his face going into his phone] Hang on. We need to call your mother.

Her: We have a sofa kind of like this. So what do you do?

Him: Oh, I'm in ag.

Her: [having no idea what that is, resuming the nod] Cool.

[Silence. Nodding continues.]

Even his TV looked old-fashioned to her. She'd never had a TV. All her screens had been computers of various sizes and shapes. She felt like she'd slipped through time to find her father and he'd turned out to be from a Smithsonian diorama, so obsolete as to be almost futuristic. And worse, he looked like he was *dying* to get away, shut out whatever was happening in the vicinity. He'd had about as much audience as he could handle in a day. This wasn't going like it was supposed to.

Him: You said you wanted a beer?

Her: I'm fifteen.

Him: Right. I'll call your mother. [pressing button] It's ringing. [raising finger] Hey, she's here . . . yeah . . . yeah . . . [glance up at Janey] Uh, I don't think so . . . okay . . . [holding phone out] She wants to talk to you.

The last thing Janey had said to her mother in her screaming tantrum after her mother delivered the news that she *knew* who her father was, and after Janey had demanded to know how her mother could have *lied* all these years, how she could have kept her away from the man who never even got the *chance* to be her father, how who on earth would *do* such a thing unless they were a *horrible* person, after all that, she screamed, "I'm never speaking to you *again!*" (little did she know), and the next morning she'd said into her phone, "How do I get to Iowa from here cheap?"

Now, sitting on her father's (?) sofa, she crossed her arms and looked defiant. She didn't want her mother to even *hear her voice.*

Him: [returning the phone to his ear] Uh, I'll have her call you back.

He put down the phone. "Your mother says you need to eat." He rocked off the sofa and padded into the kitchen.

Not to mention, *that's* why her sperm donor was white—because her mother had had *sex* with him, not because she selected *white* on a form. Janey's grandfather had been from Mexico, and Janey and her mother shared his name. Flores. Why didn't you pick Latino? she'd always nagged. This really explained so much.

"You want a pop?" he called from the kitchen. "She always told me you'd come find me someday. If you'd waited a bit longer, I would have been better situated."

"No," she fluttered back, about to launch into a show of appreciation for . . . for . . . "No, this is nice. This is . . ." She looked around for some household object to compliment. She slowed. "Wait, what?" she said. "When?"

He was back in the room with a generic orange can. "When what?"

"When did she always tell you?"

"Tell me? Yesterday."

Her head began to buzz. "No, when did she tell you I *existed*?"

He looked confused. "She always told me you existed. Since you existed."

Janey felt a sudden sickening. It occurred to her for the first time: her mother hadn't precisely said he hadn't known. The buzz in her head grew louder. She couldn't breathe. She found she was needing her full mental capacity to keep from crying. She managed, "And you didn't want to come find *me* someday?"

He cleared his throat. "Well, I . . ."

A unit of air somewhere in there clicked on.

That's when she saw it in a flash, the past, and a premonition of the future, the gravity of her error, her series of errors, her miscalculations, that: (1) He didn't want her here. (2) He'd been dreading all these years the day she'd come find him. (3) He was scared of her, his daughter, was scared of all things female. He was one of *those*, her father. (4) This apartment was way worse than her apartment, and this town was way worse than her city. (5) She wasn't going to know how to love, or like, or even how to know this stranger, (6) who was her father. (7) She was so hurt, angry, (8) (and yes, ashamed), (9) she wasn't going to know how to go home.

How long they were silent, she didn't know. Three minutes? Twenty seconds? She had her head in her hands.

He placed the soda on the coffee table, sat down carefully at the other end of the sofa. "So, kid," he said at last, "how long are you staying?"

She raised her head. She felt in that moment (how long was she *staying*? so transparent and cowardly) the value of the two splintered lives, the old Janey who'd stayed behind and the new Janey who'd left, the worth of them switching sides, whooshing by each other, the life she'd catapulted herself into dropping in worth, down, down, plummeting, and the worth of her old life lifting, rising. She felt the vinyl under her (her mother did not and never would own an ugly-ass couch like this), she could smell his old clothes, the cockroaches in the walls, and it was right then (she felt it, like a lock clacking shut) that the deadening began (though it took years), because she didn't pick up her duffel and march back to the station that night, like she knew she should. She stayed right where she was because she was going to make this man know her, or at least pay for not knowing her.

"Great news, *Dad*," she said. She kicked the duffel at her feet. "Forever!" (Little did she know.)

His expression did not change. He may have flinched a little. He scooched forward, his hand coming up between them—to hug? to smack? to point the way to the door? She leaned in. She was ready for anything. He had something in his hand. Rectangular.

Fate is not determined by one mistake, though they train you to think so, starting with the Bible—one wrong move and you're stuck outside in the rain while the ark floats away without you, or you're wandering the desert for decades. (Janey had gone to a Catholic girls' school until she turned ten and finally triumphed over her mother and went charter.) In fact we have many, many chances to fuck up. And if we figure out how to fix what we fucked, we will fuck it up again.

"Well, that's fine," her father said, his face twitching (was that a smile or a frown? It was the kind of face you really couldn't tell). "Let's just check the scores." He pointed the remote and turned on the TV.

No, it was not her only mistake, but it was certainly her greatest, as others have great loves, great ideas, or great tragedies that befall them. All else Janey could do would pale beside this error. She could kill a man. She could drown herself in a bucket. She could fail to obstruct a politician who would go on to torture millions. Whatever she did going forward would trace back to this, the nadir, the alpha.

She settled back on the sofa, the "scores" flickering across her face. She thought of the old Janey, her other self, the original, who hadn't left, five states away, shimmering in her brownstone in Brooklyn. She could almost see her. That Janey was curled in front of her laptop, working on her Malcolm X paper, and her mother was passing her a bowl of ice cream, because it was that hour. The hour of ice cream.

SHE LIVED THERE with her father for two months and hated every minute of it, but she was too proud to call her mother and say she wanted to go home. She knew they were talking, her mother and "father," trying to figure out the best means to make Janey go back quietly—knew they talked because her mother left her long messages saying they'd talked, and did Janey have any idea how she'd scared her mother, disappearing like that? Did Janey know how lucky she was that she'd made it there without getting kidnapped or crushed under a truck wheel or on the wrong bus to Alaska?

Janey and her father lived like strangers in that apartment, keeping their stuff in bags and eating fast food with ketchup packets in the kitchen. She did try to "connect" a few times. Pulled out her mini–chess set (she was in the club at school), set it up, and asked him if he wanted a game. She instituted an apartment-wide recycling program, plastic and paper in one bag, trash in the other, though she caught him throwing it all into the same dumpster.

But he never asked her to leave. Soon she was reading the *TV Guide* (which arrived in *paper* each week) and watching whatever went up on the screen. He worked as a something something for the USDA at a poultry processing plant, which meant he spent his days *inspecting dead bodies*. She slept until noon in the room he "set up" for her—blow-up mattress on the floor— and then she prowled the apartment until he came home. She went through the closets, the drawers, the sticky cupboards, looking for what? Evidence. Not only of his failure as a father but as a person, of which there was plenty: his enormous saggy shirts, his rusty nail clippers, his bent shoes, expired cans of soup, not a book in the place, not a photo on the wall. Each day at 4:50 p.m. he turned up at the apartment, stinking of offal and carrying a bag from the same cheap IHOP restaurant filled with the same items off the menu for them both. He kept plastic gallon milk containers full of water in the refrigerator and drank from one while he ate.

Her mother left daily messages. Should Janey be skipping school like this? Did Janey know her Malcolm X paper was due? Did Janey recall the regional debate was next week, after all her hard work and her debate coach was . . . Well, she'd missed the end of school, was she proud of herself?

She watched him stooped over the sink or lifting plastic plates out of cupboards with shaky fingers. She wondered what her mother had seen in this guy. And then she stopped wondering because obviously her mother had seen nothing and that's why she left and why Janey had been kept away from him all these years.

The old Janey had, if memory serves, rarely fought with an adult, but the new Janey had a mouth on her and said what she could to gall her father, or hurt him, or get any word out of him at all. The new Janey and the truant father had some spectacular fights. Once she barricaded the door. Once she threw his clothes out the window and onto the parking lot where they looked like globs of color on the hot blacktop until he eventually went down and gathered them, stabbing them up with a long cooking fork and dropping them into a bag like the convicted doing their service.

Oh why had she left home? Surely it was excusable—a girl wants to meet her father, right? People quest. People roam.

She could see her other self, her imaginary twin, the old Janey, skipping down the stairs to the street, high-fiving the janitor on the way (this was an elaborated detail, since she'd rarely spoken to the janitor, but her coastal self was beginning to seem cooler and kinder than the actual Janey had ever been).

Her mother's messages became longer. She talked about growing up in that small Iowan town, how her own father had come to the US as a teen, worked ag, become a citizen, and embarked on a (mostly failed) mission to unionize farmworkers in different parts of the country. He'd leave for months, return for a few weeks, and again leave, until one day he didn't come back. Her mother worked ag admin, spoke English, raised her daughter to never love a wandering man. But Janey's mother turned out to be the wanderer, a woman with her mother's tongue, her father's heart and name. Four months pregnant, nearly nineteen, she'd packed her suitcase and trained it alone to New York. She'd buy Janey a plane ticket whenever Janey was ready. She'd fly out herself and pick her up. She wasn't going to force her, didn't want to push her, but she loved Janey and missed her and was sorry . . .

It was July now and the mosquitoes had gotten so bad, the air so moist, Janey barely left the apartment. The claustrophobia was making her and her father yet crazier. She was so lonely, she thought she could hear her mother calling to her. Was it her fault she'd slept with this clod? her mother seemed to be saying. At least she'd gotten Janey in the bargain.

One night, her father hadn't said a word in hours and Janey thought she'd explode. She came out of the kitchen, cupped her hands, yelled, "Anybody home?"

He glanced up, then back at the TV.

She was inexplicably enraged. She grabbed his phone off the table, first as a gesture of invasion of privacy, then, when she realized she didn't know his password, as a threat. She ran over to the sink, turned on the water, and held his phone an inch from the stream. "Give that back," he roared. He jumped up and, in a rare fit of retaliation, went for her phone on the coffee table, dropped it to the floor, his foot raised above it. They paused, horrified. She dunked. He stomped.

He had no landline, so neither one had a phone anymore.

He turned off the TV that night and they slinked phoneless through the quiet rooms, more alone together than ever. The sound of cicadas came in through the panes under the long breath out of the air conditioner. Janey sat on the sofa, arms wrapped around her legs. He went into his bedroom and shut the door.

The next morning she was still waiting for him on the sofa when he came out. She followed him into the kitchen, taunting, "You can't believe I'm still here, can you? You have no idea how to run me off. Not as easy as running out, right?"

"I wish I knew how to run you off!" he said finally, his arms raised around his head in protection. "I've got a wild animal loose in my apartment. Why don't you just go home?"

She stopped. Through it all, he'd never asked her to leave. That one sentence left unuttered she'd thought proof of something, however thin, but here it was at last. Go. I never wanted you.

"Guess what!" she screamed back. "You'll never run me off!" (Little did she know.) She slammed out the door.

She sprinted at first, then slowed. She wanted her mother so badly she could almost touch her. She could see her mother's retreating figure.

Her mother! Without a phone she hadn't heard her voice since yesterday. How Janey must have hurt her by leaving, by not returning her calls, by being the worst daughter one could have given birth and devoted one's life to. Her mother had been right to leave this town, Janey growing inside her, brave to set off across the country the opposite way Janey had come. She'd been a child, not much older than Janey then, and she'd left out of love, for Janey, while Janey had left out of rage, at her mother.

Janey ran to the Shop Stop and called her mother from the

last pay phone on the planet. (Of course it would be here in this crap town.) She got change for a few crinkled bills. (How had it come to this? She didn't even have a phone anymore? And she'd gone through all her savings?) Her mother didn't pick up and Janey left a voice mail. "Hey, it's me." She leveled her voice, steadied it, didn't want to sound *too* desperate, some sliver of pride still not sloughed off. "Call me as soon as you get this." She left the number of the pay phone.

She hung up and sat on a cement parking divider a few feet from the phone and waited in the summer sun. She'd seen all she wanted. She'd made her point a few times over. She was done. She wanted to go home. Her mother would buy her a plane ticket, leaving in a few hours, and Janey wouldn't even stop by the apartment for her bag. She'd go home without a stick that she'd come with but the clothes on her body. She'd walk, if she had to, to the airport, take off, fly over the land, and she'd never see that asshole, her father, again. She waited. The phone rang. It hadn't been twenty minutes. She lunged for it.

"Janey?" a woman who wasn't her mother said.

"Judy?" said Janey. Judy, her mother's friend, the neighbor. "Judy, where's my mom?"

"Janey, thank God. We've been trying to reach you and your father all morning. We were about to call the police."

"Our phones broke."

"Both of them?"

"I . . ."

"Janey, listen. There's been an accident. Where are you?"

"An accident?" said Janey.

Her mother had died instantly. No one in the other vehicle was hurt.

So Janey flew home that day after all, though not in the way she had expected, her father driving her to the airport, murmuring apologies she couldn't hear through the roar, could only see those detested lips move in her peripheral vision. Her father, seeing her through security, handing her some twenties for a cab on the other end, cash that she dropped into the trash in the women's room, not wanting anything from that man. She sat through the wake, the funeral. People placed plates of food in front of her and removed them. People passed into her sight, touched her shoulders, looked earnestly into her eyes and moved their mouths. She was still frozen, had not even begun to thaw when, two weeks later, child protective services turned her around and shipped her right back—to her father. He was her father, after all, and he said he'd take her. She'd been living with him at the time of the accident (that turned out to be the damning fact: *she'd been living with him*) and she agreed to go, had to, because there was no one else, no other family. Her mother's will had named Janey's grandmother, who was now in a nursing home upstate and Janey saw her twice a year for a day. Other than that there were a few cousins in Mexico whom Janey had never met, and why hadn't her mother ever gone to Mexico and gotten to know them? So she went back, numb and barely speaking. Neither she nor her father seemed to know what to do about school, so she didn't go. She wasn't enrolling in the hick high with the shiny-faced locals unless someone made her. Then a social worker came by and made her. Her father enrolled her as a junior in the local high school.

The first couple of years Janey was so put down by grief and guilt and her sense of no options that she couldn't come out of her numb state without exploding. Her object was to stay as absent as possible, which was plainly like her father. But what else was she supposed to do?

It seemed a bit harsh that for the rest of her life she'd have to pay for one childish mistake she made at age fifteen, the sort of mistake anyone could have made. Surely if she'd been in New

York no one would have made her go live with a father she'd never met, who'd never contacted her, never paid support. Surely they would have pawned her off on a friend of her mother's. Other people do stupid things at fifteen and it's no big deal. They have to retake a class, or work winter break to pay for what they broke or stole or crashed, or they have to stay in every weekend for a month, or go to rehab. But her mistake was catastrophic.

It was this understanding, of her mistake, that led her to develop the game, or what was mostly a game. She'd think about the old Janey, the original, and the life with her mother she would be leading—the one where she hadn't left and therefore her mother hadn't been in the car that day (theoretically) and therefore was still alive, and everything had stayed the same between them and around them. What would the old Janey, the original, the *real* one, be doing right now?

SHE WONDERED THIS at her new high school, where her teachers halfheartedly instructed from halfhearted textbooks, though the old Janey had learned those equations two years before and the new Janey really didn't give a shit about school anymore. The new Janey had a long list of things she no longer gave a shit about: debate team, chess club, clubs of any kind, students of any kind, sports and all its subcategories, college, the future in general. The teachers left her alone after the first month, the students after the second. News of her bad luck spread and the whole school parted before her. Death-marked, city-stamped, only a quarter Latina, but not middle-American white either. She might have found a place for herself had she made an effort, but she did not. She walked the hallways in a bubble, sank into the back row. She dispensed with her virginity early and unceremoniously (four months into sixteen with a grocery clerk). Meanwhile, the old Janey, the original, was back at her original high, surrounded by chums—chums who at first wrote to the new Janey every day, but soon less, as Janey wrote less, and within a year stopped altogether since neither side was sure what to say.

She wondered what the old Janey would be doing her senior year. The new Janey ("new and improved" was her little joke) had only half a senior year. She finished early, took the exams in December with the morons who had failed the year before, got out of there fast, and wound up with a job at a massive shipping and trucking facility (at least it wasn't ag). She made the same repetitive movements nine hours a day, four days a week, while all over the country people clicked buttons and summoned to their doors pink backpacks, noise reduction headphones, discount T-shirts, sets of wooden spoons, and it was Janey's job to ensure that trucks took off across the land, drove through the night, to deliver these products with the priority citizens deserved. The new Janey contemplated the old Janey, who would be applying to colleges with her friends, her mother taking her on walking tours across quads and into gothic buildings, to sample classes at her top "choices" (that word was infected now, had pulled a nasty prank on her) and her "safeties" (that word, *safety*, too).

She wondered it when she reached the legal age to vote. At that age her mother had left this town with Janey inside her, to find a richer life for them both, but Janey was now back, unenriched, in possession of as much as her mother had had a lifetime before— a high school diploma and a fake ID—but not enough inspiration to follow her mother's ghost.

Meanwhile, the old Janey boarded a plane (the new Janey tracked the old in her mind, saw her walking down the JFK corridor), headed for a precollege summer in . . . Morocco! where she learned French and (finally) Spanish (after all her mother's urging), learned two languages in four months, plus a few decorative phrases of Arabic, wandered the architecture of a foreign land, fell in love for the first time, and so much more. The new Janey contemplated the old's smarts and passion.

The new Janey, who was now "this Janey," or just "Janey," or "same great taste" (her joke when she went home with men and the occasional woman she met online), still lived with her father. When she wasn't assisting the egress of urgent items for the public, she sat on the same sofa she'd sat on that first night, sat and watched football with her father because, well, who knows why. He passed her buckets of fried meat, coleslaw as a "healthy side" for his daughter, and enormous soggy containers of diet soda. This, while the original Janey, what should have been the real one, finished her first year of university with a perfect GPA, had an apartment in the cooler borough with her three best friends, and, oh, the fun they had. At night the old Janey rambled over bridges and down sidewalks and through the streets. During the day she pursued her dreams, which were sharp, not blurry, though the new Janey couldn't quite see them. The old Janey, sophisticated yet romantic, joined the communal spirit of the city's emergencies—the hurricanes, the blackouts, whatever wars that managed to touch the city's skirts with its black fingers, whatever causes the New Yorkers took over the streets over. She still saw her mother every week. They met at art openings, ate at sidewalk cafés under the awnings in the spring, her mother dispensing wisdom, Janey half pretending not to listen, but taking in every word.

Janey was most interested in when the two Janeys might intersect. It was a game she played. For example, what if the old Janey and the new would have said the same word at the same time? What if both Janeys said, or would have said, the word *hey* at the same moment, 2:04 p.m. CST / 3:04 p.m. EST? Or what if they said in harmony the same name? She said the names of the men she met—"Bill," "Shorty," "Bus"—said them a time or two extra, though she doubted the original Janey would have ever met, much less *slept with* a man named Bus. A woman, "Vicky," with long black hair. She whispered the woman's name into her hair. "Vicky, Vicky, Vicky," thereby giving the original Janey three extra chances to connect.

She thought it each evening when her supervisor, Manny, emptied his coffee at the sink. "'Night, Manny," Janey said. She sang the name aloud a few more times under her breath as Manny waved and left, "Manny, Manny, Manny," as if calling to the other Janey, urging her to seek out someone by that name on her crowded far-off island and thereby fasten a link between them.

"Did you need something?" Manny said, ducking back in.

It was the opposite of sci-fi. She wasn't interested in those alternate worlds where you do one thing different and the lives forever splinter off onto distant paths. Janey had done that already and was suffering the consequences. She was interested in when you do one thing different and the lives remain exactly the same.

It must happen constantly. Think of all the repetitive actions you would perform anyplace you were. All the craps you'd be taking anywhere in the world. All the shoes you'd put on and take off. All the idiots you'd say hello to. All the lies you'd make up to make people like you. All the hallways you'd walk down, all the times you'd write your name. Think of the inanities you say all day long like a song on repeat. Sentences uttered could flicker in and out, meeting and diverging and meeting again. Considered in this way, most lives are nearly identical.

She was wondering about this one night on her father's sofa, a talk show running along on the TV, her laptop open to JobLizard. Manny had quit or transferred or dropped dead or moved several towns away from her when, after six consecutive Tuesdays in a motel off exit 67, he'd offered to leave his wife and Janey had laughed. By winter she'd been fired "with cause" for insubordination by his replacement. She scrolled through the jobs site, down and down, all the inconceivably shitty work she could do, an untrained, uneducated woman, twenty years old, who had once been in chess club, on the debate team, who had . . .

There was a third life, of course, which she occasionally considered and which came to mind now: the one where Janey would be dead. In that life she had not gone off on that thirty-hour bus ride. She'd never met her father. He'd remained a mystery in her heart. (Would that have been so bad? she wondered, looking over at him, the slug. He could be counted on to be there with hamburgers and sodas, if nothing else.) She'd instead gotten into the car with her mother that day and they had been killed together on the highway going over the bridge. (Where had her mother been going? Janey had thought about that so many times and never been able to fathom. Only Ikea lay on that vast stretch of land.) If she'd died that day with her mother, the world would be silent of both Janeys. (Would that have been so bad?)

She reached the bottom of hundreds of job ads. Her father passed her a box of fries. He tossed a piece of paper onto her keyboard, folded in three, a brochure. "I grabbed this," he said. "There was a pile in the break room."

She picked it up. A photo of smiling ugly midwestern white people in uniforms on the front. "What's this?"

"It's nothing. I grabbed it for you."

"Well, don't grab things for me." She tucked it between the sofa cushions.

"Your mother would have wanted to see you make something of yourself."

"She would have wanted me to be," Janey tugged the brochure back out, read off the front, "a layer hen consumer auditor? What the fuck is that even?"

Sometimes, as she did now, Janey imagined the dead Janey, the one who had died "tragically" with her mother in the crash. She imagined the dead Janey hovering above, looking down on both Janeys: Janey not dead in New York, Janey not dead in Iowa. The dead Janey was high overhead, an over-Janey as it were, so that now, while the new Janey in Iowa was saying "consumer auditor," words the old Janey would have little occasion to say, the over-Janey could see into the new Janey's mind, could see that her thoughts had tugged to a stop five seconds before, when her father said the word *mother*. The over-Janey could see the word *mother* pressed across Janey's mind as if ironed down there. And perhaps the over-Janey could see the old Janey back in New York and, just maybe, she also had the word *mother* in her mind at this moment because, say, her (their) mother had just arrived home breathless and was shaking off her raincoat, launching into a tale, and the old Janey was looking up, grinning. The new Janey wondered fleetingly about the overlap of thoughts and whether that counted, whether the over-Janey could observe a link between them as tenuous as this, at once as strong and frail as a spiderweb, the most elemental thought, surely the infant's first thought before she could even put a word to it: *mother*.

"It's steady work," her father was saying. "They do college reimbursement. You get an education."

"No way am I going to do what you do."

"It's not what I do. You improve yourself."

"I'm improved enough and fuck you."

But who knew if thoughts counted? Thoughts, which hurry through at the speed of light—are thoughts like light?—and are accompanied by so much else. Thoughts are like nets on an ocean floor, dragging along with them sand and sadness and shells and shit. She looked at the brochure. "I don't have any of these qualifications."

"You can get around the qualifications. I know the lady."

"You know what lady? You don't know any ladies."

"She said she'd give you a job."

"A lady. This your new girlfriend?"

"Don't be cute." He cleared his throat. "She knew your mother."

The afternoon not making it through the blinds, the TV dinging a win or mock-win, smiling faces on the screen, hands raised in joy or in imitation of it, the air around Janey full of oxygen and ions, ozone, dust.

"Your mother babysat her when they were kids."

On this day Janey could feel the significance of each of her words twinkle through her. She could feel the over-Janey watching.

"You have to do the training course. It's just four days."

She was certain it was happening, that a word was about to unite the two Janeys, old and new. Both were opening their mouths to answer a question. But what was the old Janey being asked, her mother adjusting her raincoat on the chair, drops of water falling to the tile? Should they step out for rainy sundaes? Should they go this weekend to the zoo?

"Do you want me to call her?" her father said.

Even if they said the same word, Janey knew, it would have a different meaning—the context was different, the two Janeys were different—but the fact of a crossover could not be denied, the connection.

Well, the over-Janey wasn't going to give either of the Janeys the satisfaction. She wasn't going to let the new Janey say the word, wasn't going to allow the link to fasten. She was going to keep it from them both, hold it back in her tight little fist (a.k.a. heart). But the old Janey—the original, the best, the one who might have lived and gone on to greatness, or at least happiness, or at least somethingness, had she not made the one terrible error—was stronger than any of them. The rest of the Janeys were mere shadows fading in light. If anyone could do it, pull the Janeys together, it was she. The old Janey would say it and if the new Janey could hear her, she'd say it with her. The old Janey was opening her mouth. Flight, consciousness, time: so much was possible that should have been impossible. Janey strained to hear. Would she say no? Would she say yes?

CLEVELAND HAD KNOWN HER as Olivia. She'd been seven when Olivia Flores first turned up on a bright Saturday night while Cleveland was filling and unfilling a universe of buttons—galaxy M82, Andromeda, Halley's Comet in glitter—on the floor. Her mother had bent over the arrangement, "Well, what have we here?" but teenage Olivia, in a paisley dress and red lipstick, barely glanced down. "Jupiter has sixty-seven moons, not the dozen or so you have there. And did you know that outer space is completely silent? There's no atmosphere for sound to travel through." Cleveland already disliked most people, so when she dropped a bottle-cap black hole and sat up, her mother sighed with relief.

Olivia came that Saturday and then on a string of Saturdays and other days in an ill-advised attempt to save Cleveland's parents' marriage (the plan worked, but some people shouldn't stay together). Cleveland liked collecting alarm clock parts and jumping on her minitrampoline, but Olivia got her to go trick-or-treating, which she had refused to do since she was four. Olivia insisted they form their own tambourine and xylophone band, despite Cleveland's flat lack of talent. Olivia taught her Spanish verbs, the table of elements, the waltz (there still exists a video of Cleveland bravely careening around the sunroom), the sad spotted history of labor rights in this country, and the proper way to assemble a taco. Olivia was sophisticated, brilliant, beautiful, ambitious. Beside Cleveland's parents, who looked like dumplings, she was everything Cleveland thought a person should be. She sat for five years, a year longer than Cleveland's mother felt necessary (but what was the harm in paying someone to be her daughter's friend?), then she vanished and that was that.

Cleveland received a postcard of buildings, another of a statue, nothing else. She missed her sitter for years and years, heard rumors of her life far away (daughter, bright city), summoned her in her mind in times of need, mourned when she heard of her death. In sum, never saw her again.

On the day Cleveland took the hen, a numb Iowa afternoon in February, she had not seen Olivia in twenty-one years, which isn't as long as you'd think. She still contemplated universes filling and unfilling, but the universes were smaller now, empty of comets and planets, full of animals and excrement and equipment, in other words, *barns*. Not the barns of once upon a time, retro or relic, that red-planked national emblem—hayloft, chicken coop, horse stall, pitchfork—but the barns of now, the powerful machines, the massive robot supercomputers, the human-made megafauna. And on the day she took the hen, she stood before one of them: 480 feet long, nearly a football field and a half, the size of the four largest dinosaurs ever to walk the planet lined up end to end (she loved that image), this single structure filling and unfilling with forty million eggs a year—unremarkable for this type of barn, but the highest number of eggs per hen in the history of the earth.

The wind yammering over the fields. The cold sun battling it out behind the gray. Cleveland had been recently promoted to the head of Iowa layer hen farm audits. The audit: certifying best practices for consumer safety and hen welfare, navigating a star map of guidelines. Even at seven Cleveland had been good at games involving rules and organizational expertise—jigsaws over drawing, times tables over pretend. The job was a good fit.

In five minutes she would take a hen from Happy Green Family Farm and change the course of her life forever (though she did not yet know she would do it).

"If you have a moment, sir?" This was three weeks earlier in her first meeting with the regional director. She lifted her tablet. "I'd like to present a few ideas."

His eyes blinked to his screen and blinked back. "All right."

She had ideas about farmhand training. She had thoughts about feed logs. It was now in her job description to "revise for betterment all audit tools and templates."

"The sanitary procedures are undependable," she said. She tapped her tablet.

"If I may," she said, "the entire transportation section of the audit is little more than an honor code." She tapped madly, scrolled. "Now, about cage space allowance." There was the lighting section, the manure section, beak trimming.

But the director was rubbing his face. "I'm going to stop you right there, Cleveland." He dropped his hands. "See, this was my hesitation in the first place. We've gone over this. You assured us."

"In the interest of accuracy . . ." she began.

"This is not your job. You describe what is or is not in compliance. You do not participate in the problem-solving process."

She lowered the tablet, knew what was coming.

"What are we doing here, Cleveland?"

"Feeding the country, sir."

He sat back with satisfaction. "The egg is the perfect unit of nutrition." He spun a little in his chair. "Protein, B-12, D. Vitamins of the bones and the mind." He pointed to his temple. "Strength and intellect. A dozen eggs and the poor man eats like the rich. The American dream, Cleveland. The democratic solution." His eyebrows went up. "Raise the price of eggs and the poor man's family doesn't eat."

She didn't know how happy the poor man was going to be when it turned out the certification he put his trust in . . .

"It's science, Cleveland. This is philanthropic work. The ethics of survival. Sustaining civilization."

"Understood," she said.

"All right then. For the last time." His eyes shifted to his screen. "Is that absolutely everything? Are we done?"

She walked back down the hallway, the gap between the director and herself filling with carpet and drywall. She traveled across the divide, widened it. Her phone beeped.

Janey registered for the training.

Olivia, galaxy creature. She'd had an exuberance and freedom that had entirely escaped Cleveland, though she tried hard to learn it, through memorization, imitation, repetition. Olivia would have known what to say. (Olivia, lifting her chin, tossing her hair, straightening to her full height, opening her mouth . . .) Cleveland was, well, *afraid* was too strong a word, but *unsettled* about finally meeting the daughter. Cleveland wanted to measure up.

Three weeks later Cleveland was walking along a line of barns that could be seen from airplanes and rocket ships. The land piled up, stacked in the distance. The feed silos twirled into the sky like turrets. She'd just finished the Green Farm annual audit. Her briefcase was heavy with the outdated electronic equipment of a dubious, maybe meaningless task. Over by the farm office, Farmer Green waved goodbye as he shut the door. Cleveland, cheerless, waved back. (Everyone knew his sister had run off and become an animal rights activist.) She got into her car, drove out of the small lot. But there was a white blur in front of her. She slowed. A shade lighter than the gray ground, and so small.

A hen, strolling down the road, as if it was time to just walk away.

Loose hen on property. That would fall under Structural Access.

She eyed the hen from behind the steering wheel. The universe—the one full of darkness and silence and mud—thrived on coincidence and free will, error. But in the barn, error meant collapse. If hens could get out, other animals could get in, spread disease, kill off half the North American egg eaters, and so on. Cleveland would have to go back, tell the farmer he had a bio-security violation out there. She'd have to redo the audit form, subtract two points under House Security and Access, sign again, issue a Corrective Action, fill out a Biosecurity Plan form, refile the . . .

Or she could just drive around the hen and keep going.

She looked at the hen, stared into its center.

Olivia dropped into her thoughts like a stone. (Olivia raises one blue-painted nail to point out the windshield, turns her indignant face to the director, says . . .)

It may have made the difference, it may not have. The human mind is a mystery.

Hens are in constant motion. They do not freeze like rabbits. They do not "lock eyes." Their eyes work separately, have multiple objects of focus. When they cock their heads they're getting a series of snapshots from different perspectives. But this hen stopped. Her eyes "met" Cleveland's.

Cleveland pulled over and got out of the car.

HEN, ALONE, strolling away from the eight looming apparatuses of Happy Green Family Farm. Her first steps on dirt, not wire. Where was her mother? Only a little over a year old, orphan from egg crack. Who knew where she thought she was going (why did the chicken cross the road?) or whether chickens "think" about such things as destination (of course they do—not quite the way we do, but close enough). You had to root for her. Most industry hens out of a cage for the first time would never walk off into a chilly day after a life spent in a cage. Most would be crowded up against a wall under an overhang or hiding in a bush, trying to get back inside so as not to be prey to whatever the hell was up there: sky and all its certain evils. Bred to cower, you might say. But here was this enterprising (imprudent?) hen, Bwwaauk, as she was known to herself. All chickens, hell, all birds, are known to themselves and each other by individuated chirps—in other words, *names*.

How had Bwwaauk gotten herself into this predicament?

Or rather how had she gotten herself *out* of it? (The predicament being the situation of the hundred and fifty thousand layer hens she'd left behind in the barn. How had the hens gotten themselves into *that*?)

She went trotting down the road into the cold afternoon.

ANY OTHER HEAD AUDITOR might have left the hen and gone home. But Cleveland Smith had been on track, worn out treadmills. She'd won first place three years in a row in the Auditors' Hustle Up the Hancock race, where auditors from all over the country gather in Chicago on the last day of the conference and run up ninety-four flights of stairs. Woman could *run*.

The hen was fast. She dodged, weaved, but Cleveland cornered her by the wheel-cleaning station and snatched her up. She held the hen according to United Egg Producer guidelines—under the breast with one hand and holding both feet with the other, close to the body for security. She walked back toward the farm office to deliver the hen and a lecture on farm sterility.

She hesitated. A chicken couldn't go back into the barn after being exposed to the outside. A farmhand would euthanize her. A perfectly good hen, spritely. Quarantine was what was needed. Vet facilities on every farm, a half-time veterinarian, not unreasonable considering there were *millions of animals per farm*.

The regional director, holding up his hand. "I'm going to stop you right there, Cleveland."

(Olivia, in a flower dress and gym shoes, scrambles for a fly ball, holds it up in triumph, takes off whooping down the bleacher steps.)

She put the bird on the backseat and drove away.

Haha! There she went, tearing toward town (at the speed limit, of course), hen cooing in the backseat. Silly thing had dropped onto the floor. Outside, the land was the color of sand and the sky the shade of rocks, but Cleveland inside was in cartoon colors, zip-ping away. See her disappear into the distance.

She sat in her driveway. House, lawn, neighborhood were a wash of midwinter life-support tint. It had occurred to her: What was she going to tell him about having brought home *a spent hen*? (Yes, she had a husband, nice man, an admissions administra-tor at the nearby community college, specializing in sliding the young into slots as they came through on the conveyor and send-ing them back out, packaged and certified.) He'd be home in an hour, and he'd think she'd gone mad. She turned around to the backseat. The hen looked skeletal, primitive, feathers half miss-ing, filthy, cage-ravaged the way they got. This could be consid-ered stealing.

She brought the hen into the garage, cleared a little space, put down a tin of water and a plate of lettuce. By the time her hus-band got home, Cleveland was settled behind her laptop on the sofa. A fluttery panic in her chest was making her breath come out in little gasps. This was a clear violation of the Ag Facility Fraud law. She could lose her job. Well, the Green Farm was in violation, she would say. She had every right to confiscate the hen. But of course no one else would see it that way. So what was she going to do? She couldn't bring the hen back to the farm and put it in a cage in the middle of the night, let it be pecked to pieces and spread disease across America.

Her husband put down his gym bag. "Is that clucking I hear?"

Cleveland was terrified. "The Clayborns got some chickens, maybe."

"Zoning violation," he said. "I'll write the neighborhood association."

Cleveland turned on the TV.

• • •

She lay in bed, listening, eyes open, her husband breathing beside her. The only thing to do was to bring the hen to the local animal rights office. Farmer Green's sister worked there, after all. It was almost like returning her, really. She got up and went to the garage. The hen had spilled the water on the floor and was crouching under the bicycles. Cleveland got down on her hands and knees, fished her out, put her into a cardboard box, and drove to the office in the quiet downtown. The only communication Cleveland ever had with the AR people was on annual Visit the Farm Day when a few teenagers showed up in torn jeans and slogan T-shirts, passed out hysterical leaflets. So nondescript, it could have been anything, a storefront church, a dying pharmacy, a failing political candidate's headquarters. She took the box and slid it to their door.

She went back home and wrote the group an anonymous note. *Greetings. I've left you a present.*

The news refreshed itself in colorful shapes on the screen.

A response popped up. *Who are you supposed to be, our fairy godmother?*

She wrote back. *Check your doorstep, Cinderella.*

Whatever you left better not be something we call the police over.

She slapped the laptop shut.

Would they call the police over a chicken?

She slept an hour maybe, got up before the alarm, her husband still asleep. She drove to work, hid in her office, and worked on data organization. She could hear her coworkers arriving, going in and out of the break room, calling out hellos. Finally she checked, had to. And, yes, she had a new note from the group.

We see your IP address.

Could they find out who she was?

There was a knock and the door opened.

"Olivia," she gasped.

The girl was wearing some sort of hoodie and her hair seemed arranged in knots. "Dead," said the girl. "It was sudden. A car accident."

The daughter.

HAD OLIVIA MEANT TO LOSE TOUCH? Cleveland had always wondered. Cleveland had admittedly been an odd kid, but she'd been Olivia's first little charge. She imagined Olivia arriving in New York, looking up at the buildings, hand on her stomach, and thinking of Cleveland, the child she'd cared for, the only evidence that she just might be able to do this.

On the other hand, Olivia had had a lot to figure out. Alone, in an enormous city, eighteen years old, broke, smart but under-credentialed, and soon she had a *baby*. She could not have had time to read, much less answer, the many, many emails Cleveland had sent. Cleveland wrote and wrote and wrote, and finally stopped. Why should she have a permanent place in her sitter's heart? She was Olivia's job, not her sister or niece or friend.

One winter day the father of the child called. Olivia had been dead six months. He had the daughter, he said. She could use a little guidance.

Cleveland, fearful, not wanting to mess it up, put it off, waited for the right time, did nothing.

She clutched the edge of her desk.

"Five years ago," said the girl. "Almost six."

Cleveland was so rattled she couldn't think. "I'm informed about the death, but your appointment is next week."

"I changed it."

"I haven't received your course completion verification."

The girl frowned fiercely. She looked like a kid from a group home, like a teen let out of juvenile detention. But so much like her mother. "Well, I finished. Last Thursday," she said. "You haven't been *informed*?"

Cleveland was *arguing* with her? She needed to gather herself. "We'll start you tomorrow."

"I have the job?"

"Pick up your employee welcome packet at the front desk."

The girl walked out, sneakers squeaking (Olivia playing starship in an old warehouse, Olivia sweeping leaves and twigs from her clothes . . .). Cleveland's heart was banging. That wasn't at all how she'd wanted to begin. She swiveled back to her computer. She had another message from that AR group.

She knew she shouldn't read it, but she did.

She knew she shouldn't answer, but she did.

The next day Olivia's daughter came back and Cleveland shakily took her through orientation: the United Egg Producers' mission, the history of US layer hen certification, the Five Freedoms afforded to hens. She heard her own heavy voice dole out mechanical explanations, observed her own economical gestures. Olivia had made the table of elements sing, Olivia had spray-painted trig equations on the garage door (to the horror of Cleveland's parents, who insisted they were gang symbols). Olivia would have made the audit fun.

She handed the girl a uniform, a clipboard, a mono-use laptop, an armful of binders and forms. "Tomorrow we'll have a quiz."

Meanwhile, it seems absurd to say she got into a fight with these AR activists, but that's what was happening.

Where'd you get the bird? You should be charged with neglect. As a matter of fact, she's yours.

She sure as fuck isn't ours. The enduring conceptual error of our kind is believing any living creature is the property of another.

She wrote again three days later, attached twelve photos

of chickens in rusty cages that she snapped—illegally, with her phone—while Janey Flores was miscalculating cage space one row over. *Here's for your monthly calendar.*

We do targeted undercover investigations, not pet sitting. If you are in the position to conduct such an investigation, and have the courage and the will, which we doubt, come see us with your face not your phone.

That's when she stole two chickens. Drove to the Anderson Family Egg Farm, grabbed them, left them in a box with a note. *There are two million more where these came from. I'm doing your job for you. Whose side are you on anyway?*

They wrote again. *Oh excuse us that we aren't jumping up and down when strangers leave animals at our door for us to care for. Rescuing individual chickens is just stupid. If you refuse to work on our terms by whatever is crouching in your contradictory heart, if you feel exculpated by taking two hens and leaving the rest to suffer and die, let alone ten billion every year, bring them to this address, not ours.*

The address was far, sixty miles out of town, one of those ludicrous sanctuaries miles off the highway. She looked at overhead images of it online while Janey Flores sat across from her in the Anderson Farm conference room and paged through the feed log—too quickly to determine whether the guidelines had been followed.

Cleveland drove to the Spillman Egg Family Farm two nights later, a farm she'd audited every year for the past five. She walked onto the property with a sack like at the grocery and pulled six hens off the cage-free floor.

Now you are getting on our nerves, they wrote. *Since you refuse to introduce yourself, we are taking the liberty of the introduction. We have installed a security camera, for which we used scant, valuable funds. It is up and running, so whatever you do when you come to our door, whether dressed in a farmhand smock or the dark garb of an animal revolutionary, we will see it, please know.*

That was the last time she took any hens for a while.

Until she couldn't stand it anymore and took three more.

"Look around you, Janey."

They stood among angles scarce in nature. Eighteen barns. A gathering of smaller supporting buildings. The girl didn't lift her head from her ground gaze. A dull sun.

"You see, Janey, this is the story of American ingenuity. The modern egg barn is a perfectly calibrated instrument."

Cleveland delivered this speech a dozen times a year—at training sessions and 4-H clubs, impromptu at neighborhood association meetings. "Hens left to their own devices lay as few as thirty eggs a year. Eggs used to be a luxury." She pointed to a barn. "These hens lay two hundred and seventy eggs a year each. Do you know how? With one scientific discovery."

She stopped and squinted at the girl. "Stand up straight, Janey. We do not make scientific progress by slouching."

The girl straightened almost imperceptibly.

Janey Flores. Silent (sullen?), inexpressive (unimaginative?), she had an exasperating habit of tugging the zipper of her hoodie up and down, up and down, a hoodie she insisted on wearing over her uniform so she looked like (was?) a runt with an attitude problem. Still, each time the girl turned and Cleveland caught a different angle of her face, a monstrous affection and protectiveness came over her.

"Light. The discovery was light." Cleveland resumed walking. "American scientists in the 1930s figured out that light is how the hen's body knows when to lay. Long light means spring and laying. Less light means winter and rest. More light, more laying."

The girl merely needed discipline, guidance, care.

"So the scientists shined more light on the hens, and lo and behold the hens kept laying." She lifted an arm to the barns. "Enough light and these hens will just lay and lay and lay and lay. Now what do you say to that?"

"Another win for mankind," Janey said, glumly.

"For Americans," Cleveland corrected.

IN THE WEEKS leading up to meeting the woman her mother had sat for, Janey worried. She wondered whether the woman would like her. She tried to recall if her mother had ever mentioned her—Cleveland was her name, Janey loved it!—and it came to her that she remembered less and less about her mother. She had so little of her mother left—a suitcase full of old clothing, two paintings, a handful of jewelry, three voice mails, which she carefully copied along with every photo onto any new technology. So much was gone.

She tried to communicate with the old Janey. Ask her, Janey thought at her. Ask Mom about Cleveland.

She lay in her room in her father's apartment and tried to imagine what sort of person Cleveland would be. Playful, spirited, smart. She'd grown up on the prairie, so Janey could see her as a wholesome health nut—braids, sandals, strumming something acoustic. Janey knew it wasn't good for her to think like this but she imagined the two of them going camping, forging rivers, hiking through woods, sitting around a fire, Cleveland telling her stories about her mother as a teenager, acting out parts. How Janey would laugh! Then Cleveland would reach over and tuck a lock of Janey's hair behind her ear, and say, "Your mother would be so proud of who you are," and Janey would cry. Cleveland would put a big-sister arm around her and say, "Now let's figure out a plan for you. Obviously you can't keep doing *this*," and gesture in the general direction of the office where they worked (the job itself played no part in this scenario). But here Janey's fantasy would pause because that's what Cleveland had done, after all. Stayed in Iowa, taken this job, was even the boss! Janey rushed to her defense. It was understandable in Cleveland's case because . . . because . . . because . . . Janey faltered, then got it: Cleveland was a single mom! Raising a child alone and doing a great job (like Janey's mother!). A little girl holding a marshmallow stick popped up at the campsite in Janey's mind. Together the three of them explored the wilderness in a five-state contiguous region, floated over lakes in canoes, scrambled through caves. And just like that Janey was integrated into this little family (Aunt Janey!) and a *new* new Janey emerged: cutoff shorts, hair up in a bandanna, majoring in environmental science at the state university (Janey had never been one for nature, but with Cleveland by her side, she fell in love with the planet), coming home on weekends to Cleveland and her daughter (Olive!).

It had been so long since she'd thought about being healthy. Could she do it for this woman, if she had to? She would try, really try.

The auditor certification course was horrific, four long days of PowerPoints with cartoons of grinning chickens at the end of each one, quizzes with golf pencils like this was 1999, the most boring set of hours ever to unfold before her, while also truly disturbing. The vocabulary alone: "depopulation" (i.e., killing hens off by the hundred thousand), "forced molting" (i.e., reducing their food to the point where they don't *quite* die), "beak trimming" (i.e., cutting off their faces), "certification" (sanctioning, no, *requiring* a whole allotment of atrocities), "the United Egg Producers" (the middle-aged white men in charge of all this).

She was like a quester having to pass through trials of tedium in hopes of one day reaching enlightenment, and at last arriving at the end . . . Janey was so impatient, she moved her interview up five days. She drove to the address. A cube building in a landscape of cube buildings, an office "park," acres of pavement.

In place of trees, mounted signs directed you to distant lots. A receptionist pointed her into Cleveland's office. Janey knocked and walked in. The pale woman behind the desk paled further. "Olivia?"

Janey startled. "Dead."

From there it only got worse. On her first day Cleveland made Janey sit while she paced in front of a whiteboard and delivered a monologue on the topic of "duty." She spent ten minutes on the rules for the employee lunchroom. Janey was too surprised to speak. Cleveland gave her "homework."

Over the next few days they went out to do the audits. Janey donned grimly the uniform, sat in the fluorescent farm offices and paged through the documentation, tramped behind Cleveland to the barns in the rain, followed her down the rows of hens. Nearly all the farmhands were Latino. A few times one joked with her in Spanish and she didn't understand a word. She felt utterly foreign and unmoored. The barns were massive, sci-fi–level crazy, a powerful stench of chemicals and ammonia.

And Cleveland was strange. Expressionless face. A rigid way of turning her head. Why had Janey been so ignorant as to imagine the woman could be anything but what she was? This "Cleveland," a true believer in a middling cause, a ridiculous woman in a uniform, uptight, an autism-spectrum interest in regulations, named for a US president who hadn't even done anything, *twice*. A woman who seemed to sincerely believe these disgusting warehouses were perfectly appropriate places for *birds*, as if they were lawn mowers or TV sets. If Cleveland hadn't said her mother's name at the interview, Janey wouldn't have believed she had the correct person.

Something was not right about her. She was twitchy, secretive. She lived in the ugliest house Janey had ever seen, plastic sun shades over the windows, fake siding coming off in places.

No kids, a pasty husband who was already balding. Janey ducked below the windshield when Cleveland came out to the curb with the recycling bin.

Janey was in despair. She wished she hadn't built Cleveland up in her mind only to be toppled, wished she hadn't allowed a feeling that resembled hope to enter her peripheral vision. She lost her uniform at the Laundromat, lost the audit binders on a vast farm (set them down somewhere and forgot about them until Cleveland looked at her askance an hour later), lost all curiosity about Cleveland, lost her ability to fake it through this, and was well on her way to losing the job too.

In other words, Janey didn't even ask her about her mother.

"Thanks a lot," she said to her father. "Now I'm stuck measuring ammonia levels and scraping excrement off my shoes. I stink even in my dreams."

She said, "My mother only sat for her once or twice, right? They barely knew each other."

He gave the most infuriating shrug. "Does it matter?"

"It matters."

"Then why don't you ask her?"

THEN SHE CAUGHT CLEVELAND using her phone in a barn. Once, twice. Forbidden, but who cares. She caught her again. Must be checking her texts.

But, no, holy crap . . .

Janey was so disappointed in Cleveland and so sunk in her disappointment, she might have easily missed the whole thing.

Cleveland was taking video of the animals—against the law, in violation of the Iowa ag-gag law, which Janey had learned about half-asleep in auditor training and which she knew carried a possible penalty of something or other imprisonment and fines. And here was Cleveland taking photos, not of fluffed-up chicks, but of fucked-up hens. Hens crowded behind the wire, hens with raw wounds, hens with prolapsed uteruses, hens dead in a bin in a bloody heap. Janey watched this for a week. Cleveland was an undercover investigator. Who would have imagined. What an operation. Genius. Janey was impressed. Janey was almost a little frightened—Cleveland had to be a psychopath to pull this off. She had to be mad.

And the shit. She was taking pictures of it.

One midnight Janey was at Cleveland's house, sitting in her car, half-hidden by a minivan, the entire street turned down to dim, not one room lit, not a stray teen sliding out a window. Janey was dozing against the headrest, eyes lifted a slit. She jolted awake when she saw the front door open and Cleveland herself step out onto the lawn—a dewy luminescence and a shaded figure creeping swiftly over it. She got into her car and drove off. Janey waited, then followed a block behind on a slow ride through town. When she turned left onto Route 54, Janey knew where she had to be going. Janey stayed ten minutes in the Jack in the Box parking lot, then drove to the farm they'd audited that day. There it was, Cleveland's car, parked on the side of the road across from the farthest barn. Janey pulled over a way off, put on her hat and gloves, and walked down the road in the dark. She waited, her breath forming and rising in the cold.

Ammonia, darkness, fans like a plane in takeoff. Cleveland emerged from the barn with a sack.

The excruciatingly beautiful night! The tininess of Cleveland against the gigantic barn! The light inside illuminated her from behind and glowed around her. The fans sounded like *om*. Who was this woman? What had her mother passed on long ago? The same defiant spirit that had led her away from this town, that had brought Janey back? The fire of her mother, her grandfather, was a trace of it here? Janey had thought this was a dead end but now . . .

Cleveland shut the door and disappeared. Janey waited. Saw the line of shadow cross the dark.

Janey came up behind her. Cleveland was bent over the backseat, a couple of chickens climbing out of the sack.

Cleveland could be fired. She could face criminal charges. She could go to prison. She could be charged with bioterrorism. She could . . .

"Hey," said Janey.

Cleveland startled, straightened. Dropped the empty sack. She slammed the back door with menace. "What do you want?"

She was *wearing her fucking uniform*.

"Why'd you do that?" said Janey.

"Do what?" said Cleveland.

INSIDE: BARN UNIVERSE. Completely enclosed in steel and concrete, seven tremendous aisles of cages soaring twenty-five feet high, eight tiers in two stories. A system of chains bringing in the feed, a series of belts carrying out the excrement. Powerful fans pulling through and out the carbon monoxide, the hydrogen sulfide, the ammonia, the dust. Twenty thousand one-foot-candle bulbs at regular intervals, like a monstrous Christmas decoration, the sun rising and falling on a timer. The entire barn rumbling with machinery. A hundred and fifty thousand chickens stood there, waiting—for what? for whom? On a wide conveyor, eggs slowly floated by.

"WHY'D YOU TAKE THOSE?"

The hens were clucking inside the car but Cleveland didn't flinch.

Psychopath, thought Janey.

"I'm doing my job, Janey. This is the difference between an employee who will advance and an employee who will fail."

So crazy she was probably dangerous.

"Go ahead and call the regional director. I'll give you his number."

"No thanks."

"Go ahead."

"No, I don't want to."

The fans roared.

"Fine."

"Fine."

The psychopath opened her car door.

"Hey," Janey said.

Cleveland turned back.

"How many times did my mother babysit you?"

"Hundreds." She got in the car. "And I wasn't a baby." She drove off. Janey followed.

SHE AND CLEVELAND began removing animals. They turned up long before dawn, hours before the first farmhands arrived and hours after the last ones had left, when the barns were sheer machine and coo and fume, when the security lamps' glow was the only light on the land. Invisible horizon, straight roads cutting through the dark, Janey and Cleveland pulling up alongside a barn, climbing out of the car in their auditor uniforms, which they wore at Cleveland's insistence. They walked through the barns, Cleveland recording in a wrath "noncompliances"— jammed belts, crowded cages, a cat stepping along the aisles. If they got caught, Cleveland said, let her do the talking. "By all means," said Janey. Oh, she'd love to see that one. Worth the jail time. They hustled out a dozen at a time, six thin hens per burlap sack, took turns driving, tore away from the farms at three in the morning, hens huddled on towels in the backseat.

Did they talk about Janey's mother? Barely. Once, it began to snow while they were in a barn. They stepped out into a blizzard so thick, it was like peering through white mud. They couldn't see a thing. Not a road, not a building, not a car. Their flashlights lit nothing but snow. They went weaving off in one hopeful direction, then another, the sacks getting wetter and heavier (hens could stay in the sacks for only a little while or they'd die: it had happened), slush eddying under their feet, Janey cursing and shivering. Cleveland stopped, shined her flashlight on her. "Janey Flores, for the last time, stand up straight. Your mother used to say that even the most humble job should be done as if for the president of the United States. Would you slouch like that before the president?"

Janey gasped. Her mother *did* used to say that. Janey threw back her shoulders. They marched a long way. They found the car and got in.

Cleveland: "There are not two sets of numbers, Janey, one for mathematicians and one for auditors of layer hen farms. Check your calculations."

Her mother: "There aren't two sets of manners, young lady, one for the queen of England and one for little Brooklyn girls. Use a Kleenex!"

Cleveland: "Roll up that window. How do you think these chickens like being blown around like lotto balls?"

Her mother: "Shut that window. We are not lotto balls at seniors bingo!"

Janey never got used to the sound of the barns. The clanking machinery, the squeaking belts. Even the lights made a sound in these places. She'd start her long walk toward the center of the row and the fans would give way to the sound of tens of thousands of hens, a sort of roiling moaning or droning. It reached the ears in what could only be described as layers, the shallowest layer coming from the hens clucking and ululating nearby, and the deepest layer a low cooing that rose from all corners of the maze. She'd look up and glimpse through the metal a second story identical to this one. She'd crouch and see the lowest tier of birds at her feet, she herself encased between two loud walls of hens, honeycombed in, hundreds of heads poking out at all heights, ahead and behind. She couldn't see the row's end through the haze of dander. The unimaginable scale, the tiny beside the huge, the existential power of size.

• • •

Some farms had barbed wire, some had key codes. Some had a security truck coasting the horizon. Others had nothing but a dented sign to keep them out. Cleveland found ways onto them all. Virtuoso at it, really. If a barn was locked (most weren't), she knew where the keys were. If she didn't, she'd look in their audit forms and in minutes have a key or a code. A glance at their audits and she knew when the night crews would be out. "My life's work," Cleveland said to Janey's impressed grin.

("Our life's work": her mother, head in a kerchief, leaning on a mop, joking about their Sunday cleaning.)

Janey couldn't believe the eccentric people who had made up her mother's early life, first her father, and now this. And yet . . .

She could hear the echo of her mother's voice.

"The barn is the whole world as far as the hens are concerned, Janey. The earth, the sun, sustenance, rain."

(Her mother, one of her final voice mails: "You're my whole world, Janey. My sun, my sustenance. How many ways can I say I'm sorry?")

Janey didn't know when the old Janey would have occasion to say "Cleveland." Perhaps at a party in Red Hook. The old Janey would be leaning against a stove, making eyes at the closest face, a guy with a band look on, hair suitable for the latest rock and roll. He'd say he was from Ohio, and she'd say, feigning flirtation or boredom (is there a difference?), "Cleveland?" because it was the only city in that state she'd be able to think of. Meanwhile, at the same moment, a perfect thousand miles away, the new Janey held a single saved hen clucking against her chest, and was saying, "Cleveland?" because the woman was recording some "noncompliance" (what a loon!) and Janey wanted her to cut it out and come over here and open the neck of the sack so she could nestle this hen inside.

For the first time she felt like she'd rather be doing what *this*

Janey was doing than what *that* Janey, the old one, would be doing, whatever law-abiding inanity the East Coast Janey had taken up as a way to waste the day. Surely the old Janey would be an intern someplace, complimenting some asshole or writing company tweets. Meanwhile, the new Janey was a pirate, a Robin Hood, an outlaw of the best kind, smuggling a few citizen hens to safety.

What a relief. She'd thought she'd never feel alive again. She'd thought she'd been crushed for good, become just another one of the flattened personalities you encounter every day, constructed out of cardboard and cemented down in place.

So say you have been trying to dim your own lights, take it down a notch. Lessen longing. Lessen rage. Lessen. Say that has been going on for years and then *this* happens—you find this and you ride along. You revive a bit, that's all. You lessen the lessening.

JANEY CAME YAWNING out of her bedroom. Box of doughnuts on the coffee table, TV on mute, father in his spot.

"What's this about?" Janey picked a giant rubber band off the table.

"Gimme that," he said. "It's the style these days. Everybody exercises hours all the time."

Janey tossed it to him and reached into the doughnut box.

"You have a reason to look happy like that?"

"What?" Janey said. "I don't look happy."

"You don't?"

"No, I'm not happy."

"My mistake." He stretched the band out over his head.

"Why don't you look out with that thing?" Janey said. "You'll break a window."

"What are you so happy about? Does it have something to do with you getting home in the middle of the night every night?"

"Not every night."

"Often enough that I'm thinking, Why is she getting home so late every night? Three a.m.? How's that for your job in the morning?"

"I'm not happy, okay? Don't worry about it."

"Why should I worry if you're happy? I should worry if you're unhappy."

"Well, go ahead and worry then."

Why didn't she just say she was out with Cleveland? She didn't have to admit to breaking into barns to say she was spending time with the woman. It'd be so easy. He'd be pleased.

"You meet this guy at your job?"

"What guy?"

"You going to come home one day and tell me I'm going to be a grandfather? Let me walk you down an aisle before it comes to that."

"I'd sooner have an abortion."

Janey ate her doughnut and watched him pulling the band, grunting. She had a pang of guilt but she didn't want to tell him. She felt protective and private.

"What's there to be unhappy about? That's a good job."

"Torturing small animals, sure."

Afraid she might break the spell of her and Cleveland.

"You see they have college reimbursement? Not bad."

"I don't give a shit about college. Would you watch it with that thing? You're going to crack the TV."

THEY DIDN'T CALL IT "stealing" since that made it sound like notepads from the supply room and Cleveland kept insisting this was part of their job. She forbade them to call it "freeing," or worse, "liberating." Where could they take these birds where they'd be "free"? The chickens were so overbred, they no longer had a natural habitat. "You have to have a place to go where you *can* be free in order to be freed," Cleveland said. But Janey wasn't so sure. These chickens, these animals with wings, who could fly short distances, these *birds*, as in the phrase *free as a bird*, were ineligible for freedom? But Cleveland was unmoved. Likewise the hyperbolic "rescue" was out.

So what to call it?

"Releasing" sounded like a dirty massage.

"Delivering" had the religious connotation.

"Evacuating" sounded like a bowel movement.

"Exodus." Now Janey was just being silly.

Cleveland decided on the apolitical, unsentimental "removal."

They were removing the birds from the audit area.

Hen. Not quite bird, not quite not bird. Tremendous wings, body slimmer than a duck, but the thing could barely fly. A few flopping feet off the ground and an awkward landing. Not what you first picture when you think "bird." And bird itself, in the between space of mammal and reptile, a freakish mix of the two—warm-blooded and chatty, yet egg-laying, descended from dinosaurs.

They pecked at her shoelaces, hopped up on a stool, poked at her buttons, looked into her face. *Gallus gallus domesticus.* Its mammal side tame, its face still containing the reptilian wilds.

What to do with them was a problem. Janey and Cleveland brought them down two-lane roads in the dark to the closest sanctuary: off the highway, set into a patchwork of farmland. They hefted a crate of birds out onto the road by the mailbox. But that was inconvenient and took an extra two hours and on the cold nights in February, then March, the hens' fragile combs could get frostbit before they were found. So they went back to the small animal rights office in town and left them there instead. The person who ran the place wrote them swearing revenge. Cleveland was certain it was a woman related to one of the farms, but the only one ever in there was a man—Dill, they discovered, was his name. Then one night they showed up and the sign was down, a for-rent poster in the window. Janey cupped her gloved hands against the glass. Place was empty, cardboard boxes turned on their sides. They tracked Dill down to a hulk of an old farmhouse ten miles down the road. They left the birds in boxes in the yard.

The next time he caught them. Janey was carrying a box up onto the farmhouse porch, out of the chilly wind, when the screen door swung open and a lanky redheaded guy stepped out. He was enraged. Janey froze. Cleveland had the car running at the bottom of the porch. He stepped over, wrestled the box from Janey's arms. "Keep your fucking voices down," he said. "You'll wake the whole house." He slammed back inside. Janey burst out laughing.

SOMETHING SEEMED TO BE MISSING, some piece of herself receding. The old Janey: she was retreating. The life she should have lived, the one where she grew up and became all she'd ever wanted (and what had that been?), was beginning to feel faded now, and blurry.

To get the auditor job, that had been the first plan, or the first *fake* plan, since she had no interest in getting the job, only in meeting Cleveland. To *do* the auditor job, that was the second plan, or the second fake plan, since the job was stupid and she had no intention of doing it well. Then she had begun "night auditing" with Cleveland—third plan, also fake, even if she found it sort of fun.

But in truth none of those fake plans were the first or second or third. There were hundreds of fake plans, there were thousands. She had been constructing fake plans for years because any plan that involved this life in the midlands was fake. Even the plan to come out here in the first place was fake, in that it was nothing but a bedtime story, a girl's dream about coming to meet her father. The only plan she could recall concocting that wasn't fake was the day she'd decided to call her mother and go home. Since that day, it had been layers of not taking anything seriously, of seriously working at that, at seriously fucking off. Even in her imagination, even in her fantasies of the other person she'd be, far off on the East Coast, she saw herself there being too cool for it, whatever it was, because no matter where she was or what happened, that was her essential feature: herself, making a joke.

But now *that* plan was receding. That plan—to have only fake plans—was giving way, was beginning to seem like a fake plan covering the real plan. There were many layers of plans to push through to reach it, but it was happening: a plan was emerging as the real plan—fast, faster than she (the one watching all this as if outside it, the over-Janey) could keep up. Is that what one calls "growing up"? And is this—rescuing hens in the middle of the night—Janey's version of it?

Heart-beating creatures, crushed, carried away in Janey's small hands.

She wondered about this one night as Cleveland opened the door to yet another barn and waved Janey inside.

But the original plan, to have no plan, was still there, hanging behind her, tapping on her shoulder, demanding she stop. Do not pay attention to this new "real" plan. It's disloyal, the old plan reminded her, to her mother, who was the only one who could rightly claim her true attention.

But she *was* paying attention. She couldn't help it. All the fake plans were being brushed aside like branches, as if she were walking through a forest, pushing through the foliage. That's what it felt like that night, as she walked behind Cleveland, along the mad machinery, mad belts burbling and eggs drifting by like a stream, fake plans crunching under her feet like twigs. She was restless. A month had gone by since she had caught Cleveland hen-handed in the night. What now? Had they reached the dead-end concrete wall of Cleveland's dream? What was on the other side?

"Look at this. This whole barn is in violation. Are you seeing this, Janey? Every hen in this place."

Janey entered a row and stopped, like pausing in the woods to hear the birds, the tiers of cages rising like tremendous trees from her feet to far overhead, the birds humming and cooing and calling.

She saw it. The Real Plan, a vision of it: the cages falling away, the hens flinging out of them, flicking off the steel like eggshells, birds shucking off their cages, jumping out of the wire as from nests. She saw the roof open up and stars filling the sky over the canopy of swaying cages and branches. She saw the hens, hundreds of thousands of them, with a power unheard of in a chicken, fly up out of the barn and into the night.

"Cleveland," she whispered, though Cleveland couldn't hear her, "let's take them all," because the new Janey had arrived.

"I'M SERIOUS, A WHOLE BARN," Janey was saying. "A mass trans-portation of hens. A removal on a tremendous scale."

"I mean, what is the point in these random removals?" she said. "No one even knows we're taking these."

"Fifty people, a hundred and fifty thousand hens," Janey said. "We could do it."

"An entire barn. Imagine the rows of empty cages. Imagine the farmer's face."

Janey Flores, once on the debate team, in chess club, who had written half a sophomore thesis on the early speeches of Malcolm X, whose grandfather had led strikes for workers' rights, this woman had skills. Rhetoric, reasoning, civil rebellion. None of those lights had burnt out. She knew she had to think like her opponent. What was in her opponent's mind? What was their idiom? What line of logic would sway?

"I mean, who's in charge here?" Janey said. "Who's the head of audits? You or them?"

"You said it yourself," she said. "Every hen is in violation."

But she didn't quite have it. It wasn't going down.

"You're the person to do it, Cleveland. If anyone could, it's you."

"Don't laugh. I'm serious."

She tried a line from those goddamn UEP guidelines she'd had to read again and again. "Farms that fail the audit are supposed to face repercussions, right? Who decides the repercussions?"

But that wasn't it either. What angle was she missing?

THE GIRL WAS RAVING.

"We are not a guerrilla organization," Cleveland was saying. "These are not hostages. We are not making demands."

"Janey, there is a name for removal on that scale. It's called industry farming."

"Us and who?" Cleveland said. "One does not take out an ad online for dissidents."

"If I wanted to think of a farmer's face I would have married one, Janey."

Cleveland had her own set of skills. Her skills were in rule adherence, dictatorial single-mindedness. "No, Janey, you don't get to decide to change the guidelines any time you like."

Memorization, too. She was good at that. "Farms that fail the audit develop a plan in cooperation with the UEP," Cleveland was saying. "The auditor does not participate in the problem-solving process."

And yet, her skills did involve heading toward an objective at full speed, not looking left or right, not slowing. She did like fitting consequences, dramatic implications, grand gestures, universal questions. She would have been great in a cult. She hated inexactitude, hated not being listened to by the regional director. Janey's arguments were *interesting*, but not persuasive.

Janey didn't realize that the line of reasoning truly compelling to Cleveland was Janey herself.

SHE WOKE. Where was she? Still night, her husband asleep. A thought or a dream or a memory was running away from her and she leapt over the boulders of her mind to chase it.

The look on Janey's face, the smile (see that? the girl had been beaming for the first time). Cleveland had done this, was wringing that smile from Janey, as Olivia had once wrung it from Cleveland. That face was working on Cleveland while she slept. Where had she seen it?

That ridiculous girl, the one who'd followed her up and down the grates, sucked on her giant pop drinks, gotten her hair caught in hens' claws, yelled out the window, the incompetent, unruly, ill-natured daughter of the long-limbed, long-lost, lovely Olivia, this girl had, out of her misplaced disdain, thought of this. It was exactly the sort of idea Olivia would dream up (Cleveland was certainly wrong about that). Like a weed unbolting from the ground in the dawn, Olivia, coming to life. She'd been there all along.

Single-mindedness is a stubborn trait. The question about Cleveland was, which trumped: the UEP guidelines or Olivia (transferable to the daughter)?

She rose, put on her bathrobe, and went out to the patio. Too warm for March. The neighbor's hideous security light came over the fence and tossed in long shapes of harsh light. The backyard was shiny with a rain that must have come and then taken itself away while she slept. The sky was clear now, opening up, morning approaching but not yet arrived.

Cleveland knew just how to do it. Happy Green Family Farm. They had someone among them who had surely thought of this before.

She lay back in the lounge chair, pulled the wool throw over herself, and took up her phone. She texted Janey, *It would have to be a whole farm.* She closed her eyes, listened to the soft buzz of the neighbor's security light, like the soft buzz of her mind. Olivia, nodding, grateful from the grave. Cleveland curled on her side and stayed there until her husband slid open the glass door after daybreak and said, "What could you possibly be doing out here?" All she could think to say was, "Dreaming."

OF COURSE JANEY couldn't know this, but if she'd stayed, had not left her mother, had not gotten it into her head to run away and find her father, her mother still would have died in a car crash that day. Janey would have been beside her. They'd be headed to Ikea to buy flowerpots and porch chairs, but instead Janey would watch her mother die on the bridge and she herself would live on. She would not move to Iowa (though she'd eventually meet her father, and they'd have two awkward meals at IHOP when she was thirty). Instead she'd go live with her mother's best friend, Judy, who'd never had a daughter, and instead of rage, a great sorrow would underpin all Janey's doings. She'd play competitive chess and be on the debate team through high school. She'd go to college. She'd study political science and philosophy and eventually apply to law school.

One day, as a student in the Columbia University Environmental Law Clinic, she'd help file a suit against the EPA for "failing to enforce the Clean Water Act" on four Iowa-based layer hen farms. Industrial farm fans, each tall as a man, blow massive amounts of shit and dander and chemicals into nearby streams and rivers, polluting the local water. The suit would name three of the very farms she'd snuck onto with Cleveland—coincidence, fate, or divine design. So despite what Janey contended, she would have turned out to be arguably a somewhat similar person, with or without her teenage escape to Iowa. And those farms would not have seen the back of Janey no matter what.

Instead, that suit against the EPA went on without Janey. It was lost. More suits followed. And still more will come. They will all be lost. No one will be able to beat those fans.

At a five-foot wingspan, with a body weight of 280 pounds, aluminum scales, and a wire-mesh skin-like covering, those industrial farm fans are the very distant descendants of the *Archaeopteryx*, the earliest form of bird. Their cousins, the warm-blooded hens, are born with the fans' roar, they grow up with it. For the hens the fans are the sound of the earth—as sea turtles think of the ocean, as humans think of the sound of the air. It's the last sound the hens hear, other than their own voices, as farmhands stuff them at the end of their lay into the carbon dioxide cart (which according to UEP guidelines must cause "rapid loss of consciousness until death," though the guidelines do not specify how long "rapid" is—does not all life hurtle rapidly toward death?).

In fact the fans will be one of the last things to go.

In the coming decades Earth will continue to heat, irregularly at first, in patches. There'll be energy shortages, then crises. Families will spend more on energy than on rent. In the late days, air conditioners will become illegal and anyway too expensive to run. Only the richest 10 percent (so don't worry) will be able to sit and have quiet conversations in cool air (not that they will do much talking, their faces inches from their screens as they fight with people all over the world). Box fans, tornado fans, tower fans, ceiling fans, all species of fan will evolve and fill homes.

A firm of architects, coincidentally headed by a female descendant of Victor Gruen, will design an apartment complex with industrial fans making up the northern walls. Doors will roll down over them like a garage. Fan-wall apartment complexes will multiply. Around them the landscape will swirl with storms and waves. The Americas will turn into mostly desert and the islands will sink into the dead sea.

In the final decades, that sound—a low pulsing powerful hum—will take over, rise off the earth, muffle what's left.

Then one day all the fans will fall silent.

2

THE FIRST NIGHT the auditors showed up, Dill was sitting at the bay window with the lights off, thinking he'd lost it all. But he was wrong. He had much, much more losing to go. Each night the auditors showed up, in fact, he'd lost a little more, so that their arrivals marked time, each visit another tick, because that year was Dill's undoing. The fabric that wrapped him was unwinding, the layers loosening and dropping to the ground, and when the outer fabric was gone, he himself was disassembled, piece by piece, taken down, and hauled off.

When the auditors first came (though he didn't know who they were yet), their headlights lit the driveway gravel dust, so that they seemed to arrive in a cloud of smoke. He was alone at the window while his husband and the dogs and the other animals in there slept. So far he'd lost only his job, director of undercover investigations, and that had been going on for weeks already, his joblessness. He was almost used to feeling unused, unneeded, unheeded. But a few hours earlier he'd driven by the Iowa branch office and seen the sign was down. That had made it real: they were going to carry on elsewhere without him.

He squinted through the bay window into the dark at the vehicle that stopped halfway down the drive. Two figures hopped out and pulled some boxes off the backseat. Must be a couple of his investigators who had or hadn't heard the news. Or maybe some old investigators, wandering through. Or maybe even the *old*, old investigators, the original gang riding in, ready to take sides, *his* side. For eight years Dill had supervised the unruly force of undercover investigators who posed as farmhands, wore secret cameras, and recorded the various categories of casual animal abuse and neglect. But now that his eyes were adjusting to the distance, he could tell by their very postures—he could see only their silhouettes—that these were not investigators. No investigator stood like that. Besides, investigators didn't turn up in twos. They were solo creatures, more Frankenstein's monster than Quixote.

He had no idea who these people were.

They left their boxes in the yard with the trees and the stars and the cold and the dew. They got back into their car and drove off.

The second night they showed up, a week later, they were more brazen and he was in a worse mood. They pulled in front of the house, headlights flashing across the windows. A few of the dogs (there were seven) lifted their heads off the tile. The rest dreamed on, paws twitching. Worst watchdogs. He rose from the kitchen table and went out there because his husband, a banker to whom he'd been married six years, had had just about enough of Dill's "crazy animal people" but had not yet, as he had by the *third* night the auditors showed up, had just about enough of Dill himself.

That second night he wondered: Are these the same assholes as last week, the ones who left boxes of spent layer hens in the frost for him to deal with, or are these altogether new assholes? He stepped out onto the porch, where one of them, a young woman, was halfway up the steps with a box. She froze.

He raised a palm. "Lady, whatever you're selling, I don't want it."

Damn if he didn't hear clucks coming from the box. So it *was* the same assholes. She lifted her chin over the box. "These girls come free."

"This ain't no charity."

And he finally made the connection. These must be the same

assholes who'd been leaving chickens at the office. Of course. He'd been a little distracted lately, considering.

He stepped closer to get a better look. The other one, older, was stepping out of the car. They had on uniforms, but not farmhand uniforms. These were not investigators, not whistleblowers, none of the usual crowd that showed up at any hour bragging or complaining or crying.

Oh, he knew. Fucking auditors. Fuck him.

"Keep your fucking voices down," he said. He wrestled the box from her. "You'll wake the whole house." He slammed back inside. He carried the box through the kitchen to take the hens out back.

The third time they showed up, Dill got out of bed as soon as their headlights swept the bedroom where he was feigning sleep, normalcy, sanity—faking as a desperate ploy, not that the banker was believing it—and Dill leapt up because the banker woke at once, shielded his eyes. "More of your friends?"

Dill ran out to the porch, pulling on his coat, and waved his arm, *down, down*, to tell them to *fucking turn off their lights*, and then waved his arm again to tell them to *go around, go around the fucking back*, fuckers, and then he followed their car on foot to the shed and the barn, where the banker earlier that night had threatened to deposit Dill and his belongings and his eleven animals, saying, "No one on earth could take much more of this."

"More of which?" said Dill, because if he knew what piece was worst, he might be able to shut it up or turn it off or stamp it out.

"More of you." Which was really unfriendly.

The banker's esteem for Dill had been on a long steady decline, but it had started out so high and proceeded downward so slowly (Dill suspected it had begun its descent a few days after they met) that it had taken years and years. Even if Dill *had* somewhat approximated the nearly supernatural version of himself the banker had imagined on their introduction, Dill was destined to fall somewhat. Law of familiarity. Add to that, Dill had been at the height of his professional (and therefore sexual) powers when they met and he hadn't yet gone mad: the director of investigations the very month he and Annabelle had completed six new investigations and been all over the news. Their crew was small, fresh, a renegade rag-stitched team that year, not quite respectable, but better than respectable. Runaway successful. After that month, even as their little group grew, stretched, strengthened, *organized*, moved out from under him, and turned into a giant nonprofit Godzilla, Dill himself began to lose traction, and it was an awfully long way down from what the banker thought he was getting. One can only imagine the lasting (likely lifelong) disillusionment Dill had bestowed on the banker. The banker would forever see the world differently and worse because of Dill, as a place where beauty is suspect and love flawed. Well, boo-hoo, Dill thought. Welcome to the world, asshole. I never told you to love me that way.

So when the auditors showed up the third time, he thought for sure he was coasting along the seafloor now, that this was as low as it got: waved out of the game, sent home in shame with his mitt, diminished to ashes in the banker's eyes, threatened with expulsion from the (albeit rocky) Eden of his marriage. He knew exactly who they were this time—Cleveland Smith, 34, and Janey Flores, 20—had run their plates, done his research, because he was still a fucking professional.

At least he wasn't high anymore. That had to be worth something. No steps, no sponsor: he'd never been good at taking orders. No amends: the banker didn't want to hear it. That much had been explained to him. It was up to the wider public if they wanted to forgive him. He'd thought that being sober would be an improvement but it certainly was not. It couldn't get worse now.

But he was still wrong.

He walked over to the barn door, where back in the day Annabelle used to train new investigators by throwing cinder blocks at them, not that Dill recalled precisely what the point had been in that.

They got out of their car. Actual auditors, how Annabelle would have laughed!

Could they be FBI dressed as auditors? Though what could the FBI possibly want with him now? Sure, when he had investigators out all over the farms maybe. Besides, they didn't seem to know he'd been fired and that could be only inept big ag, not FBI. "A few more for your revolution," the older one, Cleveland Smith, said. She thought she was talking to the top man, which Dill did nothing to correct. Why should he?

"Since when did audits get into delivery?" he said, to let them know he knew exactly who they were.

"Cute," she said. "Funnyman."

"Tell me this," said Dill. "What is even the point in being an auditor? All you do is go and look at a place."

She was lifting chickens out of the car and letting them flap into the barn.

"Homeland food defense, right, that's what you call it?" he went on. "I bet you pulled this chicken out of a pile of manure eight feet high. That's what you're defending?"

This, while the younger one scraped excrement out of the backseat with a piece of cardboard. "What happened to the towels? I put towels back here," she was saying.

They'd brought a hell of a lot of chickens this time, Jesus. They were taking some out of the trunk now.

"I can't imagine what you're doing this for." He leaned against the car. "Getting shit on your vinyl, for what?"

Cleveland closed the trunk. "These are incidental removals."

"Oh, that's beautiful," he marveled. "What in the Jesus fuck is that supposed to mean? That sounds exactly like you morons."

At least they weren't activists. God save him from the activists.

The younger one walking around the side.

The fourth time they showed up, they'd figured it out: Dill had been fired. He was living in the shed now, where the banker had banished him, had helped him haul out a few bags of crap and said, "I'm not saying it's over. I'm saying it's almost over," and where back in the day Annabelle used to unwrap the buttonhole cameras and say to the investigators, "Equipment rule one: do not break the equipment."

The auditors drove up and said, "We hear you're not such a hotshot anymore."

Dill shrugged. "The movement spits people out."

It was true. The animal rights landscape was built on a graveyard of exiled heroes. Founders fight or fall out of fashion. There isn't always room for the old guard.

He didn't tell the auditors (because he was still a fucking professional) that if they thought they were the only ones still coming to him, they were mistaken. Investigators still turned up now and then (where else were they going to go? the needy little shits), though less, and they still left him long messages on his voice mail, "I need to talk . . ." though less because it obviously wasn't his job anymore, to talk to anyone, ever. What he was telling them all: Off duty. Out of service. Final sale over. Fuck off. And the investigators, one by one, were obeying (that was Annabelle—she had trained them to follow an order).

But the auditors were still coming. And a small part of him was grateful.

The fifth time—or was it the sixth?—they called first. By this time Dill had assembled a semblance of a living quarters back there, beddish structure, proper faucet, coffee apparatus, dogs in the yard, birds in the run, his mind flickering with memories:

Annabelle making the investigators do push-ups, drag tires. The banker opening the screen door, calling across the field, "Mimosas anyone?" wearing a T-shirt with a chicken on it in solidarity (ah, the banker loved him then), while the trainees prepared for twelve hours a day of bending over bottom-row cages, of shoveling piles of feces, faking a personality, fearing detection. A sort of *Art of War* boot camp. Investigators are half-wrecked soldiers.

Earlier that evening of the fifth or sixth time, the banker had come walking down from the main house, over the overgrown grass toward him. Dill had flung open the shed door to let in the last of the day's late-March light, and was fool enough to be excited when he saw him. Dill was kicked back on the cot, light dropping over his face in lines. A few chickens were poking around. When the banker arrived, Dill caught his face and his heart fell because he knew what the banker saw: a barely sober, jobless, rageless man. Dill had never been easy and now the banker could expect years of this at best—years, or however long it would take, if it ever did take. He stood in the doorway and said to Dill, "I don't see this getting any better."

"You're telling me," Dill said.

It was one thing, the banker explained, when Dill made so little money all those years and had an insane, overwhelming job. At least he had a purpose and conviction. It was another thing entirely now. No vision, no plans, no prospects. Who knew if he was high or not, since he was a masterful liar. His entire profession wasn't speaking to him.

"Publicly," put in Dill.

"What other kind is there? The definition of speech is that it's public."

"They talk plenty when no one's looking."

"I don't want to abandon you like everyone else."

"I think you're specifically supposed to *not* abandon me like everyone else. Isn't that the vow?"

"It's too destructive. People coming at all hours. I don't know if they're bringing drugs or animals or what. And where are all these stupid chickens coming from now? We talked about this. We had an agreement. I can't take it anymore."

"How do you think *I* feel?"

"Have you thought about looking for another place?"

"Apparently you thought of it for me."

"I hate it, I do."

"That fucking helps."

"Well."

And then he'd gone back up to the main house and switched off the lights, no wave, no call goodnight, and Dill lay there and thought, Fuck, fuck, fuck.

So hours later, when he jolted awake at the phone's buzz and knew the number, he was so weary, felt like such an emotional ruin, he didn't think he could talk without weeping.

"Not you two again," was what he said.

"Aw, be nice! You said call first. Here's your call. We're coming."

"Thanks for calling. Don't come."

"We're in a jam." It was the younger one, Janey.

"I don't care about your jams."

"He doesn't care about our jams," she was saying to the other.

"Tell him about the birds," he heard the other say. Cleveland and Janey. What kind of foolish names.

"You should see these birds. There must be twenty of them."

"I wish you two would get another sideline."

"You girls thirsty? I think they're thirsty."

"I'm hanging up."

"See you in an hour."

"An *hour*? Where are you? It's after one already."

"Yeah, and *we* have jobs to get up for."

Of course there had to be people like these two. People do all kinds of strange things.

"You are not doing this to me again," he said.

He hung up when he heard her laugh.

By the time they bumped up the driveway, it was three in the morning. They must have gotten turned around on those thin lightless roads, nothing but prisons and animal farms out there in the dark, NO TRESPASSING signs tacked up and shot.

They rolled to the shed, the dogs loping over, a couple of them letting out a weak bark, didn't even give the pretense of protection, these dogs. Dill put his face against the back window. "You couldn't let them out? They've been stuck in cages all night?"

"Their whole lives actually," said Cleveland.

They carried the cages into the barn.

"So listen," he said. "This has to be the last time." He couldn't look at the auditors, couldn't face them, or he might just crack into pieces right there.

This is what it feels like to be at the very bottom, he thought. Now I know. But even as he thought it, he knew that was wrong. Crouching on the cement in filthy clothes and broken shoes, taking out the hens one by one, he could see in his mind how much further down this could go, tossed off this land, homeless, alone.

He wasn't going to be there much longer, he explained. Unless he figured out some things fast, which wasn't a strength of his. Never had been. He was more the kind who couldn't take a hint. Stubborn. Sometimes this is called "persevering," though not in his case. Any day now the banker was going to come out that door over there and tell Dill to get off his property. The banker wasn't going to have a rifle in his hand when he said it, but the guy could get a tone in his voice worse than a gun to the head. So future hens had to go elsewhere.

He said all this while he gently lifted the hens away from one another because they were starting to clump together in the corner of the barn. He didn't know where to advise them to take the hens, he said. He'd been shuttling most of them over to the sanctuary, though they'd told him under no circumstances was he to come back. That's pretty much the line everyone was taking with him these days. And you know what? He was tired, just exhausted. Just fuck it. And now look at this, the fucking hens were clumping again. Did the auditors see this? The hens were all huddled up. They always did that when they got here. They were so used to being in those tiny cages that they were terrified of the space, all that air, the roof high overhead, and above it sky, terrible freedom, terrified, and they gathered themselves together into a clump and each tried to get into the middle. And they suffocated to death. Every time some of them died. Did the auditors know that? It wasn't that they were stupid, like the banker said. In fact there are things about birds that would shock the layperson. There are intelligences in a hen that would amaze you. You think we can breed out in a couple hundred years what took a couple hundred million to put in? No, you just had to be patient. If you made it through the first night and day with them, they were okay, they started to get it, clumped a little less each day. You got past the danger zone. Sometimes you have to just *stay* there with them, keep them from killing themselves. Did the auditors know that each time they brought hens here, he stayed with them all night and most of the next day, just like Annabelle used to do, lifting them off of each other one by one—and they were so light, little balls of feathers the layers were (not like their gentle fat sisters, the "broilers," what kind of disgusting appellation to give an animal)—and that within days they knew his hands and voice so well that they followed him around the barn as he filled their water and poured more feed? That by the time they were ready to go to the sanctuary he'd named every one?

They laid eggs all over the barn. They were bred not to sit on their eggs but one sometimes did and last time she wouldn't get up. Dill had brought food over to her because she'd never been able to sit on her eggs before and she wasn't going to get up for anything. Dill had burst into tears when he finally picked her up off her egg to bring her to the sanctuary, burst into tears because she was such an intelligent, unintelligent little birdie, thinking her job was to sit there, *stay no matter what.*

The way Annabelle used to hang around and talk to them. Annabelle always had a lot to say.

When he looked over at the auditors at last, he wasn't sure how much of all that he'd said. Not most of it, he didn't think. He was a bit dizzy. The auditors were gleaming. They spoke as if they hadn't heard a word he'd said so maybe he hadn't said any of it.

"What makes you think this guy is going to be any help? He's high on something."

"Fuck, I am *not*," Dill insisted. "For the last time, I'm not."

"Listen, we've got more than chickens this time."

He sat back on his heels. "Well, I don't have room for a fucking donkey."

"IS HE DYING or just sick? I can't tell."

"No, he's coming off some Iowa drug made in a lab by ninth graders."

"Help me get him up."

The bird mind. This is an animal whose brain has been evolving for two hundred million years.

Someone had Dill by the elbow and was leading him into the shed, though he needed to stay in the barn.

Got to unclump the hens.

"They'll be okay for fifteen minutes. Come on."

While the mammal mind evolved on one track, the bird mind evolved on another. A dynamic rolling forward, not a lizard stagnancy. Bird thought dove deep into the cortex, didn't skirt on the surface in large lumpy folds like humans. How was a bird supposed to fly with a big fat head? The bird brain is compact, has more neurons in a small space than any other animal.

He let them guide him to a chair and sit him down (because why not be a melodramatic asshole?), but when one of them came in with a bag of fast food he shot up from the table. "What is that?" he yelled. "You come in here with your hens in one hand and your bag of beef in the other? Don't you dare put that on my table."

She put napkins down in a pile. "Hey, when was the last time you ate?"

"You people make me sick," Dill said hoarsely, backing away. "Get out of here."

"You look like a junkie. You are so strung out. Sit down."

Birds. Their ingenuity and cunning, their language and tool-craft, their local cultures, their long memories, their astounding charisma, their individual personalities. Some species routinely pass intelligence tests that apes and dogs and human children fail.

"You think we don't know who you are?" said one. "It's black beans and tomatoes. A side of guacamole. No meat. No cheese."

"Hold the sour cream," said the other.

He dropped his hands. "Taco Bell? This tasteless shit? I've got a jar of peanut butter if you wanted dinner."

What a handful this guy, the younger said with her chin.

And they *fly*.

He sat down and ate.

He'd had three gooey burritos and a fistful of chips. He didn't feel like he was going to pass out anymore. The women—Janey and Cleveland, he recalled now—looked a bit overcome by the trans-formation. "Wow, you look like you just stepped out of a Calvin Klein ad."

He knew it. He'd always been like that, his whole demeanor could say, I'm in charge. Hair pushed back, I-don't-care shoulders, bad-boy stubble.

"You were starving, you idiot."

He sat back. His hair fell over an eye in a jaunty lock. "All right. I'm listening. What's the bright idea? Lay it."

They were a peculiar match, these two. The older one, Cleveland, cleared her throat. "We think we can do better than two by two like Noah's ark."

"Sorry, I don't speak Bible. What are you talking about?"

"The thing about 9/11 . . ."

The younger one looked skeptical.

"I don't see where you're going with this," Dill said.

"That was a grand gesture," Cleveland went on. "Troy. Pearl Harbor. No one misunderstood."

"This is sounding pretty radical."

"We think you might be interested in a grand gesture. And we might be interested in pulling one off."

He gave a dismissive wave. "Kill thousands of people? Sure, it's a grand gesture. But come on. Not doable. Where are you going to get thousands of people? Besides, what's the point in that? Everybody does that. That comes from uncreative minds. The same minds that build parking lots. The minds that shop the mall."

The other one, Janey, held up her hands. "I'm sorry. Who are you two? What are you talking about?"

"How should I know? You tell me."

"Pearl Harbor . . ." she said, disgusted. She leaned forward. "Okay, see this. Mysteriously from a farm one night all the chickens disappear, every single one."

"That's millions."

"A small farm. Say a million."

"You 'incidentally remove' a million birds. What are you going to do with a million birds?"

"Put a little fear in the hearts of Americans."

"They won't be afraid. They'll be confused."

"They'll imagine it," said Janey. "All those birds. *Missing.* It's wild, it's disorienting, it's beautiful. People will find something in it."

"Like what?"

"A message."

"The birds are gone?"

"The birds are free," said Cleveland.

"Free the birds," Janey corrected. "Jesus Christ. One phrase to remember."

"Free the birds," said Cleveland. "It's poetic."

"It's dumb," said Dill. "What do you do with the chickens?"

"That's part of it, the mystery," said Janey. "Where did the chickens go? Suddenly the chickens have agency."

"Where *do* they go?"

"'Free the birds.' Think of it. It's a public service announcement."

"You can't bring a million birds here."

"We come up with a plan for that."

"A plan for a million birds."

"We figure it out. You help."

"I will not help," said Dill. "Free the birds. Fuck's sake."

"We thought it was pretty catchy."

"Since when are you into sending a message? I thought you weren't into that."

"We're not doing it to send a message. *You're* doing it to send a message."

"I'm *not* doing it. But why are *you* doing it?"

Janey looked at Cleveland, who coughed a little and said, "They failed the audit."

Dill sat back.

"Farms that fail the audit ought to be stripped of their UEP status," said Cleveland stiffly, "or be subject to other measures."

Stripped of their . . .

"The audit bit isn't necessary," said Janey.

"Of course it's necessary," said Cleveland.

What in the goddamn fuck . . .

"We have a farm in mind," Cleveland went on. "A place where we know someone on the inside."

"A place where *you* know someone on the inside," said Janey.

Oh.

Got it. Goddamnit. Of course.

"Except one problem," he said at last. "She's not inside anymore, obviously."

"You could ask her."

"We don't even have any idea where she is." He always used first person plural when he lied. "Besides, no one would ever do that with you. Especially her." He could feel his voice getting louder. "Because it's impossible. Impossible to organize, impossible to get them out, impossible to find places to put them. And because it's meaningless. They'll just order more hens. They'll fill up the farm the next week. And anyway I'm through having crazy people in my life. I've had enough crazy."

"I can see that. Told you he couldn't do it. Did I tell you that, Janey?"

"I don't have to prove anything to you," he said.

"Don't worry, you aren't."

"You know what? I don't want to hear another word. We're done. Quit bringing your goddamn chickens here, and your fucking corporate tacos, and fuck you, by the way."

"Fine," said Cleveland, gathering herself up. "Come on, Janey." Janey rose, looked uncertain.

But Dill jumped to his feet. "Get the fuck out of here so I can spend ten hours unclumping the chickens you brought here."

"Maybe we should help him unclump," said Janey.

Cleveland was out the door. "You call us when you're ready."

"Never happen." He followed them out.

"Yes, it will," Cleveland called back. "You need us."

He picked up some gravel and threw it at their car as they got in. "Forget I live here!"

"Jesus, what next?" was the last thing he yelled as they drove off.

And in the morning, after many hours of unclumping, he went out into the sunshine. He was exhausted and hungry again but he'd eaten all the burritos. His back hurt. Some of the hens from the last time the auditors had come were out in the run, taking their morning constitutional. They spotted Dill and came toward him.

Moving in a line along the fence, they looked like emissaries from another planet with their thin heads and round eyes, their inexpressive faces, yet clearly on a mission of friendship. Neither side had quite figured out how to communicate beyond pleasantries, but here they all were, together. When they finally caught up to Dill, he said, "Well, what do you want?" They gathered around him and looked out over the fields.

THE BANKER WAS AT WORK. Dill snuck back into the main house through the basement, like he did every day, helped himself to a few handfuls of cereal, noted that the banker had cows' milk in the refrigerator—the poser was no longer even posing. He sat down at the computer and began scrolling through his usual sites. He used a ghost browser so that none of the world's many assholes could see what he was looking at. It was Dill's job to know what certain assholes were up to and their job to know what he was up to back.

Or, rather, *used* to be Dill's job.

While he was letting his mind skirt over the pages, thoughts relax into off mode, the door opened and the banker walked in. He saw Dill. Sighed.

Dill sighed back. Removed his hands from the keyboard. "I'll go."

"It doesn't matter."

"All right."

"I was going to come find you."

Uh oh.

"I have some news." The banker sat down at the edge of the sofa. "I've been assigned to open a branch in Egypt."

It took Dill a while to remember *bank*, branch of the *bank*.

"I'll be gone six weeks."

"Okay."

"That should give you enough time to find a place."

Ah, and there it was. At last.

He'd been expecting it for so long, he was shocked at the sharp pain, his brittle chest tightening and cracking, limbs breaking.

"I'd like you to be out when I get back."

The banker, his small body, his eyelashes, his mouth. The banker, who'd let Dill stay all this time. God, Dill loved him for that.

"Okay," said Dill.

"You *and* the animals."

Well, at least *one* of the animals was the banker's—that fucking fatass cat. Once Dill was gone he bet the banker would let the thing outside and that'd be the end of the songbirds around here. Oh, just think what this place would be like in a few years. A pool, a rose garden. Lawn. Dill didn't doubt the limit of the banker's bad ideas.

"I'm sorry," the banker was saying. "You must have known. We both did. Things haven't been right between us for years and . . ."

His voice, his moans, the way he hummed while he cooked, his brown skin. His suits, yes, even his suits. His hands. Dill loved the banker's hands. His forgiveness, Jesus, the number of times he had forgiven Dill. Dill had had no idea how much he'd needed that. His sense of humor—not that it had been in evidence much lately, but the banker could be very funny, the smarty-pants.

His name was Dev—Dev and Dill—but Dill had thought of him as the banker from the earliest hours, at first for the humorous incongruity of himself with a banker, later as an endearment, and eventually as a symbol of the alienation between them, *the banker*.

"We aren't helping each other. That's the problem. If I thought I could help—but that's not happening."

But now Dill was no longer listening. His mind was drifting, first into the past, the banker's fingers in his hair, a flash of it, then into the future and all it might hold, the horror. And then he found he was deciding. In fact he found he'd planned to all along.

Come on, it was a great idea. Of course it was a great idea.

"We need to move on, both of us."

Dill would have the old space for six weeks. Plenty of time. He'd always been best when he was working.

"Who knows. This is my fault too. I let you do whatever you wanted . . ."

The auditors were right. They needed Annabelle. Green Farm was perfect. Only she could begin to get the number of people needed together. Only she could inspire the kind of crazy necessary to pull the threads of this rug. Yeah, couldn't do it without her. Could he convince her? The auditors thought so.

But no.

No way. Not a chance.

"Maybe some of your friends could put you up for a while until you get back on your feet."

But what if he sent the auditors? Right to her place, because of course he knew where she was. She needed to see them, get a load of these two in their getups, let them ask her face to face, in her home—and Dill thought the shed was bad! He would tell them exactly what to say, and what not to (who sent them, for one, best to bring in Dill later, after she agreed. It'd never occur to her that he'd reveal her location).

All he needed was to make her intrigued enough to listen, to imagine.

It'd give him something to do while utterly falling apart.

"Hey, are you hearing me?" said the banker.

To give the auditors a chance, yes, not to put a finger on the scale or slide an ace into their hands, but to give them the slightest chance.

The banker had come and put it in his lap, saying, Here you go. Here's how you'll do it. It's all right here.

"See, this is what I'm talking about. This is exactly what I'm not going to miss."

So that night in the shed he texted them, *Let's talk*, and when they arrived, he gave them directions and instructions. To give the auditors a chance and, yeah, he'd admit, also to royally give the banker the finger and, sure, maybe to send Annabelle a little salute, a teasing wave (knock, knock, who's there?), a gesture in the form of two auditors, nudged forward toward her, to say, I see you your disappearing act and I raise you two auditors, to say, I *dare* you, and also—he realized after they'd driven off and after the banker had packed his suitcase and said, "So we have an agreement, yes?" (hey, it was his own fault if he wanted to make another "agreement" with Dill) and left in a car, and Dill heard nothing for a while, not from them, him, her, or anyone, and he was alone with his seventeen animals (he'd kept a few hens)—to say, to whisper (but to whom?), Come back.

A: No, I'm not "comfortable." You tell me how I'm supposed to be comfortable.

Q: That was a courtesy question.

A: Why don't we skip you being courteous?

Q: All right, can we bring you anything before we begin?

A: There you go again. What are you going to bring me under the circumstances? Let's get this over with. What do you want to know? They showed up and asked if I would help and I saw no reason not to. That's what happened.

Q: Were you expecting them?

A: No, the biggest surprise was them showing up in the first place. I'd been there over a year and not one person had found me.

Q: You were hiding?

A: I was . . . resting.

Q: You were "resting." On a chemical waste contamination site.

A: Yeah, and as soon as I saw them out there in the fog I thought, That's it. I'm done for. I took them for you, you see. Not you specifically, but your kind. Come to make me pay for my sins. Word had come down, I figured. My name was on the board. I was surprised by what they came in on—a plastic raft, a level up from a blowup.

Q: What did you imagine?

A: I mean, I didn't think you'd float in from overhead, blowing the trees around.

Q: Not our style. That's a myth.

A: Figures. Still I thought they'd be more professional. But no, they'd driven down the dirt road, past the signs that said Keep out unless you want to grow an extra finger. Left their car in the debris, carried the raft through the stalks to the cold muddy river. Then, my name in their fists, they pushed off the shore with their plastic paddles, drifted between low clouds and brown water, until there I was, hearing the unmistakable sound of paddles on the water. "Quiet," I told the birds, and looked out. Sure enough, the fog opened, and I saw them coming crookedly toward me. I was ready for them and they for me. We eyed one another like that—with knowing—so there was no fooling around when they lifted their paddles and let the raft float over the oily water the final few feet.

Q: And they were wearing disguises?

A: Yeah, I knew you'd have them, uniforms of some sort, but I thought they'd be different. Robes or something.

Q: Robes? Like graduation?

A: Well, no.

Q: Like a shower?

A: Just forget it. Anyway I called out, "Those are some rotten clown costumes. Are you trying to make the kids cry?"

Q: That sounds like fooling around.

A: They can take it.

Q: So they came onto your . . . house?

A: Not at first. Their raft just bumped against the side and bounced away before they could grab on. I was laughing. "Bring that scrap of plastic around this way," I said. I keep (excuse me, *kept*) a boat at the ready and a couple more in the stages of dis/repair that I like, my birds' names painted on the sides, Poquito Más, Wayway, Waygo, bobbing there in my contaminated river. I held out a plank for them to grab onto. I said a little grandly, "Come for me at last!" to let them know I knew what was happening and that I wasn't going to make a fuss, I'd go quietly, because why waste everyone's time. We were all excessively polite. They apologized for getting river water on my dress when they came aboard.

Q: Your dress?

A: The blue one with the lace edging. The perfect dress for the occasion, I was thinking, and I didn't even know they were coming.

Q: Somehow we can't imagine you in a dress.

A: Then you can't imagine much. They don't make you do research? I always wear a dress. Well, not now, of course. But this hardly counts.

Q: So they came onto your "house" and got water on your "dress."

A: Yeah, I sat them at the table and gave them each a short glass of rum because I like to see people with a drink in their hand. "You came a bit sooner than I expected," I said.

They looked surprised. "You knew we were coming?"

"I had an idea," I told them. "I didn't know when. I've been having symptoms. Headaches, blackouts. It's fine. I'm done here anyway."

They were shifting in their seats, ducking under Roy. I had the windows out. It was, what, the first week of April? Warmer than usual. Roy was flying in circles in and out the window, screaming. They looked so nervous, I felt like telling them, Relax, I'm the one who should be worried. The cicadas were making sounds like sprinklers.

"Let's start with you telling me what comes next," I said. I folded my hands. "I'd like to know how it all works."

They looked at each other. "That's why we came to you," they said. "We need your help."

Help? I studied their faces. I was confused. Help with what?

Wait a minute.

My understanding that I understood what was happening rotated ninety degrees from *yes* to *maybe*, and another ninety degrees to *no*, and then another ninety degrees back to *maybe*, until I was dizzily seeing the situation. Fucking hell. I was almost disappointed.

Dill. He'd gotten me good this time. He must think a lot of these two to tell them where I am, I thought. These two must be the second coming. They damn well better be for him to compromise my security like this. Nice of him to drop in, the asshole. I realized right then, wistfully, how much I wanted to be gone, out of my house, far from this land, the only earth I've known.

"Oh, I thought this was something else," I said.

Of course I'd been living off the grid, so to speak, for quite a while. It is really hard to be hard to find. But it came naturally to me. It was no problem for me not to be around. When I first started out, we used fake names. You invented a past, that was part of it, you did up the documentation. But that's old-fashioned now. These days the investigators go legal all the way down, birth to dying days—farm to table, as they say. But for me it was easier to have nothing to do with it. Captain Nemo style, submerge and emerge and re-submerge, let the water close over your head, sink thousands of leagues, leave only a ripple.

Q: So you realized they weren't us.

A: Yeah. Now I knew who they were. I'd been hearing about these two, and they looked exactly like that in those uniforms, like postal workers come to deliver the mail.

Q: You had been hearing about them, though you were "off the grid."

A: I hear things. Don't shut every faucet. Let one drip.

Q: So what did you say to them?

A: "You're the auditors," I said. "Okay." Not what I expected, but no doubt we all expect different from what we find out in the river with the junk, expect different from the world and from ourselves. But we learn soon enough that expectation is for amateurs.

"So you've gone postal," I said. "I can respect that. Or at least relate to it. What do I have to do with it?"

Then they piped up with their plan. Empty a farm, they explained for a while.

"That," I said, "is the weirdest idea I have ever heard."

The thin one did a thing where she looked around and said, "I doubt that."

Q: Did they say how they would do it?

A: That's what I said. "How are you going to pull off a stunt like that?"

The bigger one swiped off her hat. Dropped it on the table between us. "We're going to pick them up and carry them out," and I said, "Why?" and she said, "What kind of question is that?" and I said, "If you can't answer it, what are you coming to me for?" and she said, "Why would I be here if I didn't have an answer?"

The thin one shot down her rum.

"All right," I said. "How many investigators do you think you'll need?"

"You tell us."

"How are you going to transport all those birds?" I said.

"Are you going to answer questions or ask them? Because so far you're wasting our time."

I said, "What makes you think you're not wasting mine? Hey, you came to me." I stood up. "Get out."

Q: At which point they left?

A: No, no, I got up to get the rum bottle. I poured us out another round. Old habit. The hostess's version of "keep your hands where I can see them." I sat back down and we were all a little calmer, Roy crawling on the back of my chair.

"Do you have a farm in mind?" I said.

"Yeah," they said, "we do," and they didn't say anything else.

We sat there and I let it wash over me, the whole story. I knew. Green Farm. I could feel the air pass by me, the water swish around me and away, the sky go by, as if I'd come to a heavy stop and the earth had moved on without me.

Q: We're familiar with the sensation.

A: Yeah, Dill'd gotten me good this time. I'd followed the bread crumbs of his mind. It isn't as though it had never occurred to me, of course.

They were waiting for me to answer. "To Dill," I said at last and raised my glass. They looked uncomfortable. "What, did he think I wouldn't know how you got here?"

"Well, we . . ." said one, but the other stayed her with her hand. "So you'll do it?"

I set down my glass. "What happens to the birds?"

"That part is still a little vague," one admitted.

"You decide," said the other.

I windmilled my hair into a bun, considered.

"I don't know about this message bullshit. Birds are freedom and Helen of Troy and all that."

"Free the birds," said one.

"We can work on the message," said the other.

"No message," I said. "You take a chicken you tell no one. It's between you and the chicken and God. It's the only thing I like about you two and that foolishness you've been up to in the henhouses."

"How do you know about that?"

"Look," I said, "it's my farm. My family. We take them. That's what we do it for. We don't do it so Americans can watch us on YouTube."

"But isn't that the point?" they said.

"The point is not to use them. For a single fucking hour. Is it so much to ask? Not for their eggs, not to eat, not to make a point," I said. "Agreed?"

They agreed.

I put another rum in their hands and we moved out to the deck and watched the sun drop. The birds turned in irregular angles above us, Roy watching from the ledge. The auditors pulled their hats over their ears. It was getting cold.

On the other side of the riverbank the lost civilization begins. It melts into the trees and spreads for two miles, the village evacuated after the contamination. Rebar and concrete, rotten wood, all the categories of the plastic family, plaster walls caved in, sidewalks broken and buckled, piles of bricks. There's evidence of a former pier—cement posts and a few splintered planks.

My house looks like a waterlogged ship dragged to the far bank and left there, half-submerged, a roof of tin strips. It's part forest, part trash heap, nest-like, made from the junk I found there. It blends into the landscape like certain animals and insects. It imitates its surroundings. Architects strive lifetimes for as much. "No house here," the visitor thinks, scanning the shore. "Wait, someone's in there. Look, there's a light." Wet leaves, slow-moving water, a few trees that twist against a red sky. The contamination tints the air at a certain hour. My house leans as if it's toppling into the river, as if it's gripping the earth, barely hanging on. Like a photo snapped at the moment of landslide.

But what were we talking about?

Q: The auditors.

A: Oh yeah. Would it be all right if we took a short break? I'd like to stretch my legs, such as they are.

Q: Certainly.

A: Thanks. Ah, that's better. Will this take much longer? I should get going—

Q: You've got time.

A: Where the hell are we anyway?

Q: So how long did the auditors stay at your "house"?

A: A while. Let's see. First I fixed their shoes.

Q: Their shoes?

A: Yeah, I said, "Tell you what, you two. We have got to do something about those shoes. You can't wander around the farms like that."

"What's wrong with our shoes?" they said.

"Those soles look like they just walked out of a factory. Anyone could find you with a shoe like that. What you need is a good file to scrape the soles off." And I showed them the bottom of my Mary Janes.

I went to the toolbox to see what I could find. It was dimming by that time, night birds, dropping sky. The wind was rising, the cold settling in, Roy tucking himself into his spot. I knew they had to leave soon or they'd paddle through the puddle dark and maybe never find their way and be lost forever. But I kept them around a little. I prefer to go solo these days, but I made an exception.

Q: All right, so you "fixed" their shoes?

A: Yeah, I filed them and put in a few notches so they wouldn't slide. I could fix yours too, if you have any tools.

A WOMAN WITH LONG DARK HAIR wearing a checked dress came up the driveway on foot. She rolled a small suitcase. The dogs met her on the path. She leaned down to greet them, then walked on. At the other end of the drive, a man was sitting on the porch. He had reddish hair and boyish dimples that appeared when he squinted at the figure approaching. He had his feet up but when he saw her, he let them drop. Then he seemed to change his mind and put them up again. He held that position until the woman arrived at the bottom of the porch steps. She let go of the handle of her suitcase. The dogs lined up behind her.

"What do you think?" he said.

"I'm weighing."

"I heard you weighed. I heard we're on."

"The scale is too big. We can't plan it ourselves."

He hesitated, then shook his head. "Oh, no way. No."

"He'd know if it could be done."

"We aren't getting the fucking band back together. He was never really part of it."

"He was never not part of it."

The man said no, the woman said yes. And the man said no, and the woman said yes. Like the old days.

They both turned their faces to the sky.

SPARROWS OVERHEAD. A flock circling in uneven loops. Is it instinctual, these ovals, these spirals, this retracing of one's steps? Do all animals, even all natural phenomena, move like that, have this in common, where everything you see is moving, but nothing is getting anywhere? The solar system, time, water as it falls from the sky and rises back into it, birth and death, work and home, a father and a son tossing a ball back and forth on the lawn, chicken, egg, chicken, egg, numbers looping back to the original ten over and over with the numeral furthest to the left joining in late and slow like an old farmer going up and down the hospital corridor with his walker after a stroke. Only the universe is a long breath out.

In nature chickens wander in crooked circles through their little villages, pace out their territory, climb up and down the trees at night, prance around each other in play, courtship, battle, while the lowliest chickens revolve on the outskirts, get picked off by predators. But their egg-manufacturing counterparts, their cousins locked in cages, do not loop like the rest of creation. They stand, push a step or two through their cell mates to sip some drops of water, their tender feet cutting into the steel.

Which of these chickens do humans most resemble: the ones roaming in ovals—a school yard, a campus, a neighborhood? Or the genetically modified monsters—wobbling inside our boxes, clutching our pieces of plastic and metal, mincing and crimping in our shoes, snapping at each other in tight spaces, poking our various machines that swivel or light up or open in simulation of activity, "amusement," "exercise," "work," "love"?

· · ·

Earth has fallen a long way in hundreds of millions of years as it swept in its glaciers, spewed out its lava, glistened and blued and whitened and greened, lifted its animals off their front feet, or brought them down from the branches, or sent them into the sky.

The earliest bird, the *Archaeopteryx*, appeared in ever more astounding variations through the long Jurassic and Cretaceous periods, only to diminish with the rest of the dinosaurs, but rise again in the Paleocene and on into the future.

The *Gallus*, the wild jungle fowl of the early Eocene, or "pre-chicken," tore along the ground through the trees. The ice swelled and receded, and the *Gallus* split into species and subspecies, constellations of them spreading and splintering, until a mere nine thousand years ago, when a band of her descendants, *Gallus gallus domesticus*, began to travel the world with the great explorers looking for more than their world had to offer.

At last, around 1600 CE, *T. Rex*'s pretty little niece stepped off the boat onto the wet sand shores of North America.

THIRTEEN YEARS BEFORE Cleveland took the hen, Jonathan Jarman Jr. (24) met Annabelle Green (18) for the first time when he arrived at her father's farm with his new invention.

He had a small-size demo in his trunk, along with two fifty-packs of glossy brochures—pending patent number printed inside each one, proving that his invention was not merely a variation on the cage design already used in England, but a substantially improved version for an American audience, an invention he hoped (here when farmers imitated him—harmless teasing when his family wasn't present—would stick a forefinger into their collar and tug in a parody of nervousness) would change the face of egg farming in America.

Jonathan Jarman Jr., the only son of the Jarman Egg Farm family, was going from farm to farm peddling.

The word *peddle* raises the image of a man in a hat going door to door, but Jonathan knew that's not how it was done in this industry. Farms held a million to twenty million birds each, looked and sounded like miniature militarized cities, the largest surrounded by biosecurity trucks and fences and checkpoints. No one was going to be driving up and asking for a glass of lemonade and the kindness of strangers at the door. No, he'd done it the right way, had followed his father's advice. The right way was to hook yourself up to a research project, present your findings at egg conferences, shake hands with the farmers over a period of years—all of which Jonathan had done, while getting multiple degrees in design and engineering—then ask the farmers one by one if you can come over and show them what you want to do.

At first he had made the mistake of calling it a "sales pitch," which made the farmers nervous. He said he wanted to show his demo and explain why the farmer—all egg farmers—should replace their conventional (a.k.a. "battery") cages with the new "enriched" Jarman Star Cage Systems. But he'd had very, very little luck even getting appointments because of the unfortunate coincidence that there was no reason in the world for a farmer to change over to Jarman's new enriched cage system. It was a huge hassle, required vast conversions that were stupidly expensive, tens of thousands of dollars *per barn*, and besides that, the farmers said, the hens were fine the way they were! Jonathan's *own father*, Jarman Sr., hadn't switched to his son's design, citing these same facts. Besides, the farmers said, who knew when lawmakers persuaded by animal rights extremists would pass a law outlawing all cages, old and new and imagined, and force everyone to go cage free like communists? It made no sense to buy those fancy cages, so no one would let him come deliver his pitch.

Finally at his wife's urging Farmer Jarman Sr. intervened. He talked his son into calling it a "consultation," not a sales call— much more palatable. And he phoned all his farmer colleagues across the country and urged them to let his son give his presentation and write up his report, that's all, the cost of which would be burdened mostly by Jarman Sr. himself. All right, the farmers said, if he put it that way, okay. They understood the father and his predicament, them all having children, and knowing how hard it was to raise farm kids these days. World was a different place. Ah well. What are you going to do? Probably Adam himself had this trouble. Jesus likely gave the Father a hard time. Aw, let the kid come and do his presentation, what's the harm? The farmers would even pitch in a little, see to it that the Jarman son had a place to sleep and plenty of scrambled eggs and toast for a few days. They'd welcome him like family, cut him a small courtesy check for his final report. The farmer's world had changed, all right, but common loyalty and neighborliness among farmer families still existed.

But just so it was clear: the farmers didn't want to spend any actual *time* with the son, of course. They were busy, and in any case they didn't want to hear from a child what they should do differently, especially if it would cost ridiculous amounts of money. That kid was something else again. The farmers had twelve or twenty or even thirty barns of a hundred and fifty thousand birds each to tend to. They were trying to ship four million eggs a day. Besides, they had their own troubles. What did Farmer Jarman Sr. think *their* kids were up to? Not exactly big helpers, mind you. Fine, if the kid wanted to come, but did the farmers have to sit and listen to him too?

Farmer Jarman had an idea: What if the farmers assigned Jonathan Jr. to give the presentations to the offspring of the farmers, many of them in the same age range, give or take? They could all lead one another around and consult and write reports and have meetings when the conference room wasn't being used for company business. Similar to playdates, now that everyone was a little older and didn't require the same level of supervision. Give them all something to do. Almost like a youth group, Bible study, science club. And who knew, some of them might get interested in the egg business. (None of them wanted anything to do with it and it was just sad.) Some might, the farmers suggested quietly, find suitable husbands and wives in this manner, since the dates the kids were bringing around were, to put it mildly, preposterous.

(The farmers couldn't know at this point that the plan would backfire later, when these kids—having been schooled by Jonathan Jarman Jr., who over time would become a very convincing guy, to say nothing of Annabelle—would go on to run their fathers' businesses into the ground with the changes they made once their fathers retired. They spawned an entire expensive movement toward enriched, then cage-free, then free-range systems, which swept the country as the younger farmers grew up and took over. Some of the sons and daughters left the business disgusted. Some became undercover investigators for Annabelle. Some, combining their conscience with their lifelong lust to be unlandlocked, took to the seas on pirate ships, chasing whalers and fisher boats, and the older farmers stood back aghast and blamed Farmer Jarman for it all.

But this was much later.)

So on that warm September afternoon when Farmer Robert Green Sr. came out to reception to welcome Jonathan Jarman Jr. as a favor to the Jarman family, both men—Jonathan Jr. and Farmer Green—were feeling optimistic: Jonathan because Happy Green Farm was small, only a million birds, and might be ready to grow, which could mean a new barn with his cages. Farmer Green because he had persuaded his daughter, Annabelle, to take Jonathan Jr. around. Annabelle showed aggressively little interest in farming (though she showed more interest than Farmer Green's only son, Robbie Jr., who initiated gagging sounds every time Farmer Green brought it up). Farmer Green wondered if Annabelle might become more interested if she had to spend time with a smart, good-looking man like Jonathan Jr., and he suspected that Jonathan would behave especially smart and good-looking around Annabelle, who at eighteen was becoming a beauty.

Father Farmer Green was not mistaken in his suspicions. On that September afternoon, when he brought out his lovely daughter (*And behind door number three . . . !*—he'd come of age with *The Price Is Right* rerunning in the background), he watched with satisfaction Jonathan Jr.'s face. Annabelle smiled shyly.

"Well, I'll leave you two to it then," said Farmer Green, rubbing his hands together. "I know you'll come up with a fine plan for us." He slapped Jonathan's back and hurried them out, telling Jonathan to save receipts for meals.

Farmer Green did not consider the possibility that after a minute and a half in Annabelle's presence, Jonathan would fall irreversibly in love with her and, inspired by her beauty, manage to speak heroically on behalf of the hens and explain over the next few days his plan for enriching their lives, speak with more eloquence than he ever had so far mustered. Jonathan Jr. convinced her—and himself—of chickens' individual temperaments, of their desires and little-known sadnesses, their friendships, their surprising skill at conversation (all accurate, by the way). He got her to look at the hens in a new light, through the light of their love. Annabelle, who was already prone to tender thoughts about animals, including chickens, was awed by this older man and felt destined to love the chickens and him, to fight for their rights to enrichments. Jonathan managed to stretch the presentation process from three days to two weeks by adding several layers of evaluation, which he feverishly thought of late at night so as to be able to stay longer in the Green household. And after fifteen days, while on a visit to her grandfather's original family egg farm, now defunct and abandoned (due to certain nearby contamination) and surrounded by forest and river (a romantic spot for two egg farmers' children in love, despite the toxicity), Jonathan got Annabelle to promise to marry him. A week later he approached her father and formally, farmerly, asked for her hand.

That her father said yes seemed like a miracle to Annabelle and Jonathan, since she was only eighteen, but really it was a coup for the families. Both sets of parents were overjoyed and celebrated on the phone quietly (in fear that the youngsters might overhear their glee and repent their decision, since any idea parents approved of was probably no good). The parents were eager to join by marriage these two farms, cement these kids into the family business, and eventually leave both farms to two young adults who had become extremely interested in eggs (though they weren't interested in eggs, but rather *hens*) and enthusiastic about improving the farms (at this point the families hadn't paid a whole hell of a lot of attention to, had more or less forgotten, Jonathan's cage design, which had grown more and more avant-garde in mere weeks). The future of both farms was secured.

The families made the happy couple wait six months to marry, for prudence's sake—the kids had been dating only three weeks after all—and also because the two mothers wanted to plan the most imprudent, spectacular wedding in layer hen history. And that spring indeed the Jarman-Green wedding was a reckoning. The entire United Egg Producer membership was invited. Farmers flew in from every part of the country. Whole planes' worth of commercial egg farmers, their wives, and children landed on the tarmac and rode limousines out to the farm. (These included the small but growing group of smart young-adult children, whom the older farmers would years later say were "brainwashed" by Jonathan, and also by Annabelle, an inspiring spokesperson for her husband's design in those first years before she dismissed animal husbandry altogether and took off with some of the others in search of more radical strategies.)

The wedding was a smashing success.

Even Farmer Bristole came, representing the only large industrial egg farm in Maine (which would be raided six years later by the FBI after an undercover investigation led by Annabelle: Farmer Bristole would be charged with fourteen counts of animal cruelty, and his barns dubbed by Temple Grandin on CBS News "a filthy disgusting mess").

Even Farmer Parlin was there (he would go bankrupt after footage from an undercover investigation led by Annabelle and her evil spawn went viral and all of Parlin's major clients filed out the door, taking their business elsewhere, i.e., to other attendees of the wedding).

All these and many more arrived at Happy Green Family Farm on that spring afternoon, filled the local B&Bs, clapped and cried when the groom kissed the bride.

For about three years following the wedding, life could not have been better for the two lovebirds, the united Green and Jarman families agreed. The families waited with growing impatience for a baby to come of this marriage—though, they allowed, she was still a little young (nineteen, then twenty, then twenty-one)—and also with growing discomfort at the couple's ideas, which were spreading across the egg farmers' children like a broke yolk.

Then one day, the story goes, the son was seen driving through town, though the couple lived thirty minutes away. He was unshaven and grim-faced. He drove out to Happy Green Family Farm and pulled into the small lot. According to the administrative assistants watching out the window, he sat with his head on the steering wheel. He stayed like that for a good part of the afternoon, the sun moving across the sky, the farmhands stepping timidly around his car to their own. Finally Farmer Green came out. He got into the passenger seat. No one heard their conversation but it was clear the marriage had come to pieces.

Whatever Jonathan and Farmer Green decided between them that day was immediately revoked by the rest of the family. Both sides (for the families swiftly reverted to being sides, not a union) vehemently blamed the other.

According to her family she'd left him, and good riddance.

According to his he'd kicked her out because she was insane.

According to her family he'd driven her mad, what with his bizarre notions about chickens having confidants and dancing cotillions and doing math. He'd damaged her, perhaps permanently.

According to his family he'd had to wash his hands of a crazy wife, and he had been so heartbroken that he'd had to leave the egg business entirely and fall back on his graduate training. He went into the specifications of bottle design. More precisely, he oversaw certain design safety features in popular containers of gin, vodka, and wine coolers. He also did a line of Turkish rums.

(AS IT HAPPENS, he found out she was leaving the same day he found out he had cancer. I'm dying, he came home to tell her. But she was crying before he could speak. He could feel it coming, that she was going to leave him, though he had no idea why, had not understood her in months, and if he told her he was dying, it might change things between them, because that was how bad it had gotten—he had to hope for death to keep her around—but she said she had something to say before he could speak.

For a moment he thought she was going to say she'd joined the army, and he would tie her up and throw her in the closet. Then he thought she was going to say she'd found Jesus and was striking out on a mission. Then—God help him for this darling thought—that she'd changed her mind and wanted a baby.

Then he saw it: He didn't know what she was going to say. He didn't know her anymore at all.

This all took place in about three seconds because as soon as she said she had something to say, he said, "Don't say it. I don't want to hear it," because he sensed one way or another she was going to say, "I'm leaving," and if she didn't say it, she couldn't do it. How could you leave someone without telling them? His error. Of course the hardest part of leaving is telling the person. How did that not occur to him? And if she'd be quiet, maybe he could tell her about the cancer and then she couldn't leave. How could you leave someone who was dying?

But he couldn't bring himself to tell her about the cancer, because he couldn't take it if that was why she stayed. So they sat in silence, she crying a little. The next day she was gone. He didn't get the chance to tell her he might be dead before she came back.

As it happens, he wasn't dying. It was a mistake. Who gets a false positive the day his wife—the only woman he'd ever loved, by the way—decides to leave?

So he was dying and she was gone. Then a few days later he wasn't dying and she was gone. What a world.

"She's mentally ill," said his father.

"We're all mentally ill," said hers.)

JONATHAN JARMAN JR. stood in his kitchenette.

He was thinking, She is not doing this to me again, I won't have it.

That humorless man named for an herb was outside his door with two more of them, knocking, and now calling out, "We know you're in there, Jarman. We saw you from the lot."

Jonathan already knew they'd seen him from the lot. When he got home from work, they'd been waiting, the three of them scrunched into an old car, their faces against the glass. He had seen them see him. And he knew they'd stayed there when he went out for a run—a run he took to make certain what he was seeing. And they were still there when he got back. Then he'd gone into his condo and stood in various spots around the rooms—the "kitchenette," the "sun nook," the "half bath," his rooms castratingly adorable—wiping his face with a towel and thinking, I'm not allowing it, I can't have it, until the knock came. He didn't answer, just froze on the other side of the door, waiting and vowing.

He could hear through the door the women arguing in whispers.

"How smart is it to be doing this with a bunch of people who aren't speaking to each other?"

"Remember, this was your idea."

"Is that what you're going to go to every time? It was my idea?"

Dill called over them, "We're not going anywhere, Jarman."

Jonathan opened the door a chained three inches and let a triangle of light fall into the hall. "What do you want?"

It had been two years since she'd contacted him. He thought

he'd shaken her at last, made it out, escaped. But there was her sidekick, a little worn and thin. Dill.

"We're looking to move some chickens, Jarman."

"You've come to the wrong place. Chicken catchers are outside in the rain."

"We need more than that. We need an engineer," said Dill.

Jonathan sighed. He had no choice but to wave them inside, Dill and the two women wearing some kind of uniforms, and shut the door behind them so the neighbors wouldn't see him talking to them and mention it to Joy. What would he say? Bible people? Salesmen? He'd told her a little but really she had no idea how deep a hole he'd climbed out of to reach her. They took seats on the sofa. Where had he seen those uniforms?

"Look," he said, "you know I don't do that work anymore."

"She thinks you'll make an exception."

"You tell my wife she no longer qualifies for exceptions."

The women looked confused. He couldn't believe she'd sent them over without telling them.

"Annabelle," said Jonathan, "is my wife."

"Ex-wife," said Dill. "Divorced."

Their faces reacted, then recovered. "Who cares?" said the pretty one, pretty enough she should be on TV. "We're talking about a major removal."

"Are you even eighteen?" he said to her. "What has she gotten you into?"

"Ask me what I got *her* into."

"Even worse."

Dill said, "Jarman, up to me, I'd never see your smug face again, you know that. She insisted."

Then it struck him: auditor uniforms. That's what those were. Jesus. Annabelle was going to get into a fuckload of trouble this time. There weren't a lot of ways this could go. She'd wind up in prison for sure. He was furious. And exhausted.

"Why isn't she here asking herself?" he said.

"She's not available," said Dill.

"Neither am I." He got up. "We done?" He had to move. He didn't want them to see him shaking. "You tell her, she wants something from me, she's going to have to do better than send her little friends over here like Red Rover." He walked to the door. "You tell her to come by and say pretty please like the nice girl her daddy raised her to be. Show some manners."

AFTER THEY LEFT, Jonathan got into bed and lay in the dark thinking his life was probably over again. Every time she came back, she ruined it.

The night before with his girlfriend, Joy, he'd been so happy, so relieved without knowing it, so baffled by Joy's two little girls, who scared him, frankly. Joy had been helping one of the girls into her pajamas, but the top seemed to keep coming down backward, and then with an arm in the neck hole, and then inside out. In front of his very eyes it was becoming a hilarious, delightful, Chaplinesque game, and he was laughing, until he saw Joy's face and realized, no, wrong, not delightful. She'd played this game one too many times, and he had said, "Can I help?" in a voice that he hoped was beyond that of a stranger because the plan—which they'd discussed—was for him to "participate in family activities," for him to attach himself to them in a way other than hanging off the end as if off the edge of a cliff, for him to be enfolded, and to eventually move in, and they had decided that one way to head toward this was for him to "help." So he had said, "Can I help?"

She'd looked up gratefully and said, "Could you take her to brush her teeth?" meaning the other child, because he'd managed to do that with the child once before, somewhat successfully, so if it went well again, maybe it could be his "job" going forward. The child ran ahead of him into the bathroom and stripped off all her clothes—so now he wasn't sure it was appropriate for him to be in the bathroom with her—and hopped up onto the toilet. He stood in the doorway, uncertain. Surely he shouldn't go in? He could run back and ask Joy, but does one leave a child so small alone on the toilet? (He had messed up earlier on a similar point in an episode in the KidZ DanZ parking lot and had received shocked, angry words from Joy.)

How innocent they'd all been!

Now, lying in bed in his modern condo, where every appliance, tile, wall, and blind was the same eggshell white, he thought about that moment from the night before, how close he'd been to having the darkness of his life fully retreat. How charming that his difficulties might now amount to this: how to behave around a four-year-old girl. That was all ruined now. He'd known the minute he'd spotted Dill in the lot that his life with Joy was imperiled.

In the morning he texted Joy. *See you tonight, beautiful?* And on his lunch break he did something impulsive. He drove to a jewelry store and bought an engagement ring and, what the hell, a full wedding set for $14,000, and when the salesman asked if he wanted an inscription, he said yes, in the man's ring: NOW ONLY JOY. He went to her house, late, after the children were in bed. He needed Joy tonight, only Joy. She opened the door and let him in. They got into bed and he lay, heart bleeding in the dark, clutching her to him.

HE THOUGHT with luck that would be the end of it, but she came the next night, showed up alone in the rain. He was getting out of his car, had one foot on the ground, and he saw her there in a rain jacket, hood up. He could see the ends of her hair and the bottom of her dress, her rubber shoes. He gestured toward the door of his complex, but she shook her head—she really was one paranoid chick, probably thought the place was bugged—so he clicked open the lock and she got in. They sat in the dark listening to the rain.

"Good to know you're alive anyway," he said. "You might send a postcard now and then."

"I did better than a postcard and you sent them away."

"How do you know you can trust those two women? What makes you think they're not FBI? They look like someone stabbed those uniforms onto them with staple guns."

"I've looked into them. They're fine."

"Those are the kind that are going to land you in prison. Those people will get you killed."

"I wish you wouldn't tell me what to do."

"I wish you wouldn't live like a teenager."

"I wish you wouldn't talk like a parent."

He wanted to say, "I *am* a parent, almost." But almost is far from enough.

"Forget it," she said. "I don't know why I thought you would help." She opened the door.

Jesus, the woman gave him a headache.

"Stay," he said. "Come on. Stop it."

She closed the door.

"What do you need?"

"I thought they told you. We're moving some chickens."

"Why call on me? You know how to move a hen."

"It's a lot of hens." She let the hood down and pulled up her hair to shake it away from the hood and, God help him, he still loved her. Buying the rings seemed like a desperate move now because no matter what he did or what happened, he would do whatever she asked. He'd taken a vow in front of her father and his, and the entire egg community (his lifeblood no matter how much he resisted it), a vow to protect this goddamn cracked egg, and that's what he was going to do.

"Those two are involved?"

"A lot of people will be involved."

"I thought you hated people."

"When did I ever say that?"

"You said that."

"Well, I do."

"I thought you weren't doing this anymore."

"I wasn't."

"Looks like you are."

The thump of water was making rain stars on the windshield.

He let out a breath. "I have to get something out of it," he said at last.

"What do you want?"

"We do this one last thing and then you stop. For good."

The windows shone.

"Okay."

"Okay what?"

"I'll stop. I'm done. I'm retiring. After this one."

He didn't know what to say. "Really?"

"Yes."

What could it mean? He wasn't sure, but if there was one thing he knew about her, she kept her word, so he said, "What do you want me to do?" but if there was another thing he *should* have known by then, it was: do not make this woman any promises, because then she told him what she wanted him to do.

A: Yeah, I don't see how any of this is relevant but that's pretty much how it happened.

Q: He agreed.

A: More or less. He wanted to cut Dill out. I refused. I'd done everything with Dill from the time we met.

Q: Which was where?

A: At an ecoterrorist hangar bar outside X. He leaned in and said to me, "Who are you supposed to be, FBI?"

"I'm better than FBI," I told him. "I'm big ag."

Dill was the first person to lay it all out for me, tell me how it had all gone down. The Animal Liberation Front was over. Nothing left but vandalism and hubris and rubble. There were open rescues—people filming themselves taking animals. Little more than trespassing, and utterly ineffective. "I'll tell you this," I said. "You people are no match for my industry." I had a different vision, other areas of expertise, an alternative approach.

Q: Which was?

A: The employment-based investigation. Had never been done. We hired and trained our first two employees. Within months we were closing out investigations. In the first three years we did thirty-six investigations in eighteen states. We had convictions, raids, legislation, more press than we ever thought possible.

Q: And your husband?

A: He was the numbers man. He was good.

Q: What went wrong?

A: Yeah, the divorce. He didn't want to help after that.

Q: No, what went wrong with the investigations?

A: What do you mean? Nothing.

Q: But—

A: We grew. We influenced. Investigative units popped up all over the country. Nothing went wrong. Nothing's wrong.

Q: You left. You were, let's see, "resting." On a chemical waste contamination site.

A: Oh that, well.

THEY GATHERED, the four of them, she sweeping in in her dress, he strutting to the table, Janey and Cleveland in uniforms, walking in behind. They all sat down at a card table in Dill's shed. Then Dill and Annabelle argued for an hour.

First they argued about how many trucks they'd need. Then how many investigators. Then how many hours. Then how many birds fit on a truck. Then they seemed to be arguing about simple multiplication. Then they started saying their calculators couldn't be trusted. The calculators were "listening," even when off, at which point Dill turned to Janey and Cleveland and said, "You left your phones in the car, right?" One raised her hands, "How many times?" while the other said, "This is hopeless," and returned to the printouts she'd brought of the last audit, marking them up with a highlighter.

Next they argued about the size of the barns. Annabelle said four of one kind, two of another, and two singles. Dill said six of the eight barns were all the same now. Annabelle said she obviously knew the place better than Dill, and Dill said, "Remember Gemperlee." Annabelle lifted her chin and said, "Remember Norco." They leaned forward over the table and stared until Dill blinked.

Cleveland finally intervened. "If you two are finished, the last audit is right here." She held up the folder.

"Give me that," said Annabelle, reaching.

Then Jonathan arrived, in casual-corporate khakis. "Where's your husband, Dill?" he said. "I always liked that guy," and Dill made a horrible face.

• • •

Now Dill and Annabelle had their arms crossed in denial. Both were frowning. Jonathan glanced at his watch.

"It says so right here," Dill was saying, pointing to a page.

"I know it. I see it."

"What?"

"Barns 7 and 8 will be empty."

"Yes, that's right," Janey said with authority. "Depop, the week before our target date."

"Here are the housing specs." Cleveland passed Jonathan the folder.

"Fuck, what's the point in emptying a farm that's a quarter empty?" said Dill.

"Same point as emptying one that's full," said Jonathan. "No point at all."

"Let's wait. Put it off, say, three weeks."

"No, the timing is good," said Annabelle. "Ricardo takes his vacation at the end of April. He sees his mother in Puerto Rico."

"Who the hell is Ricardo?" said Janey.

"Oh, you guys don't have that in your file? Ricardo. He's always been there. Night security guard."

"Well, that's just great," Dill was saying. "Two empty barns. That brings it down to nine hundred K. Not even a million."

"A lot more than you ever did," Janey said.

"Wait." Jonathan was turning the pages. "No, this is good."

"Of course you'd think so."

He looked up at Annabelle. "Now it's possible. You might be able to do this."

"Okay, if your guys can depop fifteen hundred birds an hour . . ." Jonathan was saying.

"Yeah, we're not going to do it like that."

"I thought not." He sighed.

"The idea here is we want each hen lifted with two hands, one hen at a time." Cleveland demonstrated with her arms. "That's going to slow us down."

"I'll say."

"See what you can come up with," said Dill.

"One hen per hand?"

"One hen per two hands. Are you deaf?" said Janey.

"That's going to take longer. How many cage free?" Jonathan had the pages fanned in front of him.

"Two barns. So we'll need emptiers *and* catchers."

"I don't know if it can be done," said Jonathan. He ran his finger down one of the sheets. "Probably not. Any way we can shave off some time?"

"Like what?"

"How about a vacuum? For the cage-free barns?"

Dill shook his head. "Too many injuries. Anyway, these are aviaries. Vacuum won't work."

"Vacuum?" said Janey.

"Yeah," said Annabelle. "The chickens are pulled by howling wind into these giant rotating rubber brushes and shot out onto a conveyor belt."

"I'll have to do some computations. The question is," said Jonathan, "how many birds per minute need to be leaving the barns."

Annabelle took out a pad.

"You got a chisel too?" He rose. "I'll go get my laptop."

"Why don't we phone the FBI and invite them over?" Annabelle slapped down a pen. "Everything goes on paper."

Jonathan appealed to the ceiling.

"Where are you going to get all the trucks for this?" Jonathan was saying. "You're going to need poultry trucks with battery racks. Have you thought about that? You'll need, let's see . . . hand me that, would you?" He took the pad. "This pen doesn't work. Does anybody have a pen? Okay, how many trucks . . ."

"I've got twelve lined up already," said Dill.

"Twelve?" said Jonathan. "See, this is the problem with you people. You can't do simple math. You're going to need," he took a pen from Cleveland, "at least forty trucks. How many hens fit on a truck?"

"The new ones can hold up to nineteen thousand layers or eight thousand broilers," said Cleveland.

"Well, we don't have any broilers, obviously," said Jonathan, "so nineteen K per."

"We can't use commercial trucks."

"It's only for a few hours. We'll get them off quickly."

"We're not putting nineteen thousand hens on a truck."

"All right, how about fifteen? In that case we'd need . . ." Jonathan scribbled. "Sixty trucks. With sixty trucks, maybe."

They all sank back in their seats. Dill whistled.

Jonathan tossed the pen onto the table. "You've got twelve? I'd like to know where you're going to get another forty-eight trucks."

No one breathed.

"I can get the trucks," said Janey. They all looked at her.

"I know a guy." She shrugged.

JANEY WAS STAYING QUIET. She knew she couldn't do it without them. But she hoped this wasn't all a mistake. They were taking over, her authority ebbing away. She'd entrusted her vision to them, and it still felt delicate and raw.

The night before, she'd been at home with her father. She'd glanced up from her laptop to see him visibly aging in front of the TV. She thought about how upset he'd be if she wound up in prison. He'd blame himself.

"What, do I have Twinkie on my face?" he'd said. He brushed his nose with the back of his hand.

So, yeah, she wanted to contribute (though the whole dream was her dream in the first place). Admittedly, she should not have offered *this*. She'd worked trucking dispatch three years, but she'd been fired with plenty of cause and enemies.

But she'd been thinking of Manny. Her former supervisor. He might conceivably help. He called himself a workingman's revolutionary with a laugh. Talked unions. Talked politics. He'd quit a few months before she'd been fired, hadn't seen the worst of her surly antics. That night she found him online, and drove through a few towns the next afternoon. She rode past the chain-link fence onto a cracked blacktop, a low thud of building, a sign that read:

NOY'S TRUCKS
IOWA AG-PERMIT COMPLIANT

And Manny. Janey spotted him at the desk behind the counter through the storefront window. It seemed ages since she'd seen him and he looked old. She felt a press of sadness, out here on this wasteland with the trucks and truck husks that dotted the landscape like primordial crustaceans left over from when the oceans crept back. The last time she'd seen Manny she'd been counting words and dreaming of the old Janey and her mother. The world was turning out to be bigger than she'd thought, had room for more than she'd imagined. She could barely see the old Janey now. Was she there, underneath, a palimpsest? Janey put her head on the steering wheel and tried to see her, wherever she was. But the old Janey was a sheltered kid, unequal to this. Janey dismissed her. But wait. She summoned her back. She needed them both.

She got out of the car.

She walked in, a customer bell dinging the door. "Look who's come to call," she said. She shaded her jitters with a smirk.

Manny turned his chair thirty degrees on its axis and stopped. Smiled. "Now where'd you come from?"

"Nice place you've got here."

"How are you, girl?"

"Never better."

"What can I do for you?"

"Ask what I can do for you." She strode up. "I've got an opportunity for you."

He squinted, grinned. "Nah, I'm good."

"Want to be involved in something bigger than yourself?"

"I am involved in something bigger than myself," he said. "I'm the smallest thing I know."

"Manny, come on. I know you're the type that wants to change the world."

"The world is changing every minute, with or without me." Stretching back in his chair, arms behind his head, enjoying himself.

"Well, I've got a plan to make the world a better place."

"Bad idea. Each time someone tries that we have another disaster."

Damn this guy. She barreled on, told him what she came for.

He laughed. "What am I supposed to believe you could conceivably need that many battery trucks for?"

"This is a legitimate transaction, Manny. We pay you."

"Not a chance," he said. "I can't get my hands on that many trucks at one time."

"For twenty-four hours? Yes, you can. I know how this works."

"No thanks. I'll pass."

Fucking Manny. An image flashed in her brain of her going back to the group empty-handed. *Sorry. You gave me one assignment and I gave up in a hundred seconds.*

There was the racket of a truck banging onto the premises. There was shouting in the distance, the war cries of premodern man.

She remembered the city of hens. A whole generation. She remembered the vision, hundreds of thousands of hens rising out of their cages and taking off into the night.

Her mind, six feet away from his, spun through all the calculations and permutations of how this could go. (Malcolm X calling out to his Muslim brothers, raising a fist. The queen strutting forward on the chessboard. Her mother, eyes lifted, leaning in.) Janey tilted her head, pursed her lips. Had one card left to play. She stepped forward. Her face must have already changed because he leaned back. "You thought you'd get off so easy as the price of a couple of motel rooms? What would Carol think?" She folded her arms.

He paled.

She almost faltered. "It's for a good cause," she allowed. "I promise."

He rubbed his forehead. "Who's going to drive these trucks? Permitted drivers?"

"Of course." (She'd have to remember to ask Dill about that.)

"You got the money? It'll cost to get forty-eight battery trucks. Those run one-fifty a day each. You know how it's done. No shortcuts."

"That's, let's see . . ."

"About seven grand. Plus tax and gas. And insurance." He shook his head. "What do you need all these trucks for?"

"It's legit."

He counted on his fingers. "I guess I can give them to you at cost. That'll bring it down to one-oh-five apiece, plus insurance. Meet me halfway. You get me six grand and promise me you'll bring only licensed drivers. I'll see what I can do."

"Okay."

"And bring them back with gas."

"Of course."

"I don't want to hear about this on the news."

"You won't, Manny."

"And you're not blackmailing me. Is that clear?"

"Of course, Manny."

He sighed. "Christ, Janey."

She went out to her car and called Dill. "We're going to need some cash."

"Fine," said Dill. "My husband is a longtime contributor."

"We need six thousand dollars."

"I'm on the emergency account," he said. "Not after this, of course."

THE FACT THAT they never did settle on what would happen to the hens, not *each and every one*, wasn't their fault. There were simply too many. Only nine hundred thousand, since two of the barns would be empty, but still. You had to get places willing to commit to this. You'd have sixty trucks filled with fifteen thousand hens apiece, though you'd have to assume 5 percent wouldn't make it, so say fourteen K with casualties, give or take. This was all ballpark.

They had contacts. Annabelle knew people at every sanctuary and shelter in the country but still it was an awful lot of hens. She and Dill pulled together a list. Most of the places didn't specialize in birds, were more educational facility than refugee camp. They kept representative samples: you had your pigs, your cows, your turkeys. Always a nice fat barnyard for the chickens, sure. A good hundred hens running around.

"You said fourteen, right? Bring 'em. We'll make room."

"Well, fourteen thousand."

"*Thousand?*"

"Some might die on the way."

"You want to bring them *here*?"

There were the horse havens, the circus-animal rest homes, the wildlife sanctuaries for the lost coyote or the bird that hits the glass. The only way these places would take a hen was by force: If, say, an investigator showed up in a truck and refused to leave, which Annabelle and Dill were not above doing. Or if, say, someone simply released them into the sanctuary at night. Also not above doing. Desperate times and all that.

"Holy shit. Fourteen grand? What a story. Whose exclusive is this? CBS, am I right?"

"No story."

"Excuse me?"

"No publicity."

There was one place, way off in the high hills of California, a long valley full of flowers, a refuge solely for spent hens. The group had thousands of these ladies. True, the most they'd ever had was four thousand, but surely they'd take a full truck if it could get that far.

Once a lady in Woodstock flew eleven hundred hens in a cargo plane.

A farm sanctuary in Michigan had a brand-new barn, could hold a hundred hens, maybe a hundred and twenty-five.

One place, you could pay fifty bucks and get a photo of a saved hen or a goat or a turkey. If you paid two hundred you got to name one. Five hundred and you got your name scratched onto a wall for all the animals to see.

"You want to 'drop them off.'"

"We've got people to unload them."

"Someone brought fifty here once. Someone brought ten. No one ever brought a hundred. Much less . . . how many did you say? Can I ask where you are getting twenty-eight thousand chickens?"

If two shelters were fairly near each other, they could split a truck, was Annabelle's thinking. One shelter could take the fourteen thousand—the empty truck making its escape through the night—and then the two shelters could transfer half the hens bit by bit over the next week.

"In what? An ice cream truck? A wheelbarrow? How are we supposed to move seven thousand hens?"

Some said no and hung up shaking their heads. Some thought about it a little more on the toilet and called back an hour later. Some said no and determined to have nothing to do with Annabelle or Dill ever, *ever*, again. Yeah, they meant it this time. What kind of irresponsible assholes did you have to be to take that insane quantity of chickens—seventy-five hundred? Twelve grand of chickens?

But surprisingly many agreed.

"Listen," said Annabelle. "We've got to get serious. We have reached the apex of employment-based investigations. It's all falling apart. The farmers are onto us. They're a slow bunch, but they're catching on. They share databases now. They have facial recognition software, fingerprint scanning. They've got the government in their pocket more than ever. Ag-gag is old news, only the beginning. The walls are closing in, the corridors shrinking like a cartoon. It's time for extreme measures."

"We'll figure it out, bring them," they said. This generosity may have been due to the fact that an assortment of gritty animal rights activists ran the sanctuaries, from young aspiring investigators to the former underground subversives of the '80s and '90s.

"Right on," said the old-timers. They'd been around for the era of farm sabotage, they'd smashed equipment, slashed tires. "We've become tame. We're herd animals now."

"Bring them," said the young ones. "This is what we signed on for. Not leading Saturday tours through the turkeys." They'd fought hard, gone door to door for months. Won, celebrated, only to see the watery compromises. The meaningless increments. The lack of oversight. Egg-free doughnuts, four more inches of cage space, progress implemented on a fifteen-year time line, hens represented by people in suits.

These days animal activism was less revolution, more capitalism with a conscience.

"What is the matter with us, letting the enemy bulldoze us while we stammer and politely disagree?"

They had been there for the fast-food battles, had cheered when McDonald's agreed to go cage free. Now they found themselves in the preposterous position of having to approve of *eating eggs at McDonald's*.

"Fourteen K? Now that's what I'm talking about." (They didn't yet know about the other eight hundred and eighty-six thousand, since these folks could keep a secret.)

"We came from radical roots and must return to them," said Annabelle. "This is a call to arms, a revolt, a long-awaited swing away from the rich man's middle and back over to the rebel left where we belong."

"Bring them! Bring them!"

It was time to set aside childish things, they agreed. Time to wrest the power away from the oppressors. Western civilization was dead from conception if this was the end result. America may have created the first modern democracy but it also invented six out of the twelve greatest evils this earth has ever seen.

"It's time to reject the so-called Renaissance and go Dada on these assholes," they cried.

It was already too late. They all knew it. The enemy has clearly won. Soon all that will be left of the miracle of our planet will be the monocrops of damaged cows, pigs, dogs, hens, a few other practical species—and humans, horrible, unbeatable, disgusting humans.

But the sanctuaries were still run by warriors, and they would have their moment of no.

• • •

"I'm sending you a gift," she said. "I wanted to give you advance warning."

"This must be absolutely confidential," she said. "I know I can trust you."

"Yes, yes, you can trust us," they said. "Bring them."

In one case it was a new high school intern who answered the phone, agreed with little comprehension to take the hens, and left a note on the desk of the director, who read it, muttering in confusion ("who *are* these interns?") and became distracted by another problem. The note was lost under a pile of papers.

And when she and Dill had finished going through the list, had called every contact (eighty-three total), and assigned trucks to those who agreed (and to those who said maybe, and to a few who said no), they settled down to review.

Dill ran his finger down the sheet and stopped. "Oh no, wait."

What words to introduce now! No? Wait?

"That's only fifty-eight trucks," he said. "Who's taking these two?"

Annabelle looked over his shoulder. "Yeah, I'm taking care of them."

Dill lowered the sheet. "What do you mean, 'taking care of them'?"

So this whole end of the wagon was rickety before they even got started.

THINK HIGH-RISES, gated communities, all the places that give you a twitch of existential dread. The Amazon shipping facilities, the dying superstores, the prisons and detention centers, the pig farms, all the boxes that hold products and people and animals, the LeCorbusian landscape one skirts over or through, avoids. Think of the smaller boxes that we press our faces to, think of all the tiny digital boxes we touch with our fingers to signal alliance, passion, smarts, nostalgia, enmity, the whole of our minds.

Think of a guy, a lone man, sitting far below in a box of tin and wheels, a stretch of plain earth around him. Deep dawn, barren concrete, bluing sky (though the footage was black and white so the sky would look gray). The guy, Matt (but some of them don't use their real names), grabbed his plastic lunch bag and got out of the car. He walked toward the steel barn (the mic recording his breath and the sound of his steps). Inside, he pulled his time card out of the slot. His phone buzzed.

Another one, Chris, two states away, was already walking through the barn, saying hello to everyone he passed (his "character" was "friendly, helpful") over the hens' tremendous coo. (His camera was off. He flipped it on only when necessary. Early in his "career" he'd felt like he was making a zombie movie: horror with four million hens, and he'd let the camera run on and on. But these days he thought of his films—well, footage—as mumblecore: too boring for anyone to bother watching.) In his pocket his phone rang. He pulled off a glove and silenced it, didn't look to see who it was. He was supposed to leave his phone in his locker. The first rule of being an investigator: follow farm rules.

The investigators. She was summoning them.

There was Joey, an ultraprofessional—calculating, quiet, efficient, earnest, not a drop of the smartass in him—but so short that the camera, disguised as his top button, hit the farm managers at their bellies so that it was nearly impossible to catch their faces. He wore heels for professional purposes, cowboy boots (not leather, of course, but some quasi-recycled substance). The boots helped maybe a little but made his feet hot. His call came while he was still sipping coffee at the motel. It was an hour earlier there. He saw the number. What, was she back?

The investigators. Their squeaky shoes in the not-quite dawn. Their humble lunches of fake meat in a grocery sack. The time zones turning up and down across the country like a dial. Their video flickering on at 6:45 a.m., the first shot of the day the local paper (proof of place and date). They'd trained in covert operations, physical and psychological warfare. There were only a couple dozen active in the country at any time, spread out among the various organizations. A few dozen more who'd quit after a few years' run. She knew every one of them and had all their numbers.

There was Penelope. Max. Shawn. Frank.

There was the Canadian investigator, a woman with a voice like Mary Poppins. No one could remember her name. She was just "that Canadian," as in, "That Canadian can flirt the farmers into anything."

Jim, the philosopher-investigator, who, when the call came, was walking the long rows of hens. Hens and hens and hens. It was an exercise in repetition, a mathematical situation, Zenoean,

Steinian, Sisyphean. The cages, the eggs, the beaks, the long journeys down the aisles. The hours of depop, vac, debeaking, the sound of the birds, the amazing amount of excrement, the same jokes over and over, the dead birds he ripped from the floor of the cages ("mummies," they called them), an infinite series of infinite series. His phone was in his locker. She left a message.

There was Uriel. He could tell stories of shit, all right. The shit pit, walking around in it, shoveling paths through it, shit mounds eight feet high, a forest of them, stray hens running around and living in it (which would be better, he pondered, to live in a cage or in shit?), the shit being dumped in the fields and wafting into the air, turning everything white—the trees, the grass, himself, white with shit.

Ben's charisma, Mariam's charm, Tame's sense of humor, but also their deep sorrows, their solitary natures, their disturbances. They were all covering disappointments in one way or another, throwing another blanket on top.

There was JT, six foot four, former quarterback. First glance at his footage and you'd think he did nothing but bitch, a running monologue of complaints through his workday. The hours, the filth, the heat, the cold. What an asshole. But in this way he was able to talk to the farmhands all day, get verbal confirmations from managers, and be above suspicion (all farmers know an investigator never complains—it's the hardest workers you have to look out for). You'd have to admit JT was a damn professional and on top of that a great comedian.

JT got the call on his boat because he'd quit (the bitching wasn't only a technique), had taken his cash, bought this little used skipper, was sailing away to Gilligan's Island, never coming back. Fuck them all.

When she called, he was starboard, coiling ropes. He saw it was her and (he couldn't help it) answered—his first (or next) mistake.

Simon, who never went anywhere without a weapon.

Tinker, who recorded every phone conversation he had and listened to them later when he was alone. He recorded his conversations with his mother.

Pooky, who'd had it with investigating. They'd risked his safety over and over. He'd tell anyone who asked. He had proof of it all.

Mostly men, mostly white, the investigators, though a handful were women, and some were Latino. A few more than you'd think from across oceans.

They walked, the investigators, each day from their cars to the barns. Today it was Ian, Guillermo, James, Pat. Midwest flatness in the distance. Desolate earth that they saw at its most desolate hour—in the ice-dark. Or at the loveliest hour: in California, the soft dawn, leafy light, the lucky bastard investigators who got assigned there. Jonny, AJ, Joel the Jew.

Dylan, who'd captured some classic footage before he quit. A details man, skilled at showing *abundance*. He'd filmed whole dumpsters of dead hens dropping through the air into trucks. He filmed flies that were like walking on popcorn, flies that looked like piles of dirt. Dead flies all over the counters, the plywood, the eggs. And live flies in the air, swirling in front of the camera.

He was sound asleep when she called, though it was nearly eleven.

They grew lonely, the investigators, once the initial thrill wore off. They were prone to dread. Laney had nightmares. Alphabet felt sorry for himself. Terrance joined pickup games in parks in every town to stave off the sadness. They were like overseas terrorists moving from town to town. They stayed in motel rooms, had with them only enough belongings that could be packed into a duffel in fifty-nine minutes and driven away.

There was Mike, whose footage was always awful. No narrative energy. He never talked to the camera and what he did say was boring. Mike didn't seem like he even thought being a farmhand was such a bad job. Then, of course, there was the beautiful moment when he accidentally left the camera on and filmed himself leaving the facility, driving to Subway, and ordering a meatball sandwich with cheese and a cookie. That footage got around somehow and the other investigators hated him for it.

Still, he was a professional. He got his call around one, while he was tugging his fortieth dead hen of the day, tearing the skin off the bottom of the cage (carpet-pulling, they called it).

Their shoes, their forearms (or their sleeves if they had tattoos: Cean, Robert, Katie, Calvin). Their moonwalks over the tops of the cages. Their echoing calls to the farmhands, the swoop of the camera when it scanned the higher cages and then swept down. The investigator's breathing, the sniffles caught on the audio. (The dander gathered in the chest: Snake had endless colds, flus, bugs; and Rabbit, with his allergy—bad luck—to feathers.) Whatever got caught on the footage, that's all you'd ever see or hear of them.

Only a handful of directors and former directors she'd trust—Nancy, Cricket, Steve, Smoke. Then there were the investigators who didn't specialize in on-site employment but in one-off encounter work—posing as a truck driver, food service, a customer. Not really investigators, but tough enough and trustworthy. Twenty-three of them.

• • •

When a case went down PR would take over: a tele–press conference, a web page, a video on YouTube, a demand for resignations, a call to the DA, an online petition, a request for donations. The investigator would disappear. Tom would take a break to go hiking. Ula hid out in a motel room and watched TV. Jackson went to see his mother. They'd wait for the next assignment, new location.

They called PR the smile team. The webguy was the spider.

Carol. She'd grown a little weird—weirder (she was plenty weird to start). Her girlfriend had drifted away. She'd gotten a DUI and lost her license. When she saw who it was, she thought, Now what?

Donnie. He was the one who started all that vasectomy business, and it spread through the investigators like a disease. Heather even had her tubes tied, a much more invasive procedure.

Ray. He got his call at the end of the day, as he exited the barn and walked toward his car, muttering. Beyond the dumpsters, the razed fields, the sun dropping into them, the barns across the road burning red. The last time he'd seen Annabelle he'd thrown a chair at the wall and walked out. But he answered.

Ron. He was old guard, X. These youngsters pissed him off. The millennials were crybabies, Gen Z cut corners.

The investigators, their crackups and breakdowns containable, turning on a predictable cycle. Arnoldo, Sahara, Sam, Vince, Rocket, Fred.

The long stories of their demise.

When they finally quit and cut out, as almost all did (or, like Dill, were spit out), they had nothing: blank years on their résumés since what they did was strictly secret, no skills other than to perform jobs they'd spent their lives trying to abolish, alienated family, permanent back trouble. Zac had tremors, Mark PTSD, Liz lingering fears of being caught. When Sinan closed his eyes to sleep he saw behind his eyelids the barns, thousands and thousands of them, a grid stretching around the earth.

Rainey. She was sitting in the bathtub crying when the call came.

Bobby. Crouched on the roof smoking a joint. His phone sounded like a rooster's morning crow.

She called them all. Hank, Pal, Byrd, Mike. Ham, Hal, Cat, Frond. All the ones who'd quit, all the ones she'd fired, all the ones who'd stayed. Mel, Annie, Rake, Sol. Storm, Paz, Hop, Mic. All the ones who'd drifted away, said they'd come back but hadn't.

And Zee. He'd done thirty-one investigations in twelve states in six years. He'd changed cars five times, changed his facial hair over and over, changed his accent, legally changed his name twice and changed what he went by so many times he couldn't count.

One day he would marry Janey Flores, though on the day he got the call he did not know of her existence. His childhood name had been long left behind. He now went by Zee (for Zoro). And while he was still listening to Annabelle's message, his phone beeped again. It was a text from Trish (née Francine) saying, *Guess who just called*, and soon other texts were coming in because Zee knew a lot of the investigators, though he'd never felt entirely comfortable with them. Last year he'd resigned and vowed never to return. He hadn't worked an investigation in over a year.

We're planning an action. We need your help.

The world is failing but we can fight back.

Wear a ski mask when you get here. Can't be too careful, even with each other.

They didn't know what she wanted but a few days later they went. They dropped their tools, wrapped up their investigations, or got sober. They filled their tanks, filed onto flights, boarded buses. They were on the move. It was biblical, mythological, fabled. They disappeared out of their spots like the rapture but there were so few of them and they were such loners, their absence was barely noticed. An assembling army called out of reserve. For what, they didn't know, but they believed in their cause and, despite everything, they'd been waiting for the summons.

SEVEN YEARS before Cleveland took the hen, Dill stepped onto the banker's land for the first time and he felt his life might be perfect. He'd known the banker—Dev, still—for only one day.

Early July, long days of flags and flies. For Dill: summer warmth, job success, and now the promise of sex with a stranger. They'd met at a street fair where Dill had been asked to speak. They'd wound up crushed in a crowd of dancers. Dill had liked his long eyelashes, small frame, dark skin, and even the fact that he was a banker, which Dill found cute. Dev had invited him over. A mild adventure, a forty-minute drive to this small town to be surely tearing off each other's clothes within minutes.

But Dill was surprised by what he was finding, pulling up. He had not expected this cartwheel of trees, this long driveway of pebbles and dust, this toppling house, barn poking out behind. Dill, who was not yet in love, had imagined the young man to be the son of determined immigrants (he was Indian). Dill had expected a tight duplex, slab of sixteen-by-sixteen lawn, compact appliances that slid into the wall—not this rambling homestead.

Dev came out onto the porch. Dill shut his car door. The space between them was pockmarked with bugs, pollen, and moisture. The sky was so blue it seemed fake. Dev was young, shifting from foot to foot, out of place on this wide land, and he was *handsome*. You could see the hope and lust and innocence all over him.

Dill was already two years into the weeds with Annabelle at that point—director of investigations of the most renegade animal rights group in America. "An investigative unit," the press was calling them. He walked through the world with a blur in front of his face, his thoughts so loud they clouded his vision, but Dev was coming in clearly, was arriving in Dill's brain lit up. How had he ended up living on this big piece of land? Had he found himself here by mistake and managed to fall in with what had befallen him? Or had this been purposeful? Had he *wanted* more than he could handle? Dill walked over.

"I wasn't sure if you'd come."

"Me either."

He led Dill around, gesturing and chattering, through the vast house and then out into the tallgrass. They walked toward the barn, Dev pointing out the equipment shed, the tire swing, his favorite trees.

As they paused at the door of the barn, Dev's figure took on a mysterious glow. Who was this kid, this *banker*? Dill wondered. Could he handle Dill? (Because let's face it, if you thought the investigators were bad . . .)

Of course, one falls in love not because of who the beloved is but because of who the beloved allows *you* to be. What did this banker hope to be that he was now seeing reflected back to him in Dill's eyes?

Dill wanted it, whatever it was.

That day—they'd known each other only a handful of hours (and Dill was already thinking "the banker," perhaps a bad sign that he had to create distance, even while pulling in close)—they stood at the door of the barn (the same door Dill now walked toward seven years later, following the banker's ghost). Dill took the banker's face in his hands. "What is the ambition here for you?" he said between long kisses. "Are you in love yet? I want to know," daring the banker to make a terrible choice.

A week later Dill had moved in.

God, he loved the banker for loving him. He had always known that one day the banker would change his mind, recoil in disgust (how could I have wanted *that*?) but Dill had counted on being able to handle it.

That day had come.

All right, so this was one way of "handling it," but what did the banker expect? You get what you pay for, and the banker had certainly paid a lot.

Now, seven years after his first walk across the weeds, Dill crossed them again to the barn. He could feel Annabelle and Cleveland behind him, watching from the window of the main house. Inside the barn a hundred investigators in ski masks waited for him. Dill couldn't believe they were wearing the masks. She'd told them to, required it—Annabelle wanted to keep identities secret until everyone agreed—but after ten years of working with these people, he knew you couldn't just call out a command and trust they'd follow. Unruly, petulant. He'd never been able to do much more than negotiate with them and if that didn't work, curse at them, and if that didn't work, threaten (never beg). On company property they were professionals, but the second they stepped off, they were Napoleons every one, absurd figures, the fuckers. Drove him and Annabelle nuts, quitting, crying, breaking equipment, punching walls in a temper tantrum, fighting or falling in love with each other, disappearing, reappearing to yell one more taunt or piece of paranoid nonsense. Really the banker had put up with a lot of crap on his land. Really it was no wonder.

And yet here they were, a hundred investigators past and present like an end-of-the-world resurrection or reckoning, the banker installed several seas away, hating Dill at last after years of Dill goading him into it.

Dill was going in alone to make the pitch—better to hold back

Annabelle in the flesh just a little longer. If no one agreed (in fact they *all* had to agree) it was over. He was counting on them to make a terrible choice. He wouldn't put it past them, what with him there to talk them into it. It was his specialty.

He pushed the door open and walked in.

THE HUNDRED INVESTIGATORS didn't like the ski mask crap but on the appointed day they pulled the masks over their heads to protect themselves from themselves. They left their cars in the field and filed into the same barn many of them had trained in. They sat on the few benches or on the floor, or leaned against the wall, arms crossed, silent and suspicious. They waited.

Dill came in. No ski mask. They shifted at the sight of him, his many bad qualities rising in their minds. But he didn't give them time to start complaining. He stood at one end of the room and began.

He'd tell them nothing, he said. They'd need to decide for themselves. The particulars, yes. The plan, of course. The step-by-step, the exit strategy, the cut-and-run, if it turned out to go down that way—all that they'd go over and over, and yes he had an inside expert on the team. But he and Annabelle weren't interested in explaining themselves or in debating the justification, in discussing whether this would "work" in any sense other than on the physical plane, the mechanics. The investigators were not to think of this action—the evacuation of nine hundred thousand hens (it was the first time they'd heard this and a chorus of investigator-gasps, followed by curses and groans, forced Dill to pause and then go on more slowly)—they were not to think of it as a publicity stunt designed to attract attention to the cause. It wasn't a statement, a threat, or a manifesto. They were not all going to be friends after this. They would not be an organization. They were not *organizing*. If that was the only way they could think about this, they should just leave right now. Why

Annabelle had made up her mind to do this was not their concern. She was inviting them to take part in the sheer physical operation end of it, solely for the sake of the individual birds who would benefit. Annabelle herself had selected each investigator in this room. She had *chosen* them. But they'd need to have their own reasons for doing it. The masked heads of Dill's potential phalanx turned back and forth, following Dill as he paced. Now he stopped. She and Dill were asking them each to show up with two more people—trustworthy, stable, and physically strong—in two days, on Saturday morning. There were a hundred of them here and they needed at least three hundred to make it possible.

Hands were going up. They were trying to interrupt. But he shook his head. He placed a sheet of paper and a pen on the table. "Put an *X* on this page if you're in." He set a white digital kitchen timer. "We need you out in an hour." He walked across the room. "Anyone who won't be joining us, we know you'll keep quiet. You're all professionals." He went out the door, shut it. The heads swung back.

There followed a moment of silence.

They all took a private moment to congratulate themselves. Annabelle had chosen *them*. They felt a little proud.

They all took a private moment to ask themselves: Did they know two more people who'd come? Probably. They each had a handful of weirdos in their back pocket. Investigators have fans.

Then they all took a private moment to come to their senses. What kind of crazy idea was this anyway? They began saying it aloud. What would this accomplish? What the hell did Dill mean this wasn't designed to attract attention? How could you attempt the largest direct action any of them had ever heard of, that any of them had ever *imagined*, and say it wasn't designed to attract attention? How could you take a million birds and not attract attention?

One voice said, "It's impossible. Can't be done." They thought about that and reluctantly agreed he was right. The sheer logistics. It was unworkable. This made them a little angry. They'd come all this way—the dramatics involved!—only to turn around and go home? What's the big idea anyway, dragging them here? They were a little sad because they'd thought they were destined for a great act of heroism, not the fantasy of modern mad people gone madder.

Somebody said, "Ten minutes," meaning ten minutes had gone by. Already? Jesus. Well, were they going to do it or what? They looked around, faceless.

Not only that, they reflected, but this was not the sort of thing you get a night in jail and a day with the judge for. This gets you put away for years. This is called terrorism these days.

All right, in that case it made sense why some of them were there. They'd been arrested a lot. Some had been to prison. They'd done time for far fewer lives than these, for results far more humble. But were they willing to do it again? Most of them were in semiretirement these days, did little more than Feather-Free Friday protests and lunchtime leafleting, door-to-door donations, Songbird Day at the shelter. Those who were working did only employment-based operations—strictly legal, or at least arguably legal. And anyway, nobody—or *almost* nobody, apparently—did that direct action stuff anymore. There were the pet-shop parrot releasers, a handful of diehards letting birds out into climates where they'd never survive (no doubt those idiots were in there among them, face masks pulled tight) but even *they* would never come up with this.

True, Dill had said they had an expert on the inside, that there were escape plans in place. He'd said at every stage there would be at least two escape hatches. But people always say that, don't they? The first hatch turns out to be the door of a cop car, and the second the sliding gate of an iron cell.

"But how many of us could they put away, after all?"

"A good many."

"Why not all?"

"All. Of course they could put away all of us. Why not?"

Was the *point* to get them all put away?

They discussed this. Quickly. Twenty minutes had gone by. One said, "Aren't we already accessories? Aren't we incriminated just by being here? She goes off and pulls her stunt without us, couldn't we still go to prison?"

Yeah, but they had known that when they'd gotten into their various modes of transport to come here, the smarter of them had anyway, and they'd come, which made them maybe not so smart. They were all traceable, culpable. They were already in the crosshairs, gotten.

This made them unhappy. Why had they come? they lamented. They pouted under their ski masks. What fools they were. Some of them were on probation.

"At least we can't point each other out."

"Who needs a finger? I know who you are," said one and laughed.

"Oh yeah?" said another, rising. "Is that a threat?" It started to get a little heated.

"Annabelle came up with this," one of them interrupted. "She's got a reason."

Hell, of course she had a reason. They were sick of it too. They'd done dozens of investigations. They'd gotten farmers into court, propositions onto ballots, they'd single-handedly bankrupted whole egg operations. They'd ruined their own backs, relationships, minds, futures, they'd given it all they had, put their lives in danger again and again—for what? Those barns were still standing, more than ever before.

"Barns going up all over the world. The disease is spreading."

"My last investigation, they built *two more*. All I can do is drive by and spit."

"My case was dismissed in court. Judge said that chickens don't have standing."

"I'm through with those fucking shmucks at the LA office with their fancy office and their fancy clothes and their fancy food."

"Their self-congratulating books with giant pictures of themselves on the covers."

"Their fucking celebrity fund-raisers."

"Their vacations to India."

"Nonprofit, my ass."

"Making money off of our work."

"Annabelle has always been old-style liberation."

"No half measures. No compromise."

"Until she quit."

"She didn't quit. She dug in."

"Free or die."

Then one said, "I'm doing it." He got up, marked the pad with an X. He was playing it smooth but he had to be hoping another would hop up and say, "I'll go with you," be the number two. Alone you're a stranger in a sandwich board. Two, you've got a waltz. Four, you have a band. He walked to the door. "Wait," said another, "I'm coming." The rest looked after them, jealous. They'd been beaten to being first. They'd meant to go all along, right? Others went. They Xed the pad and left singly or in groups of three. Some had obviously known each other for years and performed elaborate celebratory high fives and rushed out like they were headed to the game. Some were solemn, making their mark and slouching out cool.

The hour passed and the barn emptied, until there were only two of them still in the room. A woman on the right and a man on the left. They sat staring hard at the wide plank floor, which had the sort of arrangement of lines and right angles that instills comfort in all humanity to the exact level it craves. That must be what it does or else we wouldn't see that pattern everywhere we look. The human obsession with the rectangle. Anything ninety degrees will do but a nice clean rectangle, that's all we hope for in life: to be surrounded by them, to count them, to divide our belongings up in them, to give them to our grandchildren, to be lowered into one when we die.

This here is a bad idea, the man on the left, Zee, thought.

But he'd encountered so many bad ideas in his life. His entire existence could be attributed to a series of bad choices, often, like this one, not his own. But he'd gotten away. Had left, had a job for a moving company in Chicago, a girlfriend (sort of), an actual lease. He was shakily impersonating a regular person and no one could imagine how hard that was. But each day it felt a breath more real, because it *was* real, or almost, getting close. He shouldn't have come here. But he'd come not for Annabelle, but for Dill, whom he didn't want to let down.

And he believed in it, all of it.

If he could just keep out of prison.

"Annabelle's got a hell of a shitty idea this time," he said aloud to the woman on the right. He got up, drew a *Z*, and walked out. The woman on the right was the only one in there.

That final person, the auditor Janey, took off her ski mask, frowning: It wasn't Annabelle's shitty idea. It was *her* shitty idea.

But the frown didn't last. A slow warmth reached from her stomach for her limbs. It was happening or could very well happen, they just might really do this. She closed her eyes and let the vision sweep over her: the birds lifting around her, the cages clattering to the ground like nests falling from trees, her mother's voice amid the sound of flapping wings. She opened her eyes and left the barn.

IT WOULD BE EASY TO ASSUME Dev was off feeling resolved and free in Egypt, after all Dill had put him through. But that's not what was happening.

Dev, however many thousand miles away (6,489), was washing his hands at the end of a long hallway, eighteen stories above the hot ground. He'd read that hand-washing "increases resolve," so each time he felt the urge to write Dill he hopped up from his desk, padded down the hallway of Pan Egypt Intervest to a sink of pale stone. Indeed, as Dill imagined, Dev *had* been raised by first-generation immigrants in a subdivision duplex with a square of grass out front. Dev had inherited the house and the barn and the fields that came with them from a great-uncle who had taken a shine to the boy. The uncle had been the first to leave India and come to America, had lived in that house for twenty-six years, the "roommate" of a small organic farmer. He'd helped his niece and her husband settle in America, knew Dev from the day he was born, knew what Dev was before Dev himself knew, and, recalling what his own life had been (it was a different time), he left the boy the house, barn, land, the whole situation.

And Dev had inherited Dill and all that came with *that* situation because he had been out of his mind with love, willing to do the extraordinary, put up with the extraordinary. He was dying to put up with the extraordinary Dill. But he was young then, and he'd grown up in those seven years. He was tired of having to calm the wilds around him—and he wasn't referring to the land, which was easy compared to Dill. But now, eighteen stories over Egypt (sure, send the brown guy—of *course* they couldn't tell the difference between Egypt and India), a new kind of nervousness was entering his heart. Who was he without Dill? He hurried back down the hallway to rinse his hands once more.

If he could have seen his front yard two days later, he would have been enraged afresh and discovered that rage is far better for resolve than water.

JONATHAN JARMAN JR. had come up with a plan for 303 investigators. If 303 didn't show up, it could not be done. The night before the evacuation he'd explained this to Dill, Annabelle, and the auditors. He had a stack of 303 sheets of printed instructions, each a unique assignment with its own itinerary, barn, task, getaway plan, and so on. They had asked for a plan for under 300, but the numbers and spreadsheets were all right here. Working their hardest, 303, Jonathan said, or none at all. Until Dill finally said, "Oh fucking shut up already."

Jonathan's hand rested on the sheets. Two fingers lifted and lowered in an impatient tap. All right, just so long as they understood. It was 303 or he was out.

In truth they could use a few dozen more, and he had them printed, fifty extra, arranged in order of urgency, and slid into a separate envelope, just in case these people surprised him, which they would not—but if they did, he'd be ready.

It was Friday night, late. His body had held the shape of a skeptical grimace all day. He stretched out on the sofa. He took out his phone to text Joy (because of course he brought his phone in) but then he looked up and Annabelle was there. Her hand was on his, and his hand was on her long slim body, which he hadn't held in so long. He pulled her in. His songbird, his tiger, his runaway bride.

When he woke, Annabelle curled under his arm, the investigators had already begun to arrive.

THEY BEGAN SHOWING UP at dawn, though Dill had told them ten o'clock. Dill was the only one awake.

Annabelle and Jonathan were asleep on the sofa, Janey on the banker's bed. Cleveland had gone home with plans to be back by eight, her marriage exerting its gravitational pull. Dill slept fitfully in an easy chair and got up in the predawn dark. He pulled on his jacket, let out the dogs, and walked to the barn through a mosaic of retreating shadows and rosy air to feed the chickens. Then he sat on the porch, the same porch Janey had approached with her box of hens only six weeks before. The yard was that many weeks greener now, the air that much warmer, the light coming on earlier, brighter. He squinted at the sunrise over the earth's remarkable, unremarkable spring. May in America.

Even if no one shows up, he thought, it's going to be a beautiful day.

A car turned onto the driveway.

Cleveland's husband stirred in his sleep on the other side of town, sensed weight, the body of his wife beside him—ah, so she *had* come home—and fell back into cloudy underwater silence.

Jonathan was dreaming of Annabelle—how could he reach her through all those seagulls swirling around?—though she was beside him.

An old brown dragster, dinky down at the end of the drive but growing as it approached. Dill shielded his eyes, too cool to stand. But as soon as he saw who it was, he leapt to his feet. The car rolled up and stopped sideways in front of the house, a prehistoric slab, inefficient and scaly. The door heaved open.

"Zee, my man." Dill grabbed him.

Three other warriors slumped out.

"I brought an extra." Zee grinned.

The car woke Janey. She went out blinking, her beautiful hair tangled. Zee saw her and sucked in his breath.

Janey's father had spent the night in front of reruns of cop shows. He knew Janey was up to something but he didn't know what. She hadn't come home—not so unusual—but she'd left the evening before without a love look on her face but one of determination. So what was going on? "I want to see this Mr. No One," he growled when she headed for the door. She had laughed.

He worried she was into drugs. Maybe the guy she'd gotten into had gotten her into them? Or was she pregnant? Was she off to get an abortion?

Not a day passed that he didn't think her mother would be doing a better job. Damn that woman for dying. He glared at the TV. *Blam blam.* Should he go out looking for her? He summoned her mother in his mind. Kid's almost twenty-one, he pleaded. Shouldn't he let her take care of herself? All right, all right, he promised. When she gets home, I'll have a talk with her. I'll say, "Whatever's going on, I'm there for you." (I'll kill the bastard, I'll wrap a cord around his neck.)

Of course he had it all wrong. Anyway he would have been wasting his words: Janey wouldn't have listened no matter what she was into. And she knew he was there for her.

More cars. Blues and grays and reds budding at the end of the drive and blooming as they drove up. Investigators getting out, stretching. "Long fucking ride! We drove all night." Dill greeting them with complicated handshakes, calling out affectionate insults. Annabelle rose from the sofa and went out waving, combing her hair with her fingers. Let's get this started, her face said.

Jonathan woke, fuzzy, seagulls flying to the corners of his mind. Annabelle was getting up. "Hey, where are you going?" He yawned, then remembered. Good lord, they weren't going to have to actually *do* this, were they? Was she kidding? He heard shouts.

This was exactly why he had not protested the divorce.

By the time Cleveland slipped out of the house, the field looked like it was moving.

At nine Cleveland's husband woke. Where'd she go *now*, on a Saturday morning? Had he dreamed her beside him? Where had she been for weeks now? Had he missed something? Were they fighting? He'd think she'd at least leave a note so a man knew where his goddamn estranged wife was.

Joy, at that hour, was in an aisle of soaps and cereals. She was wheeling both girls and a package of trash bags. The girls were shouting the word *help* for some reason, in unison, like a chant. She stopped to check her phone. Had heard nothing from him in two days now.

Janey was panicking. She was supposed to be directing cars but the investigators paid no attention. They bounded in like gazelles, left their cars where they liked. Cleveland hadn't arrived yet. Where was she? At last she saw Cleveland's car coming up the drive and she hurried over. Cleveland got out, spread her arms to the crowd. "Let this be a lesson, Janey, about what two women can do."

Had her mother said that?

Cleveland looked her over. "Where's your uniform?"

Janey grinned.

The hens had been up for hours by then. At Happy Green Family Farm the cage lights clicked on at 4:00 a.m. The hens were just standing there. Some of them were laying eggs. Some were caught in the wire and dying. Some were already dead.

By ten a procession of pickups and sedans and motorcycles filled the drive, were pulling onto the grass in haphazard lines. Dozens of people piled out and the place was rolling with people—jeaned, jacketed, young and old, hefting backpacks, dragging buds, hugging, hooting. A regular circus, a Dead concert. Somebody had a boom box and a handful of investigators were dancing, more joining in.

Dill was trying to keep his business face on, but couldn't help the pounding grin that kept bursting out. He worked through the crowd, allowed himself a moment to greet a few people, but wait, was that a fucking baby? He stopped dancing. Don't tell him that was a baby. He squeezed over. Fucking Penelope brought a baby. He could see Jarman up on the porch above them with a deep scowl, counting with a clicker each person. A few investigators had gotten into the chicken coop and were, what, trying to pick up the chickens? Come on. Then Dill's peripheral vision called to him and he pivoted to see, no, a *wheelchair*? How was that going to work? Some investigators were chanting, "Dill, Dill, Dill, look at us, look at us, look!" Bunch of kindergartners. They were dancing the bus stop, an old joke. What the hell: he rolled his shoulders, did a little step-to-the-side-step-back-clap, because, hey, the investigators had *come* and they'd brought their craziest closest friends from the animal shelters, from protests, pulled them out of their basement apartments or communes or group homes. They were committed, eager, vegan to a man. (In fact

Cleveland and Jonathan were the only nonvegans present. Janey had been vegan for four strong days now.) Under a tree, there was Annabelle, poised, chatting, a long dress wrapped around her, hair down her back, her hands lifted to kiss faces.

Dill could see Jarman up on the porch, counting with the clicker. He tried to read Jarman's face—how many so far? Dill moved a little closer. How many? He felt a chill of uncertainty: Jarman's face was the look of joy drained. Were there not enough people? Dill had stopped counting cars and cars ago. Jarman looked afraid, there was no denying it. Dill handed back the baby to Penelope (how had he wound up holding it?) and pushed through the people, ran up the porch steps.

"Well, our plan is fucked," Jarman was saying irritably. "We'll need to redo the whole thing. I designed it for 303 people. I said 303."

"How many more do we need?"

"You're blocking me. Move. There's another car."

"Jarman, what do we got?"

"With those three," he clicked, "421."

Dill repeated it. "Four hundred and . . ." For a moment he didn't understand, then he did.

WHY DID THEY COME? Adventure, of course, but there were other reasons. Some, like Zee, came for Dill. For all Dill's faults (many), the guy was loyal. No one could say he wasn't there for his crew, including any dogs or birds or other animals that somehow or other wound up on his porch. The investigators knew this. So did Annabelle, Jonathan, Dev, even the damn dogs, which is perhaps why so many stood by him for so long. Loyalty is hard to come by and should get its due.

More came for Annabelle, had known her all this time. Some had known her since she was a child, had attended her wedding with their parents, had walked off their families' farms when she did, had followed her through the years—habit, addiction, or faith—until she disappeared, and even then they understood why. They knew she wasn't a fool. And Dill was sharp when he stayed off the drugs—he was off at the moment, clearly. Also they were comforted by the presence of Jonathan. He wouldn't be doing this if it couldn't be done. Impossible as it seemed, he'd come up with the numbers and judged them sound.

But most of all they came for the animals, of course. They'd become activists at age four when they learned the chicken in the soup was the same species they saw on farm day, pushed away their bowls, gone vegan on the spot. Or in high school, when they'd seen a clip of Thanksgiving turkeys hung alive on the line. Or they'd had dogs. Zee had had a brother who'd died, expanding Zee's respect for all lives, including first the ones on his plate, then the ones in his bomber jacket, then the ones making hives in the walls, until he vowed not to harm any at all.

However it happened, their experiences in the barns had strengthened their convictions. They'd spent twelve-hour days placing the baby-soft beaks of chicks into hot-iron guillotines, searing off the tips, while the chicks struggled and their faces smoked.

Hens. Sweet little puffs. The solid adventure of saving them: Who didn't want to be part of it? Who wouldn't? The time had come to say *no more*.

THE OPPOSITION.

Here they are, barricaded in their concrete barns. They're dug in, ready—though they don't know what or who is coming. They wait behind ramparts of drying excrement, behind fans six feet high. The farm people, the few left on the prairie, the holdout humans.

Here's the barn manager. See him zipping up his jacket by the silos, piloting his golf cart. He's got tools and communication devices clipped to his belt like a captain on *Star Trek*. He swaggers, snaps something in his mouth. He shouts over the machinery in English and Spanish.

See the egg runners, the ones who fix the belts, the ones who do the daily hen inspection. Five or six of them step out of their jumpsuits, leaving early because it's Saturday. (An occasional investigator hides among them but not today, as they're all busy elsewhere.)

The truckers, the mechanics. The pop and depop crew. None of those are here today, or most days. This little pack off in the shadows is the rodent control squad—you can smell their poison but you rarely see their persons, only their markings: their handwriting, their traps, their baits, their bombs. You see evidence of their failures.

These are the desk people, a few to a farm. See them work their control system keyboards. Set against vinyl-partition backdrops, they lean forward on pressure-adjustable chairs. They wear uniforms of beige blouses, beige sweaters, beige hair. Their faces are beigeing with age, but do not doubt their strength. Their holiday earrings swing. Their pens bloom from a cup. They have pinned up behind them messages from God. On the sill sits the kind of plant that never dies. Only one of them is here today, the Saturday of the evacuation, and she'll be going home shortly. She presses a button and says it will be just a moment.

These are the families. The rear guard, the support troops. They stay away from the farm. They amass on holidays and eat ham, celery, hard-boiled eggs. You can see their faces on phone screens, observe their gadget gifts, read their dispatches.

The land. Its grand width, long horizon, its coordinates, its unmarked roads that cut through hand-sized towns and run flat and straight. This battle does not take place on the hilly side of Iowa.

These are the barns. They're made up of belts and birds and catwalks, ten lux of illumination and the eight-degree slope of a hen's floor. From airplanes they look like lined-up sticks of gum. Thousands of tons of feed, hundreds of acres of steel bent again and again into a labyrinth of right angles. Guests are asked to step into disinfectant foot baths before coming in, like a liquid welcome mat.

Here are the manuals, the animal movement logs, the light programs, the beak-trimming protocol. The amount of CO_2 gas used for mass extermination.

These are the farmers. An endangered species, each year a handful fewer than the year before, as the farmlands slowly depopulate (and the number of eggs grows and grows). Men built like blocks atop very clean, very white tennis shoes. They wear plain wedding bands, jeans pulled up to here. Republicans, old-style white men, Christians. An ultrapolite command, they exude a controlled calm. They can be glimpsed leaving the conference room, pausing at reception.

None of these people went into farming because they hate chickens, for Christ's sake. What do you think? It's the eggs, the eggs, so many being made that if they didn't come to work, who knows what would happen. We used to eat eggs a few times a year, but now they are everywhere, emerging from the nation's farms at an alarming rate, seventy-five billion per year. Citizens must eat as many as we can. It is our patriotic duty. We must put them into all of our meals, all of our batters and breads and spreads and sauces, our breakfasts, on top of our meat or under it, inside our sandwiches, into all of our snacks one way or another, our power bars and chocolate. But still that won't be enough. Still more eggs are coming, piling up on the belts, leaving the farms, assembling on the grocery shelves, into refrigerators, more and more and more. We must soldier on, find other ways to consume them. We must put them on our faces, in our hair. We could grind up the shells and make toothpaste. We could build rocket ships and shoot the yolks off into space, small suns, we could explode them and smear them across a daylight sky.

Here's a farmer now. He's coming out of the farthest barn at the end of the day. He's younger, springier than most. He's talking into his cell phone, the barns rising around him.

Farmer Rob ("Robbie Jr.") Green. He got ready to leave that Saturday of the evacuation, but had no one to wave to as he walked to the lot. Saturday had a skeleton crew. By four the farm was empty. The night security man wouldn't be arriving until seven. He locked the office, unaware this was anything other than a perfectly normal, utterly irritating day. Rob Jr. (he didn't like to be called "Robbie" anymore, but he wasn't ready to be called Farmer Green either), brother of Annabelle Green Jarman, was all grown up (or mostly, he was twenty-eight). He had a wife and a baby to protect—and the farm, of course. He was in charge now, though he hadn't intended for his life to work out this way. He got into his car, lifted his clean white gym shoes off the gravel, and drove away.

AT STAKE: the contested objects, nine hundred thousand white leghorn hens, their foremothers brought over from Italy in the midnineteenth century and bred in a frenzy ever since. Were they property or individuals? That's what had to be decided.

It was from this farm, don't forget, that Cleveland had taken Bwwaauk some three months before, when she dropped out of her cage and went walking down the road in search of more.

Bwwaauk had spent her life from the time she was a pullet on this farm.

You'd think that by now with all the genetic meddling, sensory deprivation, and inbreeding, a hundred and fifty years' worth, that these animals would barely have brains anymore, that their minds' dials would be set on static, a low hum, refrigeration vibration. You'd think they'd be blank-brained, a collection of impulses and flesh. Indeed some of the hens on Happy Green Family Farm were moronic slabs, but most were not. They all contained within them the DNA, if not the full expression, of the original bird intelligence. Those hardy genes pressed themselves into existence in all kinds of ways, so that most of these hens still had that feral smart-bird spark in the eye, the instinctual *Gallus* need to flock, wander, arrange themselves into hierarchies, mate, rear, befriend, follow, fly their awkward short flights, bathe and preen in the dust.

Those hundreds of thousands of brains of Happy Green Farm were ticking away in those grim warehouses, crushed into tiny boxes (or crowded into larger boxes in the two so-called cage-free barns), half-smothered and rotting alive in the oppressive air, barely able to spread their wings, unable to look up and see anything but steel and conveyor belts and low-wattage bulbs, pressed up against strangers, beaks half-severed, feet deformed by the wire they stood on day and night.

Bwwaauk had grown up in Barn 8, an old-style A-frame structure, where the cages are piled in tiers on a slant so that when the crap drops through the wire, it misses (mostly) the hens in the lower tiers. Bwwaauk had lived in a bottom-row cage, the worst spot on an A-frame because crap drops on you from above (the system isn't perfect). The whole jalopy is placed on the second floor of the barn with a large opening underneath. The excrement falls through the wire to a huge open room below called the pit.

Barn 8 was the oldest barn on the farm, built in 1990. Its cages were rusty. In places the wire had corroded and had holes in it, holes the size of a chicken. In most rows if a hole broke through the rust and a hen fell through, she simply landed in the cage below her. The hens in that cage would peck her to death as an invader, then stand on her dead or dying body to give their feet a rest from the wire. But in Bwwaauk's case, when the ammonia ate through the rust, the hole that broke open was in a cage on the bottom row. So when Bwwaauk fell, she flopped down onto a six-foot pile of excrement.

She landed with a thump. She looked up at the cage she'd just left. The hens in the cage peered down through the hole at her below. They all assessed the situation.

In the wild, chickens have complicated cliques and distinct voices. They talk among themselves, even before they hatch. A hen twitters and sings to her eggs and the chicks inside answer, peeping and burbling and clicking through the shells. Adult chickens have over thirty categories of conversation, each with its own web of coos and calls and clucks and struts. Chickens gossip, summon, play, flirt, teach, warn, mourn, fight, praise, and promise.

It is this last, *promise*, that concerns us here.

In a cage situation a hen has little use for most of these categories of conversation. Her vocabulary atrophies or never fully develops—but it's there, contained within the brain (which stores and processes information differently from the human brain—the bird's brain is more like a microchip folded inside the cortex, not like the human's bulky car motor) and will surface when necessary.

So it was that in the moment Bwwaauk turned her face up to the hens in the cage she'd just fallen from, she struggled to communicate, her mind turned on. Winked to life.

There is a particular cheep isolated by bird researchers who specialize in the *Gallus gallus*. This sound, when tagged onto the end of a vocalization, translates to something like, "It's coming." So a mother might cheep to her chicks, "Follow me up here! Danger—it's coming!" Or if a male is strutting in front of a female and he tacks the cheep to the end of a crow, he might mean, "Passion, food, babies, protection—it's coming, girl!" In other words, this cheep works as a rudimentary form of the future tense. This hen that Cleveland took, whose brain was lighting up, turning over, working, while she looked up at her hen friends in the cage (hens have long-lasting friendships and can recognize over a hundred other chicken faces, even after months of separation, and they recognize human faces too), her brain was in the toil of trying to convey the complex thought, *I'll be back for you, I promise*, not a sentence hens would generally have a lot of use for in or out of cages, since they like to stay close to one another, even in the wild. This particular cheep came to her.

She made the sound of her own name—Bwwaauk—and the cheep, "It's coming." Then she slid down the pile of excrement and marched on.

She never did go back, but she sent someone to fetch them.

JONATHAN HADN'T BELIEVED they would come. Or anyway not so many of them. But now as he shook himself awake and reluctantly followed Annabelle out with his clicker, he conceded he *had* known they would come (though he hadn't believed it, those two could coexist: an admission of fact alongside an expression of incredulity) because she had asked them to.

How did she get people to do things? Jonathan had never sold a cage. Those enriched cages? She'd been the one to convince the farmers. And when she decreed that all hens be cage free, the whole industry veered in that direction. When she decided cage free wasn't good enough, that husbandry itself was the issue, her minions filed out behind her.

Still more investigators were arriving. And more, though they could not all have been investigators. Not that many in the history of the world. They were coming up the road, filling the yard with clunkers, some roaring in on motorcycles (typical), a few came on foot, walking past the trees. He recognized some from the old days (so *that's* where they wound up—nowhere), and over there he saw her latest additions, the auditors, standing together, apart from the others, the pretty one laughing, the blond one with her usual face of stone.

His phone buzzed. Joy. He didn't answer.

He could see Annabelle out there, talking to a man whose face was covered in tattoos. Yes, she had a way about her. The sort of thing that gets people to join cults, start wars. Charisma, they called it. And Dill—who was coming up the porch steps—he had it too, Jonathan grudgingly admitted. Allure.

"How many more do we need, Jarman?" Dill was saying.

Annabelle. Her face turned for a moment from the cartoon she was talking to, rose, shining, searching out his.

"Jarman, what do we got?"

"Move," he told Dill. "With those three, 421."

His phone vibrated to let him know he had a message.

In the end the final head count was 507, fucking show-off investigators, and Jonathan already had a massive headache.

"Amazing," the pretty auditor kept saying, "far out."

"This is not far out," Jonathan said. "This is 204 too many, 204 people whose only possible function in this plan is to fuck it up."

Yes, now they had the hands, but also higher risk. This could disintegrate into chaos more easily. There could be last-moment dissenters or wafflers or weaklings. There could be unknown elements among them who could be their undoing (in fact, there were), but too late now. Everyone had to be enfolded.

Their only hope was time: they were setting out tonight. Nearly no time for the many fiascos this number of eager assholes could put together.

"I just don't see how extras can be a problem," the auditor was saying.

Dill was nodding. "Extras can only help."

"Uh huh," said Jonathan. "You watch."

When the final hour arrived, Annabelle and Dill peeled away first.

"Wait, where are you going?"

"To take care of the security guard," Annabelle called, walking backward away from him.

"What security guard?" said Jonathan. "You said Ricardo's on vacation."

"This is the temp."

"Temp?"

3

NIGHT, WOMAN, MAN. A road from farm to farm.

But there was a third farm in all this.

First farm: the one they were headed to. Eight barns, 1.2 million birds at capacity, a rumble of machinery, a stench.

Second farm: the one they were coming from. Willed to the banker on a deathbed. Seventy acres, mostly grassland at this point. A barn, a shed, a house. A farm that no longer functioned as more than a holding tank for the itinerant bird, dog, or human.

Third farm: the original. Founded by Grandfather Green just after World War II. Sprung up in the second wave of the modern American henhouse.

Grandfather Green was just Leo Green then. Back from the war with decorations, drive, and a GI Bill mortgage. He bought a piece of farmland three miles outside his home village, beside a quiet forest where a river twisted through, not much good for hunting except squirrels and birds, but peaceful. He didn't build a house on that land, that's not how it was being done anymore. He built a giant barn instead. A decade earlier a barn of over ten thousand hens was unheard of. But this was the dawn of the highway, TV, suburbs, and radical confinement. The United States—and soon the world—would never be the same (though what does that mean, really? every moment nothing is the same).

Leo Green's first barn held thirty thousand hens.

Over the decades he refitted his barn, once before the Vietnam War and once after, with all new equipment. It could hold fifty thousand birds, then seventy thousand. Then he tore the whole thing down and replaced it with the latest the '80s had to offer: a battery barn for a hundred and ten thousand hens. The country had arrived at the era of shopping malls, gutted cities, emptying farmlands, and mass incarceration. Farmer Green had the blueprints to construct two more barns in the next three years.

Instead he was pulled up short in 1986 by a Cold War surprise. A nearby weapons company, which at the time employed a third of the village, accidentally (though that word implies inadvertence and ignorance) had been leaking, dumping, and floating downstream powerful chemical agents. Everyone had to get off that land. *Now.* Dermal contact, inhalation of fugitive vapors, soil and groundwater ingestion: all held risks. So the entire town and for miles around, including Grandfather Green's farm, took their settlements and cleared out (additional payments promised for the next ten years, but were discontinued after four, the courts grown weary), leaving Grandfather Green's new battery barn empty. Green set up a new farm ninety miles away and had three barns up in three years, right on schedule.

But the original barn, long since vacant of its machinery, its cages removed, still stood. A husk, a shell, it had not detained a hen in thirty years.

Daylight was leaving, the sun shifting lower. The insects are disappearing from our planet, but on this night they held strong. All around the empty barn, insects were rubbing their instruments, tuning up, playing the preludes to the millions of songs that sound to the human ear like the authorless plainchants, a chorus of Dark Age petitioners, though in fact each cricket song contains variations that make it unique.

A hundred swallows on their way elsewhere alit on thin feet on the roof of Leo Green's barn. They checked their internal universal map, then were on their way.

• • •

A woman and a man, traveling from farm to farm, exited the highway and passed a small road. If they had gone down that road, through a twenty-six-mile stretch onto contaminated land and over a contaminated river, to the remains of an abandoned contaminated village and nearby abandoned factory, and then another three miles, almost to the edge of a forest, they would have arrived at this farm. The woman turned her head and looked down the small road as they drove by.

A: It had always been Dill and me. From the time we met, we had an understanding. We'd started something cunning and secret together and it had gotten away from us. We've been living in the aftermath ever since.

The day I resigned from the organization I told no one but him where I was going. I packed a few things and drove past the warning signs and barriers. No trespassing. Keep out. Superfund Site. Physical and chemical hazards present. No off-road travel. And so on. The barbed wire was rusted, fallen over in places, twisted and running along the ground. I remember there had been talk of designing totems to warn humans off for thousands of years but the money had not materialized. The future will have to fend for itself, I suppose. This is hardly the worst of the little surprises we'll be leaving.

I went into the original village, which had been abandoned when I was a year old. I picked through the wreckage, the houses, the factory. Nature had ravaged the place in revenge. The evacuation signs lay facedown in the weeds like fallen soldiers. I walked down to the riverbank. The whole tributary was poisoned, but a few miles up, near the old farm, in the forest preserve, it was supposed to be all right. I could bring water down. I decided to set up my home right there in the heart of civilized civilization-destruction.

Dill and I used to say what was needed were areas of human withdrawal, land and water that people would voluntarily remove themselves from and vow not to enter, allow nature to go on without us. *Wilderness*, we called it. But now I understand that will never happen. Humans won't volunteer to do anything but destroy. They will have to be forced out. And no one can make them do it—not any other animal, not even nature. But no one will have to. They'll do it themselves.

And that moment when they go? It will be an opportunity.

THE NIGHT THEY WENT to get the chickens was new spring and the smell of shit stood in the fields. A procession of seventy vehicles began to leave the banker's farm, a few at a time. They drove north down the highway, exited, a series of blinkers like Morse code in the twilight. They rode through the church-dotted towns, past pale sidewalks, long yards, little houses, streetlights winking on. They drove by pastures, thickets of trees, a Walmart on the dimming horizon. At last they arrived, hundreds of investigators (though it wasn't only investigators now—they had shelter workers, tattoo artists, vegan dishwashers, younger brothers). Across the field, silver silos jutted into the sky over a collection of windowless warehouses, like a fallout shelter for an entire city, an industrial vision of Oz.

The vehicles paused at the corners of the fields and let investigators out into the scrub. They ducked out of cars, hopped off truck beds, ran low along the tree line. They squatted at the far end of the shit, a shit expanse that stretched half a mile from their shoes to the edge of the enormous iron shit factory: the henhouses.

They waited. On their backs they had small packs of sandwiches, bottles of water, gloves. They had filed off the soles of their shoes, as Annabelle had taught them. They could hear the hum of machinery, that pure sound, the song and silencing of America. Two miles to their backs, on neighborhood side roads, no more than two to a block, the driver-investigators were leaving their vehicles, emerging to walk over with a casual nonchalance, and miles beyond that, sixty trucks at five different truck stops waited.

In the field the investigators hung back, eyes adjusting, ears twitching. All were arranging their minds into a neat stack of thought, minds that by nature are so small and poorly organized compared to the massive farm. On the top layer of their minds they placed the thickest thought: the calm necessary to move forward—no small maneuver, even for those who'd trained years.

One layer down was the mind's assembly team, which was reviewing the steps, how it would all go down, hour by hour—their feet carrying them to their assigned spots, their hands forming the necessary circles and releases, the breakaway plan, the other breakaway plan—checking off each step as they imagined its completion.

Below that layer, shoved underneath, was another layer, the nagging pragmatist: *There is no way this can work.*

Below that, the philosopher: *What does that even mean, "work"? What exactly is this meant to accomplish?*

Below that, another layer: the mind's disassembly team. It was hacking away at the steps. All that could go wrong. The plan lay in broken pieces in a muddy parking lot across the mind.

And below that was one man struggling in his shackles, shouting upward through the layers, *How many things have you fucked up in your life and is this going to be one of them?* and had to be drowned out with the clanging and stomping of the others.

Below that was another layer and another, layer after layer, descending through consciousness into what lies beneath, as the human brain becomes inaccessible to itself and you are floating past mushy desires and blurry primitive terrors, the prickly instinct territory, until you arrive and settle on the bottom, at that hard core of ceaseless longing that unites (or divides) us all.

But the night they went to get the chickens (the "evacuation" they were calling it, though the auditors insisted it was a "removal"), the investigators knew they were the least interesting aspect of what was going on. The chickens, the sheer number of them, an existentially disturbing, global-crisis amount, *they* were the subject. The investigators (and AR people of all stripes who stood or crouched, waiting in the damp shit) had to be in agreement on this, or they'd never pull it off. They had to insist (their presence at the edge of the field was mere suggestion, the insistence was still coming) that hens, and indeed all creatures, including arrogant, ignorant humans, are not ugly, stupid, or eligible for ownership. They had to stand by this belief, keep it at the front of their minds (and not the thought that they were likely going to prison, or back to prison for some of them).

They waited.

Meanwhile, unseen elements were shifting toward what was coming. The future was pulling the present into itself. Even what seemed to have nothing to do with it took part (the motes floating, the quiet wild air lifting and lowering the trees' leaves, the excrement sinking under them, the hens' minds turning as they stood in their cages, the children climbing into their beds two miles off, their parents let loose at last, their quiet wild thoughts running, though tamped down and regulated into squares by their screens) because all movement is linked and rides together.

When the signal came, the investigator Zee, whom Janey would one day marry, rose and waved an arm. The investigators straightened and followed him in three single files into the field.

FIFTEEN HOURS LATER Janey will be sitting on the floor beside this investigator, Zee. Her elbow will be touching his hip, her wrists cuffed in her lap. He'll turn to her and speak. She won't know his name but she'll know his voice, that he was the man who'd been last with her in the banker's barn, the guy who'd said Annabelle had a shitty idea. He'll say something similar now. Again it'll piss her off.

But ten minutes later he'll have her smiling.

DON'T MAKE A *SHUSH* SOUND AT A BIRD. If you must make a sound, make a *coo*. *Shush* is the sound of a snake, and birds, all birds, even freaks in cages, still know a snake when they hear one and will panic. Never leave a hen in the cold. Their combs will get frostbite. Combs are used for heat regulation, yes, but also for sex appeal, and a hen with a frost-black comb is *not* cute. Never turn a hen upside down. Never swing a hen by her legs. When you lift a hen, place one hand under her breast and take both of her legs gently with the other. She'll tuck in her wings and feel secure.

If you let chickens mix together to mate and wander as they like, they will slowly slide into the wild ways of their ancestors.

THE INVESTIGATORS ROSE UP out of the fields and walked through the dark toward the barns. Their shoes left only smooth dirt as evidence. The first trucks began to arrive, cranking their gears, their headlights throwing shapes. A lone investigator stood on the road, flagging them in, though the drivers knew where to go. They'd studied the map, and it would not be unusual for catching crews to turn up at this hour with their long trucks. All over the world farmers know to catch their hens at night, when they're ready for sleep, not a fight.

The investigators fanned out, stringing to their assigned barns with no fuss (they were professionals). The investigator Zee opened the door to Barn 2, the one Jarman had assigned him. One step into the cage area and there he was, back in the fucking barns with their racket and dim light and stink. It hadn't been so long that he'd forgotten them, but still it was a shock.

He took it all in, the rows of cages, each so long you couldn't see the other end, the *woo woo woo* of the birds, like a hundred thousand kazoos, and the low-base pulse of the fans. An extreme density of music, a concert, a long song. Grime covered the cages and hung off them in icicles. He almost allowed himself to think, This is obvious-ass impossible, but he didn't. He laughed. Well, let's get on with it. He unlatched the first cage with a gloved hand and reached in.

CLEVELAND WAS ALSO IN BARN 2. She left Janey in the row, was squeezing around the large metal carts of batteries (the industry term for transport cages), ducking by the investigators, running up the aisle, because she felt she had a responsibility to see the first hens loaded. She had taken the first hen that started all this, after all (where was that hen now?).

She stopped. It was happening, investigators lifting battery racks up onto the truck with a heave-ho, since the two forklifts were over in Barns 1 and 3. She couldn't help it, she raised her phone and took a picture (which would later be entered as evidence, along with all the other videos and photos she'd taken over the past months), though Annabelle and Dill had strictly forbade it and no one else was doing it, more professional, apparently, than the head auditor.

The photo was decent—investigators in work gloves, focused faces frozen in postures of calm. No one would have expected that she and the daughter of Olivia Flores were capable of this. But they'd done it.

When the batteries on the truck snapped into place the investigators cheered. Not all of them could see what was happening. They were spread through the barn, pulling hens, rolling carts, but they heard the cheers and knew what it meant and they cheered too (woo! woo!), their voices joining the sounds of the hens. And Cleveland raised her voice too, an auditor shouting with joy. Then she turned around and headed back to Janey.

A starter gun sounded in the collective investigator-minds, and they were off.

FOR JONATHAN'S PART, it didn't occur to him that he might be "missing" something when the evacuation began. He didn't care about seeing the first hens loaded. He was busy. And he didn't have that sensation of "missing" two hours later, when it was all going beautifully. Trucks were coming in and out, the night cool, here and there a whole aisle untenanted now, the hens' coo diminishing. It was going better than he'd hoped. Wrinkles, yes, but so easily smoothed that the plan would not have been perfect without them because perfection is not perfect without small flaws to remind us of the darkness of (im)perfection.

The architecture of the design was the most beautiful feature. At any given moment the birds were moving out of the barns at an average rate of 21,666 chickens per hour per barn, or about 130,000 for all six, the investigators doing depop at a rate of 410 per hour per investigator, which is about three or four times slower than a usual depop, not bad. And when the first trucks pulled away at nine, right on time, the shouts that went up felt like a light summer rain.

You had the flurry inside, yes. He had six crews of fifty-five investigators, each crew assigned to a barn pulling hens, all having to be on their best behavior: fast, focused, working nonstop for hours, taking short breaks (five breaths) as needed. Many (not him) had done handling work in the past. Many more had not. Still, within an hour you couldn't tell who was who. Investigators rolling empty carts, investigators pushing full carts, heavy with hundreds of hens, three-quarters capacity, which was the most he'd been able to talk Annabelle into (by arguing that if there was *too* much space, they'd bump around and be injured on the road "unless you want to install nine hundred thousand seat belts"). He noticed his cage design in Barns 2 and 3. And the cage-free barns had the latest style of aviaries. Impressive.

Of course, the hens were in no position to sit still and let themselves be lifted quickly and quietly. Hens go into a sort of stupor when they sleep, but they will eventually wake and now they were running and screaming like someone had just turned on all the lights. They attacked the investigators with everything they had, going for the arms, necks, eyes. It was rough on them all—investigators and hens—but they had only to make it to the sanctuaries. The hens would be placed in straw with gentle un-hurried hands, and from there Jonathan would be home free. (And he could get the hell out of there and go back to Joy because he never, ever, wanted to see Annabelle again, Jesus. Their passion the night before had been childish.)

All Jonathan had to do was set up the best conditions for them to make it to their destinations alive, not have trucks arriving full of dead birds. Yet there were going to be dead birds. A tremen-dous number of dead birds was involved in all this. You'd reach into a cage and one would be dead, trampled into the wire by her roommates. There were dead birds scattered over the grates. Neither Annabelle nor Jonathan wanted to leave a mess of dead birds behind, so Annabelle had one investigator running through the barns, gathering up the dead bodies to take along in heavy sacks (and eventually cremate, at Annabelle's sentimental insis-tence, their ashes blown over a friendlier field).

It looked like a siege inside those barns and that's what it was.

But if you pulled back from the nitty-gritty, a situation verg-ing on (but not quite) out of control, you could begin to see the shape, this knot of creatures, genetically twisted and stuffed into a line of dark buildings by the million, now coming out in clusters, moving in every direction away from the farm—think star ray, sunburst, firework, explosion—flowing over a pitted landscape. Inhale and exhale, birds released over the country.

That old, permanent, electric feeling of wanting to please Annabelle was unfastening from the locked depths. He'd fallen in love in these barns (Annabelle only eighteen!), walking up and down, waving his points into the air. Hens had been his life's work, the improvement of their conditions of confinement. Annabelle had cherished him for it.

And there it was at last: that sensation of *missing*. He missed that part of himself.

If you could see that (and Jonathan did) you could begin to see other things you were missing and missed, as in: it had been plain and you somehow hadn't seen it, you'd *missed* it. And *missed out*, as in: he'd *missed out* on becoming whoever that person would have been who had continued on that path. And also *missed*, as in: remembered her in a physical, visceral way (last night!), and he changed his mind (again) from his earlier repudiation. He felt the pain of loss (the wound was open again, goddamnit).

Hours later, when it was not going beautifully, when investigators were running through the fields, all his orderly escape plans abandoned, smoke taking over the sky, Jonathan had that thought again, that he'd *missed her*, in yet another sense. He was sprinting from barn to barn, calling her name, hoping he hadn't *missed* her, that she hadn't left, or more likely, gone off to do something crazy (she had, but not the crazy thing he thought), and break her promise. She had to be around somewhere. He was moving against the tide of fleeing investigators, bumping into them, calling out, screaming, "Has anybody seen Annabelle?" though no one was listening.

But that was still hours off.

JANEY WAS WATCHING THE HENS move out of the barns at an incredible speed, the battery carts flying down the rows, the racks going up into the trucks, the birds waiting in the cool night air for whatever would happen next to them.

So why the sinking feeling, the dark premonition?

It wasn't looking like it was supposed to look. It wasn't matching the vision, birds shucking off their cages, the roof falling away, the stars. The roof was still up there. The hens were going from cages into smaller cages, cages to cages, and not that gently. Some of the investigators were not skilled and were hurting the birds as they removed them. And though the transport cages weren't full, it was still an awful lot of birds per battery. Hens would be injured, some would be dead before they arrived. Meanwhile, only three hours in, some investigators were tired. They all had a long way to go.

She wondered if she'd been wrong. Had her vision not been a calling? (In fact, it had not been.) She tried to glimpse it: hens with a power unheard of, flapping into the night. She wondered fleetingly (the thought shooting through like a bird) what the other Janey was doing.

Cleveland was so wrapped up in lifting the chickens correctly (it was harder than it looked, especially when they were at the back of the cage) that she didn't notice Janey staring into space.

Zee saw an investigator just standing there at the end of a row, arms hung at her sides, not moving. What was the matter with her? Get busy! Did she think they were there to gawk? He headed toward her. As barn leader it was his job to bark her into action, but as he got close he recognized her—that girl from this morning, the one who'd walked out onto the porch with tangled hair. He stopped, heart jangling. He turned and jogged the other way.

SEVEN YEARS LATER Dill was on the phone. Zee's voice was coming through, despite a bad connection. Zee was saying, "She won't come out of the bedroom."

Yep, they still called Dill. He'd gotten them at an early enough age that they'd imprinted on him like baby chicks, the investigators. A dozen or so had anyway. They were all still vegan, and in moments of need they thought of him first.

"I don't know what to do."

Dill swiveled away from the desk, leaned back to face the ceiling. "Give her time."

"Her father hates me."

"So don't let him in. Who cares what he thinks."

"No, he won't let *me* in. It's his apartment. Her bedroom at her father's place."

"Shit, she moved home?"

"No, she *left* home. *Our* house is home. Janey loves this house. She's in her old bedroom at her father's crummy apartment. She won't come out. She's been in there for a week."

"That is heavy."

"I'm telling you. She's broken. I don't know what to do. I'm losing my mind. I'm alone in this house. Place is full of stuffed animals. Place looks like a toy chest, like a baby store. I built a fort in the backyard."

"He wouldn't have climbed a fort for years."

"I know it. I just wanted to build it."

"You guys were getting ahead of yourselves."

"Hardly. I mean, he was out of her body and alive. He was almost three months old."

"Almost isn't enough."

"It's a lot. You know she's never lived in a house before? She wanted a house. This was her idea. Now she won't come out of that fucking bedroom."

"She's in mourning."

"He was my baby too, for fuck's sake." Zee was crying. "She says I'm going on like nothing happened."

"Sounds like you."

"Of course I am. From day one that's all you do—go on like nothing happened."

Most of them had left AR, or been spit out. They'd gone back to school, become lawyers or journalists or truck drivers, reversed their vasectomies, started families. New investigators had stepped into their shoes, though the US farmers had gotten so good at keeping them out, investigator units had gone international—Mexico, India, New Zealand—but Dill didn't do that work anymore.

"We were so close," said Dill, "if not for Barn 8."

Zee sniffled. "Fuck Barn 8."

"We could have done it otherwise."

"No, we could *not* have, Dill. You need to give that up already."

"We could have."

"Not this again," Zee groaned. "I'm going to kill myself, man. It's over for me."

Dill sighed. Zee was thirty-two, Janey twenty-eight. Life is so, so long. Dill had been crushed by the banker, destroyed, and yet here he was, seven years later, loving someone else. We always think it's over for us—and it *is* over—then it starts again. Reincarnation in this lifetime.

But Zee and Janey. He thought they could make it.

"Look, you want your wife back, broken or not?"

"That's what I've been *saying*."

"Here's what you do." Dill leaned forward and the chair squeaked. "Call the power company. Tell them to turn off the power."

"Drive her out? Her father'd kill me."

"Not his apartment, you idiot. Your *house*."

"It's going to be awfully dark in here."

"Cancel the newspaper."

"We don't get no fucking paper newspaper. Kill a thousand trees."

"Forward the mail to her father's."

"He won't like that."

"Pack a suitcase. Two suitcases. Pack enough to last a long time. Go knock on her father's door. Bring the suitcases."

"I don't know if he'll let me in."

"Go into her bedroom. Don't leave. You stay in that bedroom. All day. Sleep there."

"My job won't give me time off."

"Quit the job. It's a stupid job. You can get another job just as stupid or stupider later. Go in that room where Janey is and wait until she's ready to leave."

"Both of us in there?"

"Yeah. You stay no matter what. Weeks if you have to. Months. You tell her, say, This is not Barn 8, okay? There is no Barn 8 when it comes to you. You tell her that. Nothing is burning this shit down."

"Fuck yeah."

"Now go pack."

"No Barn 8."

"Right. Good luck, man."

Dill hung up and swiveled back to his desk.

But Dill was wrong. It wasn't true that they could have done it without Barn 8. Even without Barn 8 it was impossible. There was no place they could have taken all those hens.

THEY WERE AWASH WITH HENS. No other way for Dill to put it. It was as if a sea of hens had swept in and not drained away and now they were drowning in them, hens rising far overhead, a tide of them, an undertow.

It had been going smoother than expected until about 3:00 a.m. Then they began to fall behind. Dill was outside Barn 1 passing around bags of nuts but there could be no doubt that the team was losing steam. Collectively wearying. Hens had gotten out and were running underfoot. Some of the batteries weren't fitting onto one of the trucks (was it truck 1-5? 1-6? fucking Jarman and his convoluted number system) and slowing everything down while the investigators unpacked half the truck to try to understand their error. Stacks of batteries were piled along the ground. Another truck (3-9? 4-6?) was idling in the driveway, waiting to get in. It was blocking the path of yet another truck (?) on its way out. Two investigators were waving this truck in opposite directions, the *beep beep beep* of backing so loud and long over the roar of the fans that Dill feared it could attract attention. Off to the left three investigators were pushing a cart of batteries in circles, destined for truck 2-8, which hadn't arrived, though it should have by now and might be lost.

Annabelle came over to Dill. Her face was streaked with sweat and dirt, her hair full of static, but she was calm.

"Dill, do me a favor. Put those down."

He dropped his sack of snacks.

"We need to check all the barns. See where we're at."

"Right."

"I'll take these three. You take the rest."

Dill took off across the field toward Barns 4, 5, and 6. His shoes pressed down into the dirt and shit.

Chicken shit. In this business it was once a valuable commodity. Sold as fertilizer in a competitive market, an extra dime for the farmhands—phosphorus, nitrogen, potassium, everybody's happy. But the nation's number of hens squared and squared and squared, and their shit squared with them. Supply left demand behind decades ago. A hundred and fifty thousand hens make two thousand tons of manure a year. On a farm such as this, the farmer has to contend with sixteen thousand tons of shit before Christmas. Meanwhile, chemical fertilizer has become cheap and is a hell of a lot easier than hauling around thousands of tons of shit. Farmers pay for their shit to be carried away and put into landfills. Some of it winds up in our waterways. Some is spread out in the fields around the chicken farms as a sort of superfertilization. That shit sinks into the earth over a period of years and more is spread over it, tamping down the shit beneath it to form a thick crust of chicken shit to stay for all time.

Now the heel of Dill's shoe pressed down onto one piece of shit in particular. That shit, a bit denser than most shit due to the mysteries of biology, pushed past the shit around it, and sank. It continued to sink, bit by bit, through the other shit, over days and months and years, until it arrived at pre–Green Farm dirt. From there its slight heft began a slow historic—then posthistoric— descent. As the earth made its rotation, as the planets moved on their skytracks, as humans raised and lowered their civilizations, the shit traveled a hundredth of a millimeter at a time farther below the surface of the world, sucked by gravity, until it broke free into the cavern of the water table. It drifted down through the soft mud, landed on the bottom, and kept going, grinding through tertiary layers, chalk, carbon. Finally one day this extraordinary piece of shit stuck fast in the Paleozoic era, its cellular makeup joining its ancestors and imprinting a fossil into the rock.

Far above the shit, in the shifting sky, the stars were the only objects humans could see and not destroy. They could destroy only the sight of them, which they were doing, dot by dot, the stars blinking out over the planet, dimmed by human light. But from where the investigators were that night, they could still look up and see some, and Dill did, before entering Barn 4.

BARN 4 HAD ENRICHED CAGES. Dill walked through. The aisles were like funhouse mirrors, cages until you couldn't see, columns of infinite regress, multiplying overhead onto a second floor identical to the first. The first rows were empty and filthy, cage doors hanging open, grime floating through the air like the aftermath of a nuclear holocaust, the belts still churning and squeaking and rolling. It was like wandering the wreckage of an abandoned city or like climbing out of a smoking volcano, the air ready to kill you with whatever was gathering in your lungs. At the far end the investigators were packing up the final quarter of the birds. They were covered in excrement and dander, coughing, shirts torn, bleeding at their necks and arms. The survivors of a catastrophe.

"Is it over?" one said, hollow-eyed.

"Almost," said Dill. He patted his shoulder and dropped a bag of peanuts into his hand. He ran through the corridor to Barn 5.

And Bwwaauk? Where was she during all this? She'd walked off. The investigators, a few hours before, back at the banker's, had left open the gate to the run. But only Bwwaauk had been brave or oblivious or quixotic enough to ramble out before dark, while the others huddled in awe. Bwwaauk hopped onto, then over the fence into the neighbor's yard, and trotted away. By the time the sun set she was fast asleep in a tree.

Dill went into Barn 5, a cage-free barn. It was in chaos. A tower of batteries had knocked over, surely birds injured, investigators shouting, a fight on the verge of breaking out. The middle of the tremendous barn had somehow flooded with water and investigators were walking around on the tops of the aviaries. They were singing, dropping down, and sloshing from island to island like in a musical. At the other end of the barn, Dill spotted an investigator with an eye patch, rolling down an aisle on a cart, waving a black shirt like a flag. "I run this town," he was shouting.

Dill stepped out in front of him, held up his hands. "Where are we at with the birds?"

The investigator raised his arms and flapped. "Flew away last year." He rolled by.

"Get down from there!" Dill yelled after him.

The last barn, 6, was another cage-free barn. Birds had gotten out and were running around on the grates. The investigators had gotten the worst of the hens' attacks, their arms and necks spotted with wounds. They looked like they'd joined an ancient culture, war paint on their faces, rags tied around their heads and arms like giant wings. Birds were flapping all around them, the dim lights tossing shadows.

"Who's in charge here?" Dill demanded.

An investigator, bent like an old man, pointed up, nodding slowly.

Dill looked up, puzzled. "Ceiling?"

The investigator shook his head.

"God?" he guessed.

The investigator recoiled.

"Who then?"

The investigator choked hoarsely. "Sky."

But the next day Bwwaauk was lonely. Hens are social creatures. She traveled along the streets and came upon some hens, a little group of so-called backyard chickens (named, as usual, for their relation to humans). She stood outside the fence and looked in but she couldn't get into their enclosure. The owner (though you can't really own another being) came out and said, "Well, what have we here?" and invited Bwwaauk in with some lettuce and corn. Bwwaauk, strutting, bobbing—nobody's fool, but reaching for the leafy romaine—followed her in.

Dill came out and turned to head back to Annabelle. He stopped. Beyond the road that cut through the farm stood Barn 7, free-standing and older. Barns 7 and 8 had been depopped last week and were empty—Cleveland had it in her records and Annabelle had confirmed it—but . . . he hesitated. He was a professional, after all. He ran across the shaved grass and dark road to Barn 7, swung the door open. He could already tell by the silence that it held no birds. He walked through to the hen area, an old-fashioned battery barn. The machines were quiet, belts still, fans switched off, cages open and cleaned but rusty. The emptiness felt guillotine-final. He went back out.

Behind Barn 7 was Barn 8—it looked older than 7, an antique really. He shouldn't be wasting time. But . . .

He ran across the field and opened the door. He could swear he heard machinery. Then, no, please, *no*. The sound of birds. He staggered in with the awe of a condemned man. A full barn. Buzzing flies, grime as thick as it ever got piling up in statues, spent hens crouched in their cages, their feathers half gone, combs poking through the bars.

Somebody's fuckup. Whose, it didn't matter, because here they were, Dill and a hundred and something thousand birds, their sisters in the other barns shuttled out while they were left behind.

HERE'S A QUESTION: Who cares? It's just a bunch of stupid chickens.

But chickens did not always have the reputation of being dirty, ugly, and dumb, a practical version of the pigeon. That's a uniquely twentieth-century construction. Until recently chickens commanded respect. Roosters, of course, were warriors and leaders since the earliest images of them on the pharaohs' walls in Egypt. Hens were devoted mothers, teachers, and nurturers—in India, China, the Mediterranean.

The hen in ancient myth, scratching through water and sand to bring the world into being.

The hen, protector of creation. Her egg, a symbol of life, resurrection. Inevitable yet fragile.

All through the Middle Ages and the Renaissance, it was always the hen—her loyalty, her vigilance, her love. She came out the other side of the Reformation as the Protestant hen—thrifty, tidy, industrious, pious. Observe the way she used every stick and morsel in the barnyard and woods for nesting and caring for her babies! Admire the compact egg with its perfect chick nutrition!

In nineteenth-century England, people went mad for hens and the vogue spread to the United States. The era was known as the "hen craze." Her beauty, her plumage, her proud vanity. At the first Boston Poultry Exposition in 1849, ten thousand people paid four pennies each to stroll the Public Garden, study a thousand chickens of all breeds and sizes assembled in tents a hundred feet long. These shows were wildly popular for decades across the country and abroad, straight through the First World War.

Only then, at the business end of history, did the hen's standing begin to fall, correlating to when we began putting them into cages and out of sight.

ZEE WOULD REMEMBER the moment Dill came tearing across the farm. Zee was loading hens into truck 2-9 (really it was a very simple number system) when he spotted Dill running toward him.

Zee would think of it in the coming years, while he tried to find some other kind of employment (the absurdity that his only skills were in an industry he despised so much that he'd stopped his life to stop it). There was the trucker job. The hotel job. Landscaping. Dill appearing in the distance.

Zee would think of it while he waited for Janey to get out of prison. He wooed her from the other side of the bars because once he met her no other woman would do (sharing Oreos with her from the visitation vending machine and laughing). He remembered it on his long drive to the prison each Saturday, and when she didn't make parole and they had to wait another four months, there it was: Dill sprinting, growing larger. In moments of adversity, when he faced an unreasonable challenge, that's what he thought of. Dill running.

So, seven years later, following Dill's command (he was still a professional), he showed up at Janey's father's apartment, where she'd retreated into her teen bedroom. He knocked on the front door and called, "I've come to get my wife."

Dill cutting across the gravel, veering Zee's direction, getting closer, and finally upon him. Dill stopped, gasping. He dropped a heavy hand on Zee's shoulder. "Barn 8's got hens," he said before running on.

Now *that* was a situation, Zee thought seven years later, rolling his suitcase past Janey's father (he'd had to buy one to bring over—no, he'd never owned a fucking dumb-ass suitcase). *That* was a catastrophe. That was basically crazy and was probably why he'd laughed. *This* was nothing—his wife encased within a room, her father frowning, waiting to see Zee's next move and it better be a good one since Zee had agreed to take this on, had sworn before God and plenty of investigator-witnesses not to give up on her no matter what (although they hadn't used words like "give up" in the ceremony because that would have been inappropriate). This beside *that*, he thought, another full barn! *This* beside evacuating nine hundred thousand hens in the first place (what kind of shitty idea?)!

Seven years after the discovery of Barn 8—a prison sentence, a string of dispiriting jobs, a marriage, a birth, a death, and so much more behind them (and so much more ahead)—Zee held the handle of his suitcase, tilted his head to Janey's bedroom door, placed a hand lightly against it, only his fingertips touching the wood, as if touching the side of her face. (Where the fuck was Cleveland when they needed her, by the way?)

"I'm here, Janey," he said.

He stayed quiet when she cried, "Go away! I hate you!" and her father shuffled angrily behind him.

But they'd gotten the other hens out, hadn't they? They'd gotten them all. Almost.

Well, almost isn't enough.

But almost is damn close. Sometimes almost is all you need to go forward. To throw yourself out there, ask for more, say it one more time, *More*, demand it. His hand encircled the doorknob (he prayed for more). "I'm coming in, Janey," he said, and walked in, pulling the suitcase behind him.

MEANWHILE, FARMER ROB ("Robbie Jr.") Green knew nothing about it until the next morning. Yes, he slept through the whole fiasco—in his bed, with his wife, baby in the next room, because there was a trained security guard on the premises and an expensive, perplexing alarm system, and Rob didn't realize he needed to be there *literally* twenty-four hours a day. He thought twelve were plenty enough, which were how many he put in and put up with most days, since his father had gone into so-called semi-retirement after the stroke, and his cousin was the most incompetent man Rob had ever known.

Rob's cousin Jack, back from Los Angeles, recalled from the west like a defective appliance, there to "help," since Robert Sr.'s illness. Jack had done nothing right since he'd arrived. The chore list Rob drew up for him grew shorter each week in inverse proportion to the list of his cousin's deficiencies Rob discovered.

As an example. On the Saturday morning of the invasion (though Rob did not know there would be an invasion, God forgive him for thinking he might be able to stay away for a few hours without an army of lunatics coming along and taking the whole place down), Rob woke with a heavy heart because although he'd planned to take off all of Saturday and Sunday, he knew he ought to check in with his cousin, since Rob had been at an egg conference in Des Moines on Wednesday and Thursday, and had barely seen his cousin Friday, what with Jack's interpretation of casual Friday: long lunch and early departure. He reached for his phone and called.

"Jack, what's this I hear about Barns 7 and 8?"

"How should I know?"

"Why did I have a message from cleanup last night saying they were done with 7 and to let them know about 8?"

"Am I God, Robbie? Do I solve the mysteries of the universe? I'm busy here."

"They were both depopped, correct? The computer says they were. Did you not sign the paperwork? I saw depop Tuesday inside 7. Were they here Wednesday doing 8? Did you see them do it? Did you check?"

"Yeah, I checked."

Rob could tell by his voice that he hadn't.

"Look," Jack said, "I'm doing the opening shots of that documentary for you guys today."

Documentary.

"You mean the promotional video?"

"I'm doing it now."

Rob sighed. "Where are you?"

His Hollywood cousin was making a promotional video to go on the company website, a public relations effort to counter the bad effects of one of his cousin's major screwups: Jack had let a journalist onto the farm last month, had not run it first by Rob, who had already told him to never let a journalist onto the farm. Chase them off with a stick if you have to. With a gun. Call the police. Did he really did not know that? Did he not know that animal ag was under siege by the liberal media? But there you have it: while Rob was gone for a few hours at a pullet farm, Jack had let the journalist come. Mr. Hollywood, unable to resist a reporter, especially a female one. The result was the article spread open on Rob's desk, a nasty "exposé of the egg industry," specifically of Happy Green Family Farm. Jack had read the article open-mouthed and stunned, and said finally, referring to the journalist, "But she was so *nice*."

To make matters worse, a "famous writer" (whom Rob had

never heard of) "tweeted" about the article to the reading public—fortunately almost an empty set at this point, but still catching the attention of a "famous spiritual leader" (so famous that Rob had never heard of her *or* her religion), who then posted a link to the article that her "followers" shared 186,512 times, urging a boycott of any establishment that used Happy Green Farm eggs (which luckily was extremely difficult for anyone outside Green Farm to determine). It was so unfair because Green Family Farm was pretty decent as far as egg farms go—six of the eight barns under a decade old, two of them cage free with more conversions planned—not a superfarm of thirty barns. Green was practically barnyard.

This had all settled down in a week (people aren't going to stop eating eggs, after all, or pay attention to where they come from), but Jack still wanted to put together a promotional video. Jack, who'd been in Hollywood six years and not made so much as a commercial, insisted on "saving the company money" and making it himself. To this end he hired an (expensive) cameraman and offered his neighbors—a woman and her daughter—a hundred bucks each to take part.

So on Saturday morning, mere hours before the farm was invaded by hundreds of insane people, Rob dressed and, instead of spending the morning in bed with his beautiful wife watching their chickadee baby curl and uncurl her tiny fists, he kissed them both and headed out.

When Rob showed up at Jack's neighbor's, Jack was ordering around the "crew" (one man with a video camera). The woman and her daughter were debating who was the star of the "movie."

"Promotional video," Rob corrected. He tried to figure out which—mother or daughter—his cousin was trying to sleep with.

Jack put on the mics, arranged the mother and daughter in their living room over by the doilies and stuffed chairs, and then

Jack said to the mother, "What do you think you'll see on the farm today?"

Now, as Rob said to his wife later, if your plan was to be filmed about a visit to a modern egg farm, do you think you might do five minutes of research online about what a modern egg farm is? So as not to sound like a complete idiot?

Her first take: "Well, I know I'm going to see an awful lot of chickens running around!" A big smile.

Rob motioned to shut the camera off. "Really?" he said. "Running around? Keep in mind that at capacity we have 1.2 million hens."

She and her daughter exchanged frightened looks.

"Maybe they'll be inside barns," he said gently.

For the record, Rob had said this was not a good idea. Rob had not wanted to use strangers. Rob had said they should have the business manager, Mary, do it. Mary had two daughters and they would have been perfect. Rob had said they should forget humans and have a cartoon of a chicken who puts up her wing and shows where she lives.

"Let's roll," said Jack.

Had Rob wanted to be a farmer? It had not been first on the list. When he was young he detested the idea. He'd wanted to be a soccer star. Later he thought fireman—ride the truck, run into the flames (he'd been twelve when the Towers fell). After Annabelle left, detective. He'd been an imaginative boy, but not a driven one. In the end he'd majored in business and was working for his father by age twenty-two.

He thought about this while the women talked on about the farmer strewing grain on the barn floor, about the hens' chicks making *peep peep peep* sounds, though there would be no hens raising chicks *on an egg farm*. He looked over at the cameraman.

He left and drove to the farm. Jack had had one chore to organize that week. He merely had to oversee the depop of Barns 7 and 8: arrange for the depop crew, a matter of paperwork, a few emails and calls, a single brief appearance on each of the two days it would take, a walk-through when they were finished, a couple of conversations with cleanup.

Rob arrived at the farm and walked over to Barn 8. He went in and saw them. A hundred and fifty thousand spent birds. How depressing. He called Jack. "What happened to the depop crew?"

"They came," said Jack. "They left."

"They forgot something." Rob turned off the call before he could hear his cousin's irritating voice.

So Rob understood that he had to spend not only twelve hours a day each weekday but part of Saturday, too, but he didn't know this included the middle of the night. That Saturday evening, while a crazed battalion led by his sister gathered to march over the land toward his farm, he spent two hours and twenty minutes with his adorable daughter before she went to sleep, instead of the full day as he'd planned. Then he ate the vegetable-tofu dish his wife set down before him (she was making less and less meat these days, since his father's stroke and his own rising pressure). He went to sleep having no idea that hundreds of raving criminals were at that moment removing every chicken from the premises, until the barn manager arrived at 6:45 the next morning, while he was eating breakfast beside his beautiful baby dropping Cheerios from her mermaid chair. The barn manager walked in, a police officer behind him, and said, "They've taken the ladies." The first thought Rob had was *Annabelle*.

BARN 8 WAS THE FIRST THING to truly go wrong. Later everyone would say so. The mistake of Barn 8 would endure. Barn 8 would go down as the colossal error that ensured the defeat of the greatest animal heist in recorded history. Politicians would refer to it, comedians would joke about it. Barn 8, what transpired there, who fucked it up.

That night, or early the next morning, in the hours before the sun set itself to rise, the fact of Barn 8 spread through the barns. The words "Barn 8's got hens" were shouted down the aisles, called up into truck cabs, passed along the lines of investigators, from the ones who ran the Friday Feather protests, to the ones who'd grown up in Cuba, to the ones who usually dealt with cows and secretly felt chickens beneath them. The investigators, all with their own reasons for being there, reasons that were honorable (according to them) or exasperating (according to their parents) or criminal (to the farmers) or hilarious (the commuters who heard about it Monday on the radio on their way to work).

But in fact few of the investigators' motives were that simple. It is difficult to be honorable for more than a flash of time. Darker or more complex motives are always banging around under the surface. Investigators *are* exasperating, but only to each other and to whoever is trying to herd them. Exasperating people tend to be loud and dumb, while, in public, investigators are intelligent and watchful, trained. You could be looking into their faces, talking to them every day, and have no idea (and maybe you are). Almost none of them were insane, as Robbie had said (though they had their moments) or criminal (they prided themselves on following the law with the exception of the ag-gag laws, which they considered unconstitutional, a violation of the First Amendment). And they certainly didn't find any of this funny.

However, one group was sifting among them that night that indeed *was* criminal, and a few of its members were possibly insane. This group was not made up of investigators proper. Their training had been in methods not sanctioned by any of the major AR investigative units (they had split off during the Investigator Wars of 2013). This group felt a bit shunted to the side that night, their expertise unappreciated (they almost always felt that way). As dawn approached but had not quite arrived, and as hundreds of investigators stomped and fumed over Barn 8, this little group stayed silent.

The investigators, still loading chickens, still emptying the final rows, shifting the last trucks into gear, were muttering. It was impossible to get *another* hundred thousand or whatever out. They didn't have any more trucks, they were out of time, and anyway whose fuckup was this? Who was in charge? Annabelle and Dill? And anyway, *of course* it was fucked, the whole thing. Why had the investigators been so naive as to believe Annabelle and Dill could organize one simple rescue? A big one, granted, but elementary in design. Those two had basically abandoned the movement months, years, before, to say nothing of that suit, Jarman, while the rest of them had carried on. The investigators would just have to leave one barn full. Maybe they could come pick up the rest next week, when Happy Green Family Farm least expected it.

Ha! other investigators were saying. They'd all be eating off metal trays next week!

While this was going on, the other group, the silent one, the only true criminals among them—even the anarchists would have nothing to do with them—made a decision on their own initiative: no one gets left behind. This small fringe group should not have been invited to begin with, which hits at the deeper, fuller, longer flaws in the plan, a plan that had appeared (somewhat) doable under Jonathan Jarman's direction, but was a damaged cart rolling along, shaky, a broken wheel, riddled with bullets, dropping pieces of metal on the grates, hens falling out, bound to collapse.

These stubborn radicals at least had the decency to wait until all six barns were basically empty and investigators were assembling in clumps, cursing and demanding, Now what? Should they leave or wait or what? Then these fringe rebels pulled on their face masks, trotted single file across the farm in the dawn that was just beginning to light their silhouettes, and, skilled arsonists all, set Barn 8 on fire.

FROM THERE it was only a matter of watching it all self-destruct. Barn 8 went fast.

At one time Barn 8 had been Meadow Barn, its cages shiny and able to hold more hens than ever before. In 1990 Leo Green had led a local reporter over to it, raised his arms, and prophesied, "This is the future." But decades had passed. Barns went up and came down around it, more barns were added, technology advanced. Twenty-six years later it was Barn 8, set at the end of the farm, filthy and fetid, a disgrace, scheduled for demolition after one more cycle of hens. It was so old it had wooden rafters, it had plywood walkways, not to mention the hens themselves, fluffs of ratty feather and skin. Setting it on fire essentially involved setting the belts on fire, setting the pit on fire, setting the walkways on fire. It essentially involved very little, because once the feathers caught, the hens were packed in so close, the fire leapt through the barn and soon was raging, smoke billowing out the ventilators and seeping through the roof. Smoke led into the sky like a train.

Thanks a lot, Bwwaauk.

By this time the little band of rebels—a semicharismatic leader, her childhood friend, and the five young people who loved them— were gone.

Of the sixty trucks, fifty-nine had left or were leaving by the time the flames hit the hens, but hundreds of investigators still were on the scene.

Some of the fire alarms were out of service, but not all. When the working ones sounded, the investigators, still cursing, heard a sound different from the fans, the trucks, the hens, and their own voices. They heard bells. The investigators tilted up their heads, mouths open, and saw smoke in the sky. For one collective-investigator moment they paused, watched the poof of white grow. Then they dropped what they were doing and went streaming into the fields in all directions. The final truck heaved off, leaving a few loaded batteries on the pavement.

Sixteen minutes later, four minutes longer than in drill practice, the town's single fire truck came whining up the road. The firemen looked out in astonishment at all those people running away under the tall white flume rising before the red sun.

Meanwhile, the hens in Barn 8 were burning alive—cooking, some would say, well-done, charred. But the firemen, leaping from their truck, were more concerned with preventing a spread to the other (empty) barns than in saving a bunch of the dumbest sort of bird (who were supposed to be saved already by Annabelle, or at least depopped and dead).

Because the fire alarm was set to trigger a call to the elderly sick Farmer Robert Green Sr., *not* Robbie Jr., Robbie wouldn't know for another hour.

PERHAPS IT WAS BETTER that the hens died, rather than live another moment in those cages. Later the AR community mourned those Barn 8 hens with candles and songs and a website. For a five-dollar donation, you could give a deceased hen a name—beyond the individuated clucks by which they were known to one another—and six hundred grand was raised for animal sanctuaries across America.

The company, Happy Green Family Egg Farm, for their part, posted a report on *their* website, saying that there were no deaths or injuries in the fire, meaning humans, of course.

In fact nearly all the farm's hens died, about a million. The police chased the trucks and ran a few off the road, the investigators hopping out and making a run for it, keys swinging in the ignition. Some pulled over of their own accord, hands up in surrender. A few trucks, those that had left earlier in the night, made it to their destinations—the sanctuaries scattered around the neighboring states. The hens were being unloaded by nonplussed volunteers when the police caught up with them. It all took a little time because there were simply not enough police to chase down all those hens. They needed dozens of cars in a town that had four police officers and two police cars and one police bicycle. The sanctuaries had police at their doors and in their driveways. Volunteers were hiding in the bathroom, peeking out the window, calling the investigator-truckers and saying, "Don't come! Don't come!" so those trucks rode on with no destination but the sunrise, until the police stopped them too. The trucks were rounded up and impounded, chickens and all, a few towns off, in a vast megachurch parking lot, which was coincidentally empty on this Sunday, the entire congregation, twelve thousand congregants, having gone off on a field trip to Washington, DC, in protest against government spending on health care for the poor, and the church had its own caravan of buses winding through the hills. The trucks full of hens were driven to the church parking lot, a few more arriving each hour, and left there, forming irregular triangle-family shapes on the tarmac. The plan was to empty the trucks just as soon as the police could find enough people to unload all those hens and figure out where to put them—surely not back on a criminal investigation site still smoldering with fire? But where else? The chickens would be all right for a handful of hours while they unraveled this.

But, as Rob Jr. knew, they would not be all right. He kept screaming this into the phone from the farm, which was streaming with officers and journalists and photographers and townspeople, and then in person at the police station. Hens cannot sit in those batteries with no ventilation, Rob Jr. said. The trucks need to be moving, sifting the air through, or the hens will die. And on that sunny Sunday in God's parking lot, all of them did, in accordance with God's plan presumably, suffocate and die.

BUT TWO TRUCKS RODE ON. Trucks 2-5 and 1-4: shiny, silver, gleaming, flames painted on the passenger doors, palm tree silhouettes on the wheel flaps, HOW'S MY DRIVING? stickers slapped on the back like a taunt. Trucks 2-5 and 1-4 had pulled away from the farm wreckage hours before it was wreckage. They left at midnight, while the evacuation was still going the way it was supposed to, when the trucks that left contained heroes in their cabs and the rescued on their backs. They drove away to cheers. With those cheers echoing in their minds, mingling with the clucks and the coos of the hens, the heroes forged ahead into the dark, following a less obvious route than the others. They turned off the highway and onto a small side road not meant for trucks of that size, trusting the directions Annabelle had given them. Signs flashed in the headlights—DANGER. NO TRESPASSING. SUPERFUND CLEANUP SITE. They passed the barbed wire, passed the second set of signs, passed the single totem that had been erected as a sample, though they couldn't see it in the dark. The road split in two, one dirt and one gravel, and into two again, and then again. The heroes were soon lost in the night, forbidden to use their GPS. They wound around and around, the tall trucks teetering on the bumpy mud roads. Now and then they pulled to a stop and an investigator jumped down from one truck and ran to the other, pointing and swearing. Finally, after much too long of this, they dragged up a long hill and found in their headlights where they were supposed to be: Grandfather Green's original barn, empty thirty years.

The investigators tried to send Dill the code that confirmed their arrival, but service was weak that far out and their message didn't go through. So not only were they unable to report their success—that they'd finally found the goddamn place—but they learned nothing of what was happening back at Happy Green Family Farm. They arrived in the dead of night, four investigators, interrupting the silence with their cargo of thirty-eight thousand hens.

Sore, hungry, exhausted, grumbling, these investigators, professionals all, knew better than the police that the hens couldn't stay in those batteries. Wearily they began to unload.

AS SOON AS DILL SAW THE POOF of smoke rise over Barn 8 and heard the bells that he knew would bring fire trucks roaring up the road, he thought of gasoline. Where had the assholes gotten the gasoline? Had they brought it along, had it been their plan, or did they just drive around with a trunk full of gasoline? (Neither, as it happens. They found it when they banged the lock off an equipment shed.)

The bells sounded, a dinging in the barely dark, and the investigators froze across the farm. They were outside now since the barns were empty (at least the assholes had had the decency to wait). They looked up, pricked their ears, sniffed the air like dogs. In the next instant every investigator on the premises fled.

They went leaping and tripping over equipment, escaped into the field of shit, set off at a dead run down the road. Dill, for his part, headed for Annabelle. She and Zee had been securing a battery onto the final truck on the premises, but when Dill reached them, she had her hands on her hips and was watching the cloud of smoke in the sky, investigators bumping by her.

"Now there's a temporary solution," she said and gave a nod. Did she mean the fleeing investigators, the fire in the barn, the evacuation itself, or perhaps the entire project of animal and environmental activism? Annabelle walked to the cab of the last remaining truck. "Let's go." Dill, who was winding himself up to throw the biggest tantrum of his life—*these goddamn fucking no good unprofessional investigators*—dropped his arms and followed.

NOW THAT IT WAS NOT GOING BEAUTIFULLY—smoke taking over the sky, investigators streaming through the fields—Jonathan thought again of this concept of *missing*. He was hurrying around the barns, hoping he hadn't missed her, that she wasn't trying to do something ridiculous, get into Barn 8 and save the chickens or who knows what. He spotted her climbing into a truck with Dill and another investigator. He called to her, began jogging over, but she shut the door and faced away. Why? So infuriating. How was he supposed to protect her if she was always running away?

It occurred to him in that moment a fact that seemed so obvious, he wondered why it had taken him so long to understand: she was protecting Jonathan, not the other way around. Every time she left, every time she refused to let Jonathan follow, that's what she was doing, and every time it was a hard choice. Now, riding off with Dill, she'd done it again, protected Jonathan, because no doubt the biggest trouble was going to wind up wherever she was, and he'd taken enough steps to walk out in his own tracks, follow the exit path he'd cut for himself, but he couldn't pull her behind him. Instead she chose Dill. She let him do the protecting. Dill in the getaway car, Dill climbing the fence, Dill destroying the computer. Dill was the sacrifice. She counted on him for that and it had ruined him and his life and they'd both let it.

Why didn't she let Jonathan protect her? The very thought enraged him.

A month later Jonathan would be at Dill's grand jury hearing for arson (the Greens had to charge *someone* for the insurance, though Jonathan knew they had the wrong guy). Jonathan would be on the stand as a character witness. He would be thinking, Dill hadn't done his job. Why hadn't he protected her after he rode off with her in the last truck? (Of course, Jonathan had it wrong. She'd chosen Dill not to protect *her*, but to protect the animals. The fact that Jonathan didn't know this is one of the reasons she left him in the first place.)

Jonathan considered Dill over at the defense table, in a crappy suit, bruises on his face from who knows what behind bars. Cool despite everything. Fucking sentimental dangerous asshole. Look where it got the lot of them. How Jonathan hated him. Dill belonged in prison. But Jonathan didn't say this to the grand jury and judge because he knew they had the wrong guy. Dill hadn't started the fire, not his style, a wormy pacifist in the extreme. He'd never kill a bunch of animals. His fingerprints weren't on the gasoline cans or the shed. They didn't have a shred of evidence.

Besides, if Annabelle were there, she would never forgive Jonathan if he didn't help Dill. So he'd hired a lawyer for Dill, a damn good one, and he spoke on the stand with conviction. And Dill, a little battered, walked free.

INSIDE BARN 8, as the smoke choked the hens and the fire raged around them, the spirit of each hen came forward. She shook herself, fluffed her wings, and miraculously all her missing feathers, pecked off in the ravages of radical confinement, grew back. One at a time the hundred and twenty thousand hens (thirty thousand had already died in their cages) stepped to the middle of the barn and curtsied, while the rest of the hens cheered and clapped their wings. She gave a final wave and then looked up into the smoke and ash and flames. It looked like forest up there, like rain, flickering leaves, stretching branches, changing seasons, whirring bugs. When the roof collapsed, the spirits of a hundred and twenty thousand hens shucked off their cages like twiggy nests and soared into the sky.

If this strikes you as similar to the vision Janey had in the barn—perhaps even the fulfillment of that vision?—you would be correct. For this is what chickens believe happens when you die, it is their unified spiritual prophecy: The flock gathers, bids goodbye, the departing hen does a final little two-step dance and a curtsy, while the ancient forest trees of their origins rise around them. Then she calls out her own name and flaps into the sky, her soul on its final journey. As humans see a tunnel with a light at the end, as turtles see a misty underwater tow gently tug them away from all the fauna and faces familiar to them, so hens see this. The vision Janey saw in that barn six weeks back, while night-auditing various farms around Iowa, and which inspired her to pursue all that came after, was the collective death wish of the seven million hens on that particular farm. Those hens wanted nothing more than to die. They were wishing it so strongly (praying, some might call it) that somehow Janey stepped into it, caught a glimpse, saw what they saw, and mistook it for something else (this).

Did all those hens' spirits really rise? I don't know. Either the hens were right and the graceful flight that evolution denied them in life was granted in death, or they were wrong. I might be all-knowing about these people and animals, but even I do not know what comes after death for chickens.

CLEVELAND AND JANEY? Meanwhile, where were they? They had run. They were out on the road, slowing to a jog. The last truck rolled by and Janey waved.

"Why is this funny?" Cleveland kept saying. "Stop it. It's not funny."

They walked along side roads, Janey sobering. They watched the sun coming on, lighting the sheds, the fences, the posts, the distant houses.

A police car drove up alongside them and slowed. "Good morning, ladies. Would you please stop right there and put your hands up?"

Janey again started laughing.

JANEY WAITED FIVE YEARS—until Cleveland got out of prison—to go back. Janey had gotten less time (some said it was because of her looks). Then one afternoon they went. They drove over, left the car, and walked into the fields alongside the old barns. Cleveland had been out of prison only a few weeks—divorced now, with a job at a grocery (in three years she would be an assistant manager, her skill at organization overriding her record). They stood in the wild grasses, untended for so long, and surveyed the barns, including the eighth, which had never been demolished or repaired. It was blackened, roof caved in. A cool breeze rippled the grasses. The sky seemed as remote as ever.

"I'm going to marry him," she told Cleveland. "I want you there." She'd waited until Cleveland was out to say yes.

They kept walking.

Even now she felt traces of the vision returning. She could see it hovering at the edges of her sight. Was it the past or the future? she wondered. Memory or promise?

They turned back toward the barns, which were empty and desolate. Cleveland took a few pictures. "We did it," Cleveland murmured, though obviously they had not. Had *any* of those hens made it? Where would they have made it to? Were any of them "free"? Janey now knew what it was to be imprisoned. Janey thought she saw a movement, a figure, and turned quickly but saw nothing. Maybe just the vision. They walked back to the car and got in.

4

Price Securities
Assignment: Happy Green Family Egg Farm
Security Officer: 063507
Log: 6/26/2028, final entry

She was here my second night on the job. I saw her.

This is not part of the public record because I told no one. I did not record it in this log, did not call the emergency number taped to the desk, or mention it in the morning to the gruff barn manager, because I did not think it necessary to report a glimpse of what was clearly a family member in a family business. Later I did not report it to any of the assortment of authorities because, for one, my English wasn't and isn't that good, and for another, how was I supposed to know the woman was a terrorist? Perhaps it is beyond this security officer's station to suggest that if the company suspected violent, criminal relations might be coming by to do reconnaissance, invade, pillage, and then burn the place down, the company executives might have put up a picture with the word *wanted* underneath, in lieu of a framed group photo with the perpetrator as a teenager smiling into the camera, the owner's arm protectively around her, the words *Our Happy Hen Green Family* in fancy script below.

My first night on the job I had studied this photo while sitting at the desk, noted the unsurprising blinding whiteness of the family in contrast to myself and the workers I'd met. Hard not to study it since the photo was posted three meters from my head.

My second night I was on an 0400 hours walk-through (not

required by Happy Green Farm, but recommended by Price Securities). I strolled the perimeter, then walked between each long, loud barn in the howling dark, an unsettling experience, no matter how well trained the security officer. I turned a corner and my flashlight's beam caught a figure, a woman in a brown dress about twenty meters away from me. It was only an instant. I saw her face turn toward me. I was so surprised to see a woman out here in the night that for a moment I did nothing. Then she was gone. I ran after her. I went down the length of the barn, thought I saw her, swept my powerful flashlight. A spring fog had descended and lit up under my beam in a spooky haze. Nothing. I turned and went around the other side. Didn't see her. I double-backed the other way. In my mind I could still see her shape and that pale face turning, the shine of her dress off my flashlight. I ran around the next barn, swinging my light. I kept going.

It was only much later, after I'd returned wet with sweat from running, that I realized it was the girl in the photo. Had I even seen her out there in the dark or was it a mirage? Perhaps a ghost or a spirit? Or had I invented her, having stared absently so long at the framed group?

I considered whether I should put it in the log. Either she had been there or she hadn't. If she had, then surely she was allowed on company property, right? A little strange at that hour, but still. If she hadn't, well, I didn't want to go around writing in the log about ghosts, which I do not believe in, my second night on the job.

I decided to leave it out of the log.

Two nights later, Saturday, half an hour after my shift started, she walked right in and stood before me. I almost ducked. I knew immediately she was the woman who'd slipped through my flashlight beam. I didn't greet her, because, being Nicaraguan, I understand hierarchy and family aristocracy, and how even on a chicken farm the boss's daughter may or may not wish to acknowledge the existence of the workers. But she paused beside the photo, said pleasantly, "Is Ricardo here?"

"No, ma'am."

"And who are you?"

"I'm from Price Securities."

I now see what she was doing—she stood there by the photo long enough that I could be damn sure the girl in the photo and this woman were one and the same. "That's right," she mused. "He's on vacation."

"Yes, ma'am. I'm the temp."

She shook her head. "What a waste of money. Actual night guards, you know? While the alarm system is always off." I stiffened. It wasn't very nice to call me a waste, and we are called "officers," not guards. She leaned an elbow on my desk in a languid, flirty pose, which I now know was a guise to have a look at the board of green lights that I sat by. "See? Off." The green lights twinkled. I'd been told not to touch them.

"Anyone else around?"

"I am alone, ma'am."

"Except for the birds."

"Excuse me?"

"A million birds. Alone except for them."

"Yes, ma'am," I allowed, "alone except for a million birds."

She straightened. "In that case, could you help me with something?"

Not having much choice, I stood and followed the wayward daughter, perpetrator, enemy-terrorist—though I did not know she was any of these things—a few steps around the corner. I can still see myself behind her. I sensed there was something off but there I went. No, don't go! I call to my younger self, who never listens.

"I keep telling them we need a stepladder in here." She opened a door, pointed. It all happened very fast. "Could you reach that box for me? That one there?" not saying what it was or why she could possibly need it on a Saturday evening. I stepped in and reached up toward the boxes on the shelf. I was shoved hard from behind and I stumbled. She or one of her cohorts slammed the door shut and the light went off. "Hey," I called out and pushed on the door just as I heard the clack of a padlock. "Hey," I yelled and shouldered the door, once, twice, a few more times in terror. It was absolutely dark. I heard a male voice. "Sit tight, amigo. Nobody's going to hurt you."

Man, I *hate* being called amigo. What kind of amigo do you lock in a storeroom? Anytime someone calls you amigo in this country, watch out. I shouted and kicked the door. Damn thing was sturdy. I fumbled around in the dark determining the co-ordinates of my confinement. I had been a fool, yes, but she was benefiting from a very lucky coincidence. Since I was so new to the job I had left my phone in my car as I'd been directed. "No phones on campus," the barn manager had said. She was banking on me following the rules. I can tell you I never did that again.

I looked for something that could help me escape. I did this for a long time, taking apart what turned out to be rolls of toilet paper, reams of paper. I kicked the door a few more times. I sat down on the floor. I could hear nothing beyond. I thought I heard trucks but I couldn't be sure. I waited.

I will not disparage myself for falling asleep. Did you know that hostages often must be woken when they're found? It's true. In prisons it's part of the training. I worked in a prison before I came to Price Securities and the handbook instructs: *If you are taken hostage, remain calm. Stay positive. Focus on a soothing image—a seashore, a quiet forest, a loved one. Try to sleep.*

I curled on the floor and dreamed of my girlfriend. Followed protocol even while unconscious.

I woke face down on the linoleum tile, three feet into the

storeroom, to the shouts of a man I recognized in the doorway—
the barn manager. "Where the fuck are the chickens, Smirnoff?"

At that hour there were no live chickens on the premises.

They called me Smirnoff because on my first day I'd had a bottle
of water. "No drinking on the job," the barn manager had said
and let out a laugh. The next night he called me Vodka, and the
next night Smirnoff. No one ever said my actual name, which is
Muñoz. First name: Alejandro.

The police, the FBI, the firemen, the reporters, they were all there
when I came out blinking into the light. Someone had set up a
TV and I could see the aerial shots and hear the perpetrator's
brother making a statement. They all lined up and asked me one
by one, How could I have slept through it? How tired did a man
need to be to sleep while criminals burn the place down? How
did it feel, they marveled, to be responsible for the misplacement
of a million units of company property? And though my English
is not good, I said in answer to every question, "But I was locked
in a closet."

No one told me to leave. I came back the next night.

I figured the next batch of chicks would arrive by the end of
the week but they were calling it a criminal investigation site.
No chickens allowed. The workers were sent home to wait for
the trial. I waited for orders from Price Security. I heard nothing. Weeks passed. I kept coming—I was on night shift, which
is probably why no one noticed me. My paychecks arrived in my
account every other Monday. I wrote to Price Securities and received no answer. I wrote again, said I'd taken the initiative to
move to the day shift, since technically there was little need to
protect the hens at night, seeing as there were none.

• • •

In the second month I asked my girlfriend to marry me—there's something about being locked in a closet that puts things in perspective. When she said yes, I'd never been happier, more sure of the future.

The brother was in charge. He showed up now and then, paced the barns, muttering and shaking his head. Once he turned around and said, "You're still here?" I opened my mouth to reply but he walked away down the grate, as if he'd forgotten me even while I was still before his eyes.

Why didn't he bring in more chickens? He had people in to discuss it. They walked up and down the rows, outside around the barns, sat in the office, feet up on the desk. I kept close by, a room away or a few meters behind, wanting to show them that I was wide awake and on the job, not asleep this time! When the birds arrived, I'd be ready. They seemed to have no idea who I was, despite my uniform. When one got into his car, he *tipped* me. Then a handful of workers came and carried out the equipment that might be useful elsewhere, though they left a great deal behind. Some of it is still here. They shut the door and were gone.

We had a small but jubilant wedding. I carried her up the stairs to our apartment. Our friends had filled the cupboards with chocolate kisses, champagne glasses, confetti.

In the years since the last hen left the premises, my job has grown dull. I try not to let on. I tossed away the last book I was reading for fun a year ago, pages from the finish line. I send emails, requests for reassignment, but it seems to go to an automated system, no one on the other side.

I think about the daughter: Did I really see her my second night here or was she a ghost? If I had reported it, none of this might have happened.

But it did happen. She came, took the birds, and left, and everything else seemed to cave in behind her, like tugging the end of the tablecloth and it all came tumbling to the floor. The farm's ruin, the decay in the fields, the ash, the echoing barns. The sinking of this beautiful country. Even the mass extinction over the earth seemed to choose that moment to kick in in earnest. The slide downward—we all knew it was coming, and now it was here and staying. As if the woman were a black hole, and everything fell into her and was destroyed. All that was left was the wind blowing over the flat fields and these cavernous barns, the crevices sealed up so tight according to FDA regulations that not even rodents can get in after all these years.

The only one who survived the demise was me, a lone security officer, curiously left untouched, padding down the aisles, looking up through the steel grates to the second story. The silence is so powerful, it presses against my ears.

The second year the electricity went off. Stretches of months went by without anyone driving up, stepping out of their car. The third year only the brother came once in a while, sat in his car and stared out his windshield, drove off before dark. By then he was not surprised to see me because he didn't. I stayed hidden and watched.

So when those two came back, they had no idea I was there.

But they came, a few years ago, the two auditors who went to prison. I was doing my last security walk-through of the day, getting ready to leave. I'd gotten into the habit of knocking off a bit early so I could pick up my son at preschool. My wife doesn't get off until four.

I was circling the silos when a car came up the road. I ducked behind a barn. Two women got out, spent a moment stretching their legs, raising their arms. At first I thought, Hummm, prospective buyers? Then I recognized them from their pictures in the news years back. The older woman had her phone out and was taking photos. She turned and caught me, I think, though I tried to dive out of the way. They walked, then stopped, the pretty one staring up at the barns, the other facing the fields. They spoke. I saw them laugh, one gestured sideways with an arm. They stayed a little longer, turning serious, somber even. The older one crossed her arms and spoke into the wind. The other turned her head toward her. Then they walked back to the car, drove away.

Sometimes I come in early. I try not to wake my wife as I sneak out while it's still dark and the bats are finishing their hunt. At dawn the whole valley comes alive here. A certain set of crickets begin their song at the exact moment the sun touches the horizon. Birds begin to swirl, fewer than before, but still a lot. They call to one another, circling, and fly off.

It's a good job. Temps don't receive benefits, which is a downside when you have a family. My wife wants to leave this empty land, move closer to her siblings, to a place that's bigger, louder, colder, more expensive. I want my son to have every opportunity. I tendered my resignation to Price Securities, effective this Friday. I hope for a good reference. We'll leave this bank account open for any bonuses that may come my way for my constancy all these years.

ANNABELLE, ROB THOUGHT, then said aloud when the barn manager and a police officer appeared in the kitchen. Rob was sitting over his bowl of cantaloupe and cold cereal (his wife rarely let him eat eggs these days, what with his father more or less dead of heart disease at sixty-four). It was a quarter to seven in the morning. The baby had woken at six.

Even before the men spoke, the name was rising in his mind to greet their stricken faces because the only times he'd encountered faces like that were when news of his sister arrived.

Annabelle. His earliest memories were of her carrying him on her back or under her arm like a heavy duffel, her waking him in the dark for a backyard midnight adventure of building a night fort or looking for bats.

"You've been invaded," the cop said, his heft and stance alarming in the pastel quiet.

"They've taken the ladies," the barn manager said.

Rob lowered his spoon into his milk (almond milk, since his wife contended dairy caused diabetes) and got up from his seat. He kissed his wife and baby at the door.

It was a short ride to the farm, a route he'd known all his life, first from the backseat with his sister, later the passenger seat beside his father, and later from his own house three blocks west of his childhood home (though he hadn't planned for it to work out that way). He listened with half an ear to the men, but his attention was on the plume of smoke he could see even from here: evidence of Annabelle. His sister's thumbprint on the sky. The car crossed the fields into the breaking day.

• • •

He had the door open before the car had come to a complete stop behind the line of emergency vehicles. He maneuvered with excessive politeness, "Pardon me, please" and "Might I get by?" through the reporters and firemen and civilians, until he reached the barricade of police tape and cones that held the public away from Barn 8, still partially on fire and smoldering. A police officer who seemed to be in charge tapped him and said, "You're going to want to see the other barns." Rob followed him.

At the door to Barn 4 a cop held up his hand, but the one in charge said, "That's the son," and they all parted. Rob was certain he heard snickering behind him.

Annabelle had always outwitted him, and he'd adored her. What kid doesn't look up to his big sister, especially if she's lawless and beautiful? He counted the day Jonathan Jarman Jr. arrived on the farm as the day he lost her. Before then, her pranks had been for Robbie's benefit, either as target or coconspirator. Once Jonathan showed up, she cut Rob out. Within twenty-four hours he was permanently uninvited. Everything that came afterward seemed an extension of that, she leaving by degrees while he watched from afar. It seemed everyone who loved Annabelle stood back and watched her betray and leave them. It was her most unique feature—after, of course, the obvious. And sure, he'd gotten over it, dismissed her in the same tone they all did, with the same scoff.

Then how to explain this? He paused just inside Barn 4. The fans were off, the belts still. He heard nothing. On the drive over they'd said the birds were gone—but what does that even mean, "gone"? He walked past the entryway into the hen area. Not one coo or cluck. Silence. *All* of them? He turned into an aisle, saw the rows of empty cages (*how the hell, Annie?*). He strode past several. Nothing. He stopped and rocked on his heels, let out a whistle. He actually felt delight.

"They're all like this," the barn manager was beside him saying. "Well, except for Barn 8."

"I see," said Rob.

"We're finding the trucks," the officer in charge said. "We're rounding them up. It's a hell of a thing. We're still looking for the security guard." Rob could tell the officer was too polite to say Annabelle's name but everyone knew the family history. At last the officer tipped his head in confidence. "Do you know where your sister might be?"

A residual protectiveness kicked in. "What makes you think it's her?" he demanded. He could tell by their faces that his face was arranged wrong. "I have no idea where she is," he said. He stepped back into the sunlight, the posse scurrying after him. He walked toward the cars. He stopped in the middle of the pavement. "Wait, where are you taking the hens?"

But it wasn't until a couple of hours later, while he was shouting into his phone, all the maturity and rage of his twenty-eight years returned, that it occurred to him: he knew where she was. He lowered the phone.

A: Of *course* I went to check Barn 8. Who has security guards these days? The alarm systems are more sophisticated and cheaper. Our alarm system was *off*. It was my father. He'd always had Ricardo. If Ricardo had been there, he never would have seen me. Ricardo sat for hours and played solitaire with an old deck of cards. If *he* had seen me, he would have sounded the alarm. He knew what I was about. But he wouldn't have seen me because he'd never be out walking around like a zombie. Besides, Ricardo was on vacation. I knew that. My father would have just let it go for the three weeks. We had an alarm, I'm telling you. But my brother, Robbie, was running things and he'd gotten a temp guard.

I'd just come out of Barn 7—empty—when I felt myself light up under his beam. I ran but he was determined. He stayed out there for an hour, swinging that flashlight around. I worried the other workers might start showing up. They come early on Thursdays. I couldn't believe they'd empty one barn and not the other since both were scheduled for the same time. I had seen the depop crew on Tuesday. They take at least three weeks between depop and pop. This was a formality on my part. That damn temp. What a mess.

Look, are we almost done? I've utterly lost track of the time. Can I go?

Q: We have just a few more questions.

TWENTY YEARS BEFORE ALL THIS, Farmer Robert Green Sr. drove down a small road, Robbie and Annabelle in the backseat. He went past the barbed wire and end-of-the-world signs, the familiar path unrolling like an ace bandage. The old boat of a car tugged up a hill and stopped in front of a large barn. His daughter ran across the grass, Robbie following. Farmer Green got out and stood there, hunched. He sighed.

Farmer Green was prone to fits of melancholy. Anything could trigger it—a holiday, a rainy morning, autumn's late dawn. He'd fall to missing his father, the original chicken farmer of the family. He'd steer the kids into the backseat, tell his wife he was taking them to "a game," and drive here, to the farm of his childhood, though his wife would be furious if she found out.

He walked toward the barn, stooped to pull up a few handfuls of weeds that overran the path. The worst of the contamination was closer to the village a few miles off, but here the earth and air still supposedly contained its traces: trichloroethylene, tetrachloroethylene, chloroform, and other chemicals. His wife didn't want him bringing the kids. And she sure as hell didn't want the kids climbing onto the barn's roof, which, she said, was surely rotting after years of neglect and could crash in under a child's weight at any moment.

Well, it had held up so far.

But Robbie Jr. knew their father wasn't watching. He and Annabelle ran through the tallgrasses and weeds to the barn, climbed the ladder bolted to the wall. They sat on the rooftop, stringing their legs over the side. They lay back and looked at the clouds. They sat up and took in the trees of the forest beyond. Robbie liked this part.

He did not like the next part, when Annabelle insisted they "roof race," meaning whoever reached the edge of the roof first without falling off won. The urge to slow down as you neared the edge contrasted with the urge to speed up to win. It was a version of the game chicken (meaning the one who lost was "chicken," implying that chickens scare more easily than most animals, though that is not the case—hens will fight fiercely to protect their young, and don't even get us started on the pluck and courage of the rooster, famous for his skill in battle). It was the sort of game Annabelle liked, and Rob, worshipful, followed.

ZEE WAS IN THE FINAL TRUCK beside Dill. Annabelle drove.

Texts were coming in like heartbeats, the investigators violating the radio silence pledge, minutes into an emergency, fucking unprofessionals. They were all getting what they deserved, Zee thought, for following Annabelle into yet another scenario she'd concocted. Look where it got the lot of them. And since Annabelle and Dill didn't want to look, Zee took it upon himself to tell them.

He read the texts aloud, described the photos—the fire trucks, the investigators in handcuffs. He showed them to Dill, who kept shouldering Zee away and muttering about it being the investigators' fault, as if *she* hadn't orchestrated the whole thing, flat beginning to billowy end.

Annabelle turned off the main road and kept going. They left the service area and his phone fell silent. They drove past the contamination signs. Oh lovely. Just what he wanted to do this morning. Wallow in chemical waste.

But wait. What was *that*?

A massive barn, two trucks standing stupidly on the horizon.

So if he was understanding this correctly, and he wouldn't put it past her, they'd brought the hens *from one factory farm to another.*

They stopped alongside the trucks. Annabelle turned off the engine. He could hear the hens cooing like morning birds. A hum of insects. A wide plateau of silence underneath, the sound of no sound of machinery. Four investigators came walking out of the barn looking like they might fall over. Annabelle hopped off the truck. "What are we waiting for? We've got to get these hens off the trucks."

One of them cupped a cigarette. "What the hell do you think we've been doing?"

Zee took this opportunity to stretch his long legs, step down, and ask rhetorically, "Ready for prison?" The investigators looked disappointed. They hadn't been getting the texts, they didn't know what was up all over town, but they could tell by the postures of the group removing themselves from the truck that the plan wasn't cool anymore. They got it fast: it was fucked and it would get further fucked still. So, this knowledge in their hearts, together they finished the unloading. It took a couple more hours. They took down the batteries and released the birds into the barn, over forty grand in there now between the three trucks.

"You starting an egg farm?" said Zee.

When they were done and standing by the trucks, talking next moves, talking imminent escape, Annabelle came out and said, "You all scoot."

Fine with Zee. "You coming?" he said, meaning Dill, because no fucking way was Annabelle getting in—she'd already walked off. The investigators started up one of the trucks. Dill and Annabelle, they stayed. Zee looked into the rearview and saw her heading back into the barn. What a loon.

"WE CAN GET SOME PEOPLE UP HERE to take them tomorrow," Dill was saying, wiping his hands on his pants. He followed Annabelle to the back of the barn. "We need to get some water set up," he said. "Do we have any supplies?" He watched her unlatch the barn doors, a set of old-fashioned affairs that you dragged through the dust, the entire building made of wood that had had decades to soften. What was she doing? "They'll get out," he said, while she dragged the door, sunshine breaking into the darkness and the faces of thousands of hens. They were startled by the light and backed off. He said, "It's dusty in here, but . . ." She started wading through the hens to the other end of the barn.

"Jesus." He saw now. "Was this your plan all along?"

She reached the dark end of the barn, raised her arms, yelled, "Let's move it out," over the heads of forty thousand hens.

THAT FIELD. Once fallow, now flower. Tallgrass, clover. A forest on the other side.

They'd never been invited onto the land before. No one had ever asked them to come have a look at the sky, and they couldn't see it from their cages. They'd never felt space around them, never dirt or grass under their feet. The hens paused just inside the crowded barn and gazed out, heads tilting and turning. The sky glinted—surely full of predators. But the ground might have something to eat. With their left eyes—the eye they use to see distance—they could see the trees that began on the other side of the grassy prairie. The air was moist and clear in ways unfamiliar to them. Pollen floated through it. That's the thing: they want the air—cool, bug-filled, quiet—and they will soon love the rest, if you just give them a little time. Let them adjust.

The haze of sunlight met the barn's darkness in a swirl of motes.

These voyagers, descendants of the ancient forest dwellers, hesitated. White leghorns are a jittery breed. Yes, Bwwaauk had nonchalantly strolled out of Plato's Cave, but these hens were not in possession of the same wandering spirit, the devil-may-care insouciance of that odd hen. These hens were afraid.

No thanks. We'll stay inside. This is good right here.

Suddenly, like everything else in their lives, someone made the choice for them. There was a horrible noise and then the hens at the door were shoved out by the hens behind.

BACK AT THE POLICE STATION Janey was cuffed on the floor. She was a few hours from falling in love with Zee, who seven years later would come for her in her teenage bedroom, wait with her there for three months, and then walk out beside her, as if out of a dark barn, blinking in the sunlight. Zee, with whom she would try again. Demand more.

But before all that, while she was still cuffed on the floor, Janey had a strange sensation, but what was it? Ninety miles away, Annabelle was lifting her arms, and Janey was somehow feeling the drag of the barn door, she felt the air rushing in, the shocking daylight, she felt the crumbling of the world made up of steel and wire and bulbs and belts and food flakes. The illusion of the barn was scattering into bits of light.

Janey. She had had the original vision of hens leaving the barn, but it was Annabelle who'd imagined them arriving, dreamed it those long nights on her houseboat, concocted her scenario, but didn't know how it would happen.

Sitting on the station floor, Janey felt the prairie wind and sun on her face, but she would never find out what it meant. Only three humans ever knew where those forty thousand hens went, and they told no one.

DILL HAD WATCHED MANY HOURS of raw footage of farm-hands chasing hens from one end of a cage-free barn to the other in preparation for depop. It used to remind him of predator apocalypse movies—thousands scrambling, shrilling, panicking, piling—and this was no different from that, but to be amid it, to be in the investigators' shoes, among hens going into hen meltdown, was a jolt. Some would be trampled and injured, some killed. But there was no other way to get them to leave, so he lifted his arms and shouted along with Annabelle, and the hens flowed around his feet like a wave in water. He and Annabelle followed them as they left the barn and went screaming into the field.

They wove through the grass for the cover of the trees—the forest preserve that began at the edge of the field. He walked around the side of the barn to look for Annabelle, who'd disappeared, but he stopped when he spotted a line of police cars snaking up the hill. They were a long way off, dots in the distance, turning lights. He went back into the barn to hurry the remaining hens.

"WE ACCELERATED UP THE HILL. I could see two more of those ludicrous trucks at the top. Not until then was I even willing to grant we were going the right way. We'd been driving in loops for an hour. Brad in the front car supposedly had the coordinates locked into his system but I had my doubts until we saw the trucks, two of them just like the others, dull in the sunshine, and who knew how many trucks there were altogether. A lot.

"I told myself, Hey, I've had worse assignments, maybe not dumber, but this isn't as bad as it gets. It's not nearly as bad as standing down a drug addict or breaking up a wife fight. World can get ugly.

"I know what you're thinking, and, no, I never had to shoot to kill. You won't see me in the papers.

"So we drove toward the trucks. We weren't in a hurry. They weren't going anywhere. The forest at the border of the contaminated area unrolled along the horizon. We pulled up, three cars' worth of us. We didn't bother with sirens, but our lights circled forlornly. I opened my door. The trucks were empty. I heard clucks some way off but I didn't see any chickens. I don't know what I heard anymore after the morning we'd had.

"I ran my keys along the metal sides of the truck as we passed. *Clack, clack, clack.*

"'Do we know how many are in there?' I said.

"Brad shrugged. 'Could be thousands.'

"'Not chickens. Fuck's sake,' I said.

"We gathered in front of the trucks. Fred got out a bullhorn and stood there with his feet planted. 'All right,' he called. 'Who ordered an omelet?' He lowered the horn and bent over laughing. That went on for a while. We heard clucking in the distance, and then a couple of chickens came strolling around the corner, heads bobbing. I thought again what I'd been thinking all morning: what a pain in the ass.

"I'd never been on that side of the contamination line. You? Once when I was in grade school the science class a year ahead of mine rode through on a school bus without stopping but some parents objected and it never happened again. If the place had been easier to get to, more of us might have wandered in to see if we'd come out as werewolves. But by the time we could drive we had girls on our minds and I had a stepfather to fight with. Even with a car it was an hour and a half away.

"I don't know what I expected it to look like—burnt out like napalm Vietnam movies? My father was a vet. But it looked like nothing. The trees and grasses on one side of the fence looked as boring as on the other. They say it's sunk into the earth and air, invisible. A few lungfuls won't grow you a fifth limb, but don't touch anything. I didn't like being there even an hour. 'Man, this is one creepy place,' I said. 'Come on, Fred.'

"Then Brad said, 'Whoa, there's one on the roof,' and I thought he meant a chicken but I squinted and there was a woman, hands on her hips, her dress rippling like a goddamn superhero. Like her plan was to hold us off from taking her chickens. I was like, Lady, you think I'm going to have a face-off over who gets the chickens? I got kids at home. You take the chickens.

"Hey, I'll have another. Thanks.

"These animal extremists, I'm telling you, they are something else. You ever see the videos they put on YouTube? They look truly scary running through the dark, carrying crowbars and chain saws. Machetes. Ski masks over their faces. They're scaling fences and kicking open doors and bashing in equipment. All this, and then at the end they reach into a cage that they just violently pounded the lock off of, and they pick up a little bunny or a puppy and cradle it, pet it between the ears with a thick black glove, give it a kiss through the ski mask. They have got to be criminally insane. I can't think of any other explanation.

"You know, I've had worse assignments—you get dose deaths, you get kids that a dad broke their collarbone. You sign on for it all. From my angle, the sun was in my eyes so I couldn't see it that well, but I did see her go down."

ALL THAT NIGHT only a single human was injured, and she wasn't injured that night but the next day, after all the trucks had been found, and investigators were in handcuffs all over the state and some beyond the state's borders, and most of the hens were melting at the church in accordance with God's plan, and Rob Jr. had his head in one hand and with the other was holding his phone to his ear, shouting, while pacing outside the tiny police station of Al, Iowa, and would let up only when someone tapped his shoulder and wore that grim Annabelle expression that all his adult life told him to stop whatever he was doing.

Meanwhile, Jonathan Jarman Jr. was on the highway, going one mile under the speed limit (professionals all), heading back to Joy and the two little girls.

And Dill was waving the final few chickens from the barn, sweeping them out with his hands and feet, collecting the ones in the corners and letting them flap from his arms out back, and watching them head across the field for the forest like baby turtles head for water when they push out of the sand. He wasn't paying attention to where Annabelle was because he knew his job and did it well.

Zee had been pulled over and arrested with the others in the truck. He was jostled into the station, lined up along the wall with a hundred more like him (the four cells were filled to capacity). He found himself seated next to that girl, the most beautiful woman he'd ever seen. He thought, My God, my elbow is touching the woman I'll spend my life with, though I'll have to wait until I get out of prison to talk her into it.

He exhaled slowly. Please let me get this right, he prayed. He smiled at her in what he hoped was a winning way. "Fucking Annabelle," he said. "This has to be her worst idea yet."

The beautiful girl scowled.

SURPRISINGLY, none of the investigators went to prison, only the auditors. This was partly due to a team of defense lawyers assigned to the investigators pro bono by the Humane Society of the United States, and partly due to the fact that the Green family had no intention of sending the only daughter in the family to prison—only men as far as the eye could see across the various cousins and uncles, except for Annabelle (and of course the newest addition, Robbie's chickadee)—especially since Annabelle was in a coma and might never wake. But they had to press charges against *someone*. They needed the insurance money. They had loan payments, contracts, employee paychecks due.

Robbie's incompetent cousin, Jack, took charge. He gathered the dazed family into the hospital cafeteria late that night after Annabelle's fall through the rotting roof, and devised a plan that somehow worked. The family refused to press charges against the investigators, claiming after the fact that the evacuation was "services rendered" and that it had been their very own Happy Green Family Farm idea. They insisted they had planned to retire the farm, since Farmer Green Sr. could no longer run it and farming had changed beyond all recognition, didn't contain the attractions it once had and couldn't be profitable without five times the hens they'd had. A tiny farm like theirs couldn't compete. They had *asked* the investigators to empty the barns, they said, and bring the hens to the sanctuaries. Only the investigator who had set fire to the oldest barn had acted against their wishes, and violated fire code and state regulations besides. Dill, whom they'd always hated and blamed for Annabelle's radicalism, was the arsonist, they claimed, and they wanted to press charges. In addition Happy Green Family Farm sued the Al, Iowa, Police Department for a dozen allegations from wrongful injury to illegal destruction of property in the seizing and impounding and destroying of nine hundred thousand units of company property. Indeed they did eventually receive a sizable settlement for God's melted birds, due in part to a video Jack put together of the hundreds of thousands of chickens, dead and piled on the church's blacktop. The town's prosecutor was left scrambling for charges to bring against the investigators and wound up with watery ones like resisting arrest, driving a category D vehicle without a proper license, or littering. Most got probation, community service, and fines. For months teams of current and former investigators and sanctuary workers could be seen along the roadsides, picking up garbage and putting it into gray plastic bags, or on their hands and knees weeding the woody public land on the median strip, or painting lines in the parking lot in front of the courthouse. Only Dill was charged with arson, for which he spent twenty-nine days in jail awaiting a hearing, after which the charges were dropped: the mismatched fingerprints on the gas can and equipment shed, his long public record of nonviolence and animal protection, the many witness statements, and his excellent attorney all helped. Luckily for the Green family the insurance did not require a conviction for payment, only a charge.

Cleveland and Janey did not fare as well. Their employer confiscated Cleveland's company BlackBerry, discovered the photos and videos of the past several months, brought every charge they could think of against them—violation of the ag-gag law, breaking and entering, burglary, false representation. Janey received a five-year sentence, out after two, and Cleveland ten years, out after four and a half.

WHAT ELSE WAS EXPECTED OF HIM? he'd like to know.

He'd shown up in court in his suit and tie. He'd worn a suit and tie to the prison every Sunday, and let that punk have Saturday. He wore a suit to each parole visit—he'd insisted on accompanying her. There were an awful lot of suits and ties involved in all this. He wore a suit to meet the punk's family, and a brand-new one to her wedding, and another to the bank when he cosigned on the mortgage. He wore one to the hospital when she was giving birth, and one to the funeral. He'd done it, he'd been a father, not that he got any credit.

Now after all that, they were right back where they started, she shut up in her room like a fifteen-year-old. And she wouldn't eat the food he set out for her. Not even her old favorites.

Okay, he shouldn't have put out the chicken. That was on him. He'd set it down in front of her door in its takeout container, along with a diet pop—truly used to be what she liked—knocked, and went down the hall to the sofa. He leaned back, could see the box and drink sitting on the floor. He saw the door open a little and the items disappear. About a minute later he heard the door slam open, saw the box fly out of the room and hit the wall.

Well, *goddamn* it! How was he supposed to know what she ate? And why did she have to *throw it at the wall*?

Was he going to have to clean up every goddamn mess her mother left behind? He never asked to be a father. She'd come looking for *him* and hadn't given him *one minute's peace*. "You have to eat!" he yelled. No answer. He called Cleveland and left a message. "She's starving to death, for all you care!" He stormed down the hallway, stood outside her room. "Now I've had about enough of this, young lady. You come out here and clean this up!"

"Go to hell!" she screamed back.

He was so mad he stomped all over the chicken.

He swore all the way to the supermarket. He picked out potato chips, pretzels, and miniature carrots in a bag. He swore all the way back to the apartment. He stepped gingerly around the smashed chicken, placed the paper bag by her door. He put down one of his jugs of water, too, so the goddamn girl wouldn't die. He knocked. Nothing. "Aren't you going to see what I brought?"

"Go away!" she screamed.

"There's carrots!" he bellowed. He stomped down the hallway and banged himself onto the sofa. When he leaned back, the bag and jug were gone. A little while later he brought a trash bag and sponge over and cleaned up the mess.

A couple days later her husband showed up and he thought he was saved but then the worthless crazy-haired hoodlum joined her in her room, coming out only to pee and stand for a minute gangly-armed in the hallway.

Now he would feed them both. Cleveland said Taco Bell, which happened to be fourteen miles away, but fine. He would manage.

"I'M SAYING IT, JANEY."

Janey had her hands over her face.

"It's been three months."

"Don't," said Janey.

It wasn't Zee or her father who eventually talked her out of the bedroom. For all Zee's mooning and her father's shouting it was Cleveland who impatiently spoke common sense. "I'm saying it. You'll have another one." Cleveland pulled Janey's hands away from her face. "The heart lives on whether you want it to or not."

Janey didn't remember her mother ever saying that, but she knew from hard experience that it was true. So she cried in rage and sorrow but she left the room at last. And Cleveland was right. They named her Olive.

Olive had quite a collection of people raising her—an odd grouping of former investigators, her *tías*, Zee's six sisters, and their families, and Janey's grumpy father.

But Cleveland took charge of Olive every Wednesday afternoon, first playing with her on the floor, later picking her up after school. Cleveland bravely took her to do the things Olive wanted to do, even the ones Cleveland didn't like. They identified insects on cropland, played chess at the homeless shelter, busked the town streets with her violin (the proceeds went to AR organizations). She did get Olive to make a papier-mâché replica of the solar system and they turned the garage into a universe of star systems and comets.

"Did I ever tell you about the time your grandmother and I

formed a band?" Cleveland would say. "I played the triangle . . ." Janey would listen from her office.

"Stand up straight, Olive," Janey heard her say. "We do not foment revolution by slouching."

Janey had not lived the life of the girl in New York. She had chosen to go to Iowa, chosen to stay, chosen to follow Cleveland into the barns, to join Zee after prison, to come out of the dark bedroom and into the light, to try, try again. She had authored her life. There *was* a better life than the one she lost and it was the one where she chooses.

BUT THERE WOULD BE MORE GRIEFS for Janey, there always are. One day, when her father was old, she and Zee would take him to Florida. Olive would be away at college. His Alzheimer's would be fairly advanced by then, more so than when Janey had booked the trip two months before. She'd imagined him sitting on sand in the sunshine, waves dashing by, him ducking and complaining as Janey ran up from the water and shook drops on him, laughing. Instead, every unfamiliar sensation brought him discomfort and fear. He couldn't recall anything she said, even five minutes later. He wouldn't come out of his room except to eat.

The last day of the trip found them waiting at the airport. Her giant father was rigid with panic, not knowing where he was or with whom, not knowing how he'd get home, and Janey's pain was so great, she couldn't look at him. It was Zee who, as usual, was so good with him. Zee sat beside him and repeated over and over in a low voice near her father's ear, "We're on a holiday in Florida. Your daughter is with us. We're going home, waiting for the plane. The flight information is right there on that screen. Flight 632, see it? Departing at eleven fifteen. We've got forty minutes to board," while her father's cloudy eyes fixed on the screen. Each time his lips began to move and sounds to emerge, Zee would quiet him with the mantra once again. "We're on a holiday. We've had a wonderful time. Your daughter is here. See, you can read the flight information right there, flight 632 . . ." Janey bit her lip because, despite what she had predicted her first night in her father's home, she *had* learned how to love him.

Bonnie K—, Iowa State Park Ranger

Some died. You'd walk through the forest and see white puffs lying on the ground, like pillows turned inside out. A pile under a tree. A bundle in the bushes. They'd all gotten on top of one another and smothered. But then I'd see a whole group poking up a path, pecking at the roots, and another dozen gathered under a tree, tossing dirt around. Frankly, I was surprised so many of them were still alive.

But if you think about it, the little ladies are underrated. These hens have been bred through so many generations—a sort of sped-up evolution—that they've become genetically strange and powerful animals, designed to live through rather bizarre trials. I read about it all online. They have to be able to just stand there in those cages for months and months, their lungs filling with dander. They have to be able to take the onslaught of massive doses of inoculations, to endure sensory overloads and deprivations, clown-car crowding, the vicious pecks of their cell mates. They have to be resistant to disease. They have to tolerate violence, noise, panic, and not drop dead of heart stress (as many do, apparently). These birds are practically radioactive, if you understand what I mean. Superbirds in some respects.

So yeah, I knew they were there. I saw them alive and dead out my window. But I didn't do a thing. I told no one they were here, I ignored them. I lied.

I figured, on the one hand, you've got their lack of practice at finding food. They had that going against them. On the other, you've got that they've been bred to fast through those low-calorie molts. If they could smell, they'd find the river that twists through here, banks of bugs, gushing water.

On the first hand, you've got their lack of practice at fleeing predators. Chickens are oblong balls of feather and flesh, water-logged-looking compared to most birds. Can barely climb or fight, can fly only a few feet. Are best at walking or flapping uselessly, windmilling on the ground. But, going for them, you've got that this forest was overhunted for so long, an army of gunmen tramping through, dropping any warm- or cold-blooded creature in its tracks, that, save for an occasional squirrel and a smattering of swallows, these trees were shaken empty of animals decades ago. Besides, you'd be surprised how fast instincts kick in. They were hopping short awkward flights into the trees within days. They were sleeping in the branches.

Yeah, I'd say it was a closer call than you might at first guess. I was curious about how it would play out.

Against them, you've got humans. No animal stands a chance against us. We'll kill anything alive, right where it's standing, wherever and whatever it is, and we'll have plenty of excuses for it.

Against them, you've got that any rangers coming through here, not to mention calm citizens taking their state park con-stitutionals, were going to notice tens of thousands of chickens. Humans are a damn unobservant, cross-eyed crew, but that many hens were not going to slip by.

But, in their favor, you've got the fine coincidence that this state park's boundary happened to run up against a forty-square-mile region that, due to a certain chemical waste incident, was declared uninhabitable three decades ago, cordoned off for the next thousand years. And even though this patch of forest itself supposedly fell outside the contaminated region (whether it did or didn't is a matter of debate), no one wanted to buy it or even get near it, which is how it became a state park, and how I wound up here and understood with a grim finality that my supervisors despised me. To see a visitor here was rare.

The so-called noncontamination may be the cause of my lethargy, headaches, and disorientation. In fact, initially when I saw the hens, I thought I was hallucinating.

They are excellent climbers, as a side note, once they get the hang of it. I glimpsed a few lurching around in the lower parts of the trees, somersaulting out of them, stringing through the leaves. Bravo!

Against them, you've got winter.

For them, you've got that it was spring.

Against them, you've got that it was spring and that if there *was* a time humans would brave chemical contamination and its subsequent potential cancers and neonatal disorders, it would be then, when humans are let outside.

In the hens' favor, you've got the local economy—and the fallout from its demolition. This was the year the state went bankrupt. The senate elected to reduce benefits, pensions, library hours, and—most relevant to the hens—funding to state parks. All state parks were hereby shut down indefinitely. Humans in search of weekend entertainment would not be coming this spring. No rangers leading nature walks, no peanut brittle in the welcome center, no PowerPoint shows of rocks. Not that we ever had much of that anyway, what with the contamination.

Against them you've got that, despite the park's closure, the state did still employ individual rangers to monitor the parks and do low-level maintenance—not to keep the paths free of brush and prevent nature from taking back what's hers, which takes a whole team, but to drive through from time to time, make sure no vandals—or chickens—were taking over in there. You would think the ranger of this forest would spot tens of thousands of chickens, but, in their favor, the ranger in charge of this patch of forest happened to be *me*, and I had become delinquent to the very highest degree. I was through being the codependent mediator between human and nature. I didn't really give a fuck anymore. I'd spent my adolescence and young adult life trying to obtain the position of head ranger and, first, in what could only be a cruel joke, I was put in charge of a contaminated forest empty of animals and, second, within a year the park was cut in a line budget item. The handful of other intrepid rangers and volunteers left and I was alone.

So in the hens' favor you've got that I did not, as I was supposed to, drive through my assigned amoeba-shaped piece of forest each afternoon, the piece carved out to abut and buffer the contamination. Instead I sat in the state park ranger trailer and watched tremendous amounts of TV. I was working through every season of every show I had ever heard of.

I'd never been able to do this before. As a child raised by a public librarian and a high school history teacher, occupations as adorable and close to extinction as my own, I'd lived under a severe, screen-restricted regime. I'd missed every media event essential to a healthy social childhood, and I continued to as a young adult out of loyalty. But now in the weeks before the chickens showed up, I'd decided that these state park fucks could go fuck themselves. I was going to catch up on my shows.

At first I watched out of loneliness and boredom. But gradually I began to feel pleased with my little radiant porthole. I had no actual TV set, of course. The state does not outfit the ranger trailers with them, but I had the internet, which they *had* to give me since cell service is spotty out here and I had to file the reports online. I had access to hundreds, thousands, of shows. Shows about war between planets, shows about people wanting to be married, shows about being black drivers, shows about people jumping off of cliffs and into cars, about dogs, zombies, France. Then there was porn, which had me sidetracked for a week before I let myself be dragged away by the whole genre of shows about comedians enacting themselves having embarrassing sex, failing children, being funny in a world that doesn't understand them. I began to understand why people rushed home from work to sit in the glow, bits of color touching their faces, the room darkening and lightening not in response to the earth's daily churn, but to the hourly TV one. I could nestle the state-issued laptop between my knees, the show two feet from my face, which was better than having it across the room with all that dull, hopeless "real life" space between me and the screen. The room faded out of existence and it was almost as if I was there with them, inside the show.

I had to send the daily reports, yes, on the defunct state of the state park. I filled out the reports online while I watched the shows on the other half of the screen. A perfect setup, because no show—no matter how good or how much I dreaded or longed for its characters—took up more than 70 percent of my concentration and usually considerably less (and honestly couldn't one say the same for even the most passionate affairs in "real life"?). Between the report and the show I came close to having 90 percent of my attention attended to, leaving only 10 percent to wave alone in the wind, thinking or racing with irrational fear or fury.

Who says that what we experience while watching TV isn't every bit as real as what we experience while watching what *isn't* on TV? If TV creates the same emotions—sadness, desire, rage— and if the emotion is sincere, and frankly a hell of a lot less work, why shouldn't it count? Isn't it true that in "real life" people and promises disappear with less ritual than on-screen anyway?

I was in this condition when the superchickens showed up.

Now and then I'd glance up from my laptop and find the room still there. Through the smudged trailer window along the couch where I reclined, I could see green getting greener, light failing, dark falling, light returning. I'd look back at the laptop.

Then one day I glanced out and saw a trail of chickens, all puffed up, poking around.

What the hell is that? I thought. A chicken?

I looked back at the show. I thought nothing at all.

I looked out the window a few hours later and saw more of them, *hundreds*.

I looked it up online while watching a show about vampire women—an unbelievable number of episodes to this one, I'd be safe for months—and there it was, an article about an entire farm's worth of chickens stolen by radicals. Did anyone realize they'd dropped some off here?

Why didn't someone come looking?

Ah, I'll tell you why. Because I said the hens were dead! No one wanted to come onto this land unless they had to. The ranger association wrote and asked me if I'd *spotted any domestic white leghorn chickens*. I looked out the trailer window at the group gathered around the cooked brown rice I'd put out there. *Yeah, some*, I wrote back. *They all died in a day. Probably the contamination. I bagged them up and buried them.* Then I added to keep them from coming: *I'm still getting those headaches, by the way.* And: *Could you add a bit more to the supplies account? I'm almost out of food.*

Meanwhile, outside the trailer the superchickens ran over the grounds. Even the local boys, who might conceivably drive in looking for something to torture, stayed away, more interested these days in their heroic exploits as oxy-morons. You can imagine.

The chickens nested, laid eggs, so they had that going for them too. After a couple of days, I walked through the forest and looked at the chickens and the eggs, the enormous number of eggs. Eggs everywhere. I thought, Neat, maybe I'll have some chicks. Maybe this is the start of a new generation of chickens, right here in my radioactive forest. Then it hit me. Wait, there aren't any roosters. Don't hens' eggs need to be fertilized?

I looked it up. Yes, the chickens had to get fucked in order for this to happen. I was researching all this while I wrote reports and watched season three of the vampire show that by then was taking up only 30 percent of my attention. Then I watched season eight of a show about a hospital (20 percent). Then I watched a show about a supernatural firefighter (40 percent). And I began to think, This is a tremendous roadblock, the absence of a rooster. Not even a roadblock but a dead end. These eggs were not going to come out fertilized. Tens of thousands of hens, each laying eggs every thirty-two hours, according to the United Egg Producers website. And it was spring, the perfect time. Still, no way. Scientifically impossible, unless you wanted to count on a virgin birth, which hasn't happened in a while. I did discover in my browsing, while watching season four of a show about a family that sits on sofas all day (10 percent), that occasionally a chicken does change its sex from female to male. A hen becomes a cock! It happens in one out of ten thousand birds. The hen grows a cock on its head and starts to crow. Why do they do that? I do not know. Proves something about something. But the trans cocks do not produce sperm and so will never be able to fertilize a chicken.

No, the lack of sperm would be their defeat.

I didn't like that. It seemed an unfair disadvantage.

Even more, these superchickens weren't supposed to want to sit on their own eggs! This is the kind of breeding that had been going on. Bred to breed themselves out of existence. Humans had screwed them but good.

I could see them out there. I watched with binoculars, while watching season two of a show about a family with sick kids that keep getting better and better (8 percent).

So that's the only thing I did. The human mind bends toward action, though we like to pretend it leans toward lethargy. Guess how easy it is to buy roosters. You press a button during the closing credits of a show about bombs that go off in deserts or underwater (25 percent). Available for pickup next business day. I ordered two dozen roosters. I had to agree to terms and conditions that included promising I would not turn them against each other for a fight. The farm called in the morning and said I could come pick them up.

I drove into town in the state park truck for the first time in a month. I loaded up on feed, then I drove to the farm an hour away. An old farmhand helped me put the crates of birds in the back. Each rooster was in its own separate compartment, two per crate with a divider between them. Back at the park I hoisted the crates onto the ground but did not open them. I considered.

Even with the roosters I was going to have to depend on human error. Humans had already erred so much, it seemed too much to hope that there could be yet more, and also inconceivable that there wasn't a hell of a lot more to come.

I was going to have to hope that humans had not been able to make every single one of these chickens insistent on not sitting, that a suppressed gene would leap forward, assert itself in a chicken who was here and alive and who would meet up with a rooster, and that the two would find enough in common to want more than friendship, to each be searching for more, for love perhaps, or at least sexual or biological satisfaction.

We were going to have to hope that primitive gene was strong, stronger than humans, and that the hen would sit, not one day or two, but that she would desire the whole situation, to create, nurture, tend, protect (*stay no matter what*), to conquer all that humans had done to her, that she'd sit and busily poke at her nest, pull bits of twig and leaves around her, pick out bugs, gently turn her eggs, and that the other hens would watch with interest and envy, that they would feel their own stirrings within them and imitate, and that after a few days the hens would begin to feel the shuffling of their babies beneath them and be moved enough to break into the ancient twittering song that hens sing to their embryos, songs that the embryos sing back, whatever transmission of information occurring in that music forever unknown to us because, no matter how smart we think we are, the simplest things are still sealed off.

Maybe the chances of this were low, yes. But surely not as low as the original spontaneous creation of life, however many million years ago. Not as low as the routine daily occurrences happening all around us, sperm swimming up canals, genes mutating, and so on, the evolution of animals, human and nonhuman. Before I could change my mind, rule against myself skewing the odds, removing a handicap, and instead let the hens rise or fall on the vicissitudes of fate, not man, I opened the crates. I released the birds one by one. The roosters put out their heads, clucked. They stepped hesitantly into the trees.

JONATHAN SAID, "Annabelle, can you hear me?"

Joy and the girls were at a birthday party at Holy Moly Cheese, where they would play Cyber Robot and Cracker Cracker. Joy had been so patient with him about this. He was worried about her family, he'd told her.

"Annabelle, I know you can hear me."

She had promised to resign for good after this. They hadn't discussed what that meant. She'd been in a medically assisted coma for over a month now. The doctors said she was ready to come out.

"Annabelle," he said, "come on." If she'd just open her eyes.

Q: Name?

A: Didn't I answer that already?

Q: This is for the form.

A: I can't even feel my feet anymore. I can't feel my shins.

Q: This last part won't take more than a few minutes. Then all you do is sign and you're done.

A: All right, fine. Just hurry up.

Q: Name?

A: There you go again.

Q: For the form.

A: Annabelle Green Jarman.

Q: How long were you involved in the organization?

A: In what capacity? I had, let's see, eighteen years as daughter, three as wife, eight as investigator, two as outlaw, or depending on how you're—. Hold on, what was that?

Q: What was what?

A: I heard something.

Q: We didn't hear anything.

A: All right.

Q: So would you admit that during your involvement—

A: There it is again. Did you hear that?

Q: No.

A: It's gone now.

Q: We can skip some of these. Final question. Could you tell us—

A: Hang on. There. Did you hear it? Someone's calling my name.

Q: Sorry, nothing.

A: I'm going to go see. I'll be right back.

Q: You can't go back out there now. You already signed.

A: I haven't signed anything.

Q: You almost signed. It's right here. We just need your initials really.

A: I have to get my legs off this. I don't know if can—

Q: Wait.

A: What?

Q: We can't promise what comes next for you, if you go.

A: No one ever did before and that didn't stop me.

Q: He won't stay with you.

A: You just said you weren't going to tell me.

Q: He'll go back to the other woman. Dill won't stay either.

A: Oh. Well, what if I stay here? What happens then?

Q: We can't tell you. Not until you sign. Right here.

A: Do I go before a judge?

Q: Oh no, nothing barbaric like that.

A: Do I come back as something else? A cow, an insect, a tree, a boy?

Q: [to each other] They can't help it. Earth is all they can imagine.

A: What then?

Q: Just sign.

A: Hum, tempting.

Q: Here, use this.

A: Hang on. I hear him again.

Q: No, that's not him.

A: I know his voice.

Q: He won't stay. In fact everything you love will soon be gone. Fish and elephants and birds—especially birds. It all gets worse from here on out. Earth will be covered with contamination.

A: Oh . . . Is there anything left for me if I go back out there? Anything at all?

Q: No.

Q: Aw, come on, tell her.

Q: It's not our place.

A: Tell me what?

Q: Nothing.

Q: There will be a moment.

A: A moment?

Q: A gathering of humans.

Q: Mostly humans.

A: Where?

Q: A room.

Q: A household.

A: And I'll be there?

Q: Yes, you'll be among them.

A: Among what?

Q: Music and chatter and light.

Q: You'll be older.

Q: Older, yes, still slim, your hair will be up.

A: I wear it like that sometimes.

Q: He won't be there.

A: What will I be doing?

Q: Passing a platter of food.

Q: Laughing.

Q: Grilled vegetables. You'll be a little high from a glass of wine.

Q: In fact if you concentrate now, you can almost see yourself outlined in the human blur. See it?

A: I think so.

Q: There you are.

A: Will it be enough?

Q: Almost.

A: I hear him again.

Q: He'll go back to her.

A: I'm going. Excuse me.

Q: We thought your legs were numb.

A: They seem to be working now. Or not quite, woops. No, I've got it. I'm coming, Jonathan. Wait up.

I BELIEVE IN THE AUDIT, even now when I know it's not possible. One cannot enter a barn and look at every object and animal, leave no spot unexamined. Can't do it.

Therefore I regret to inform my superiors that I, Cleveland Smith, in sound mind, resign from my position as head auditor. I was fired, prosecuted, imprisoned, but some positions one has to decide for oneself to leave. But insofar as the auditor is one who looks and reports, I do not rescind my right to look, only my duty to report, for I believe in the beauty and horror of small corners, forgotten faces, wide expanses. I will continue to look. I will watch the world molt.

I, Janey Flores, resign on behalf of the old Janey Flores, the one who stayed behind in New York. She will no longer be reporting for duty in my mind. Henceforth there will be only one Janey Flores (in addition to the 1,883 others currently alive worldwide, not to mention Jane Flores [12,921] and J. Flores [1,164,046]). With the old Janey Flores goes the entire apparatus: the friends she would have made, the words she would have spoken, the moments she and I would have met. From here forward, there will be no echo, no stereo. My words are mine alone.

Salutations, Perpetrator:
I represent the 295 million layer hens currently alive in the continental United States. This cease and desist order is to tell you that your persistent actions—including but not limited to locking my clients into indoor boxes, feeding them foods unnatural to

their dispositions, chopping off their beak tips, destroying their social systems, and subjecting them to death by gas at an early age—have become unbearable. They have submitted an average of seven letters of resignation each, and yet find themselves still in your employment. You are hereby ordered to release them.
Carter Dillard, attorney

I, Dill, resign. It is a forced resignation but I will go—not from the animal war, of course, you don't resign from that, you just switch positions. I resign from my former position as director of investigations. I will finally let go and find more elsewhere. I'd like to thank you for the many years of service I was able to provide.

I, Rob Green, resign. I always hated this job anyway. My wife works at the YMCA, where there are openings. I've also been offered a job as a guidance counselor at the Al District Community College. But you know what? I'm thinking about opening a bicycle shop.

I, Investigator Q, resign. I've been doing this for so long now, I no longer think of myself as anything but a farmhand. I don't even know if I'm reporting to anyone anymore. I'm just moving from farm to farm, west and east toward a far-off horizon. A farmhand, a familiar sight, fewer of us every year. Now one less. I quit.

Epilogue

THE CHICKENS OUTLIVED THE HUMANS. They outlived any other bird, all of whom the humans permanently displaced after another hundred years. But those chickens—whose ancestors ran across a contaminated field into a less contaminated forest and fell in love with the roosters they met there—they outlived them all. Fifty thousand years later they were still making their annual pilgrimage back through what had once been a state park to what had once been Grandfather Green's first barn, to see their origins. As turtles crawl back up the sand, as children come home after they go out to seek their fortunes and fail (divorce, lose, sicken), as creatures return before they start back out for more, so do the chickens, to mark the land with their eyes. Instinctual, biological, psychological, spiritual—anything but intellectual—it is what we living things do: look back.

Every year the superchickens trekked through the original semicontaminated state park. For the first thousand years they stopped to puzzle over the runes left by an earlier time. They did not disrupt these runes with their dirt baths or nesting, left them generation after generation, somehow sensing that the rocks, so carefully arranged, belonged to their creator, who might come back—that phantom limb, that missing *om*. They hoped they might one day understand the message left for them, arranged in bright white rocks:

SMorEs YAY!!!

And after the rocks weren't there anymore, the chickens kept the tradition of stopping in that spot, seeking to understand a mystery whose object is unclear and clues are lost. In this respect they had more in common with humans than they ever did when humans existed.

The chickens knew nothing of the cages they'd once lived in. The original ancestors had not yet developed sophisticated means of storytelling. They passed down only the imagery and sensation of claustrophobia, rotten air, debilitating hopelessness, and pain, so that a sadness lived within their tribe and gave them a more complex personality than other wild chickens, who died out with the humans long before.

Also within them lived the time that chickens had been celebrated by their previous masters. All the centuries they'd been admired for their dazzling plumage, when they'd been held up as examples of proud mothers, mighty warriors, resourceful families, spiritual companions to accompany the dead in the afterlife, symbols of spring, rebirth, renewal, strength. Their genetic history was so bound up in their human connection that they felt something missing, though they didn't know why. Much like the dog's loneliness, which the humans, so long before, never understood or even tried to, that the dog was saying, "Master, it is not because you are going to the movies that I am sad, but because in a far deeper way than you will ever experience, my clan is gone and I am alone."

But the future chickens will not be alone. The evil humans will be gone for good, and the chickens will never evolve hands, will never rise to such heights where mass destruction is possible. They'll take only what they need. They'll run over the land, eating the grasses and the bugs that survived and revived and thrived. They'll live.

ACKNOWLEDGMENTS

Many people agreed to be interviewed for this book. I am grateful to the commercial layer hen farmers and industry scientists who spent a tremendous amount of time teaching and talking to me about modern chicken farming. My thanks especially to farmer Robert Knecht for taking the risk of bringing me inside the enriched and battery barns of Vande Bunte Egg Farm. Thanks also to Dr. Darrin Karcher, farmer Mark Oldenkamp, Mitch Head, David Inall, and the United Egg Producers.

I am also indebted to Matt Prescott, Gary Francione, Daniel Hauff, Marla Rose, John Beske, Vandhana Bala, Mary Beth Sweetland, Ingrid Newkirk, Matt Rice, Twyla Francois, Paul Shapiro, Kim Sturla, and Joel Bartlett. Thanks to Carter Dillard and Harry Moren for legal advice and aid. Thanks to Christine Wagner and the hens of SASHA Farm Animal Sanctuary.

Extra gratitude to the investigators TJ, Chris, Liz, Cody, and Juan, who devoted many, many hours to answering my questions, and who gave me access to hundreds of hours of raw footage of their layer-hen investigations.

Some of the research I did for this book appeared in *Harper's Magazine* in the essay "Cage Wars." Thanks to Ellen Rosenbush and to the dogged fact-checker Jesse Barron.

I read many articles and books while researching this book but it wasn't until I read *Chicken* by Annie Potts that I was able to imagine the independent mind of the hen. I also could not have done without *Chickens' Lib* by Clare Druce and *The White Leghorn Chickens* by H. H. Stoddard.

Thanks to the John Simon Guggenheim Foundation and the University of Texas at Austin for their crucial support, and to Liz Cullingford.

Thanks to Carlos, Terrance, Calvin, Kevin, Patrick, Joel, James, AJ, Jason, Jose, Steven, Shawn, Chris, and Alfredo for joining me beyond the cage. Thanks to Ms. Heather Crabtree. Thanks to Dylan and Arnoldo.

Thanks to Clancy Martin and Terri Kapsalis for their essential early reads, to Lucy Corin for her insightful advice, and to Lydia Davis for her encouragement. Thanks to Diane Williams, always.

Thanks to Ethan Nosowsky for his brilliance and faith.

Thanks to Yana Makuwa, Katie Dublinski, Marisa Atkinson, Ill Nippashi-Hoereth, Caroline Nitz, and all the Graywolves. You are my pack.

Thanks to my soulful agent, David McCormick.

Thanks to Olive Nosowsky.

Thanks to Paulo Zerbato, who created the chicken tattoo I now find on my back, and to Yvette Watt, who painted in her own blood the portrait of Took-Took, which hangs a few feet from where I sit.

Thanks to Bob and Nancy Unferth, and Katiebird and Cean Colcord.

And, Matt, there is no Barn 8 when it comes to you.

Dear readers,

As well as relying on bookshop sales, And Other Stories relies on subscriptions from people like you for many of our books, whose stories other publishers often consider too risky to take on.

Our subscribers don't just make the books physically happen. They also help us approach booksellers, because we can demonstrate that our books already have readers and fans. And they give us the security to publish in line with our values, which are collaborative, imaginative and 'shamelessly literary'.

All of our subscribers:

- receive a first-edition copy of each of the books they subscribe to
- are thanked by name at the end of our subscriber-supported books
- receive little extras from us by way of thank you, for example: postcards created by our authors

BECOME A SUBSCRIBER, OR GIVE A SUBSCRIPTION TO A FRIEND

Visit andotherstories.org/subscriptions to help make our books happen. You can subscribe to books we're in the process of making. To purchase books we have already published, we urge you to support your local or favourite bookshop and order directly from them – the often unsung heroes of publishing.

OTHER WAYS TO GET INVOLVED

If you'd like to know about upcoming events and reading groups (our foreign-language reading groups help us choose books to publish, for example) you can:

- join our mailing list at: andotherstories.org
- follow us on Twitter: @andothertweets
- join us on Facebook: facebook.com/AndOtherStoriesBooks
- admire our books on Instagram: @andotherpics
- follow our blog: andotherstories.org/ampersand

This book was made possible thanks to the support of:

Aaron McEnery
Aaron Schneider
Abigail Charlesworth
Abigail Walton
Ada Gokay
Adam Lenson
Adrian Astur Alvarez
Ailsa Peate
Aisha McLean
Aisling Reina
Ajay Sharma
Alan Hunter
Alan McMonagle
Alan Simpson
Alasdair Hutchison
Alastair Gillespie
Alessandra Lupski Raja
Alex Fleming
Alex Hoffman
Alex Ramsey
Alex Lockwood
Alexander Barbour
Alexander Bunin
Alexandra Citron
Alexandra de Verseg-
    Roesch
Alexandra Stewart
Alexandra Stewart
Alfred Birnbaum
Ali Conway
Ali Smith
Ali Riley
Alicia Bishop
Alison Lock
Alison Winston
Aliya Rashid
Alyse Ceirante
Alyson Coombes
Alyssa Rinaldi
Alyssa Tauber
Amado Floresca
Amanda
Amanda Greenstein
Amanda Read
Amanda Silvester

Amber Da
Amelia Ashton
Amelia Dowe
Amine Hamadache
Amitav Hajra
Amy Benson
Amy Bojang
Amy Savage
Andrea Reece
Andrew Kerr-Jarrett
Andrew Marston
Andrew McCallum
Andrew Rego
Andy Marshall
Andy Turner
Aneesa Higgins
Angela Everitt
Ann Menzies
Anna Corbett
Anna Finneran
Anna Glendenning
Anna Milsom
Anna Zaranko
Anna-Maria Aurich
Anne Carus
Anne Craven
Anne Frost
Anne Guest
Anne Higgins
Anne Ryden
Anne Sticksel
Anne Stokes
Anne Willborn
Anne-Marie Renshaw
Anneliese O'Malley
Annie McDermott
Anonymous
Anthea Morton
Anthony Brown
Anthony Cotton
Anthony Quinn
Antoni Centofanti
Antonia Lloyd-Jones
Antonia Saske
Antony Pearce

Aoife Boyd
Archie Davies
Asako Serizawa
Ashleigh Sutton
Ashley Cairns
Audrey Mash
Audrey Small
Aviv Teller
Barbara Mellor
Barbara Robinson
Barbara Spicer
Barbara Wheatley
Barry John Fletcher
Bart Van Overmeire
Ben Schofield
Ben Thornton
Ben Walter
Benjamin Judge
Bettina Rogerson
Beverly Jackson
Bianca Duec
Bianca Jackson
Bianca Winter
Bill Fletcher
Birgitta Karlén
Bjørnar Djupevik Hagen
Bobbi Collins
Brendan Monroe
Briallen Hopper
Brian Anderson
Brian Byrne
Brian Callaghan
Brian Smith
Bridget Gill
Brigita Ptackova
Briony Norton
Bronx River Books
Brooke Williams
Bruna Rotzsch-Thomas
Caitlin Halpern
Caitriona Lally
Callie Steven
Cameron Lindo
Camilla Imperiali
Campbell McEwan

Carl Emery
Carla Carpenter
Carol McKay
Carole Burns
Carolina Pineiro
Caroline Lodge
Caroline Smith
Caroline West
Cassidy Hughes
Catherine Blanchard
Catharine Braithwaite
Catherine Lambert
Catherine Tolo
Catherine Williamson
Catie Kosinski
Catriona Gibbs
Cecilia Rossi
Cecilia Uribe
Chantal Wright
Charlene Huggins
Charles Fernyhough
Charles Raby
Charles Dee Mitchell
Charlie Cook
Charlie Errock
Charlotte Briggs
Charlotte Coulthard
Charlotte Holtam
Charlotte Ryland
Charlotte Whittle
China Miéville
Chris Gostick
Chris Gribble
Chris Lintott
Chris Maguire
Chris McCann
Chris & Kathleen
    Repper-Day
Chris Stevenson
Christian Schuhmann
Christine and Nigel
    Wycherley
Christopher Allen
Christopher Homfray
Christopher Mitchell
Christopher Stout
Christopher Young
Ciara Ní Riain

Claire Riley
Claire Tristram
Claire Williams
Clarice Borges
Cliona Quigley
Clive Bellingham
Colin Denyer
Colin Matthews
Colin Hewlett
Collin Brooke
Connie Muttock
Courtney Lilly
Cyrus Massoudi
Daisy Savage
Dale Wisely
Daniel Arnold
Daniel Coxon
Daniel Gillespie
Daniel Hahn
Daniel Ng
Daniel Oudshoorn
Daniel Pope
Daniel Raper
Daniel Stewart
Daniel Venn
Daniel Wood
Daniel Jàrmai
Daniela Steierberg
Danny Millum
Darcy Hurford
Darina Brejtrova
Darren Lerigo
Dave Lander
David Anderson
David Ball
David Bevan
David Hebblethwaite
David Higgins
David Johnson-Davies
David Kinnaird
David F Long
David McIntyre
David Miller
David Musgrave
David Richardson
David Shriver
David Smith
David Steege

David Thornton
David Willey
Dawn Bass
Dean Taucher
Debbie Ballin
Debbie McKee
Debbie Pinfold
Declan Gardner
Declan O'Driscoll
Deirdre Nic Mhathuna
Delaina Haslam
Denis Larose
Denis Stillewagt &
    Anca Fronescu
Denton Djurasevich
Derek Taylor-Vrsalovich
Diana Digges
Diana Hutchison
Diana Romer
Diane Humphries
Dimitra Kolliakou:
Dinesh Prasad
Dominic Nolan
Dominick Santa Cattarina
Dominique Brocard
Dorothy Bottrell
Duncan Clubb
Duncan Marks
Dyanne Prinsen
E Rodgers
Earl James
Ed Burness
Ed Tronick
Ekaterina Beliakova
Eleanor Maier
Eleanor Rickards
Elie Howe
Elif Aganoglu
Elina Zicmane
Elisabeth Cook
Elizabeth Braswell
Elizabeth Cochrane
Elizabeth Draper
Elizabeth Franz
Elizabeth Leach
Ellie Goddard
Emilie Charnley &
    Simon Jones

Emily Webber
Emily Williams
Emily Yaewon Lee &
     Gregory Limpens
Emma Bielecki
Emma Coulson
Emma Musty
Emma Page
Emma Perry
Emma Reynolds
Emma Rhymer
Emma Selby
Emma Teale
Emma Turesson
Emma Louise Grove
Eric Anderson
Eric Reinders
Eric Tucker
Erin Cameron Allen
Erin Louttit
Esmée de Heer
Eve Anderson
Ewan Tant
F Gary Knapp
Fatima Kried
Fawzia Kane
Felix Valdivieso
Finbarr Farragher
Finn Williamson
Fiona Davenport White
Fiona Galloway
Fiona Liddle
Fiona Quinn
Florian Duijsens
Fran Sanderson
Frances Winfield
Francis Mathias
Francisco Vilhena
Frank van Orsouw
Fred Nichols
Freddie Radford
Frederick Lockett
Friederike Knabe
Gabriel Vogt
Gabriel Martinez
Gabrielle Crockatt
Garan Holcombe
Gareth Daniels

Gareth Tulip
Gary Clarke
Gary Gorton
Gavin Collins
Gavin Smith
Gawain Espley
Genaro Palomo Jr
Geoff Fisher
Geoff Thrower
Geoffrey Cohen
Geoffrey Urland
George Christie
George McCaig
George Stanbury
George Wilkinson
Georgia Dennison
Georgia Panteli
Geraldine Brodie
German Cortez-
     Hernandez
Gerry Craddock
Gill Boag-Munroe
Gill Osborne
Gillian Grant
Gillian Spencer
Gillian Stern
Glen Bornais
Gordon Cameron
Gosia Pennar
Graham R Foster
Grant Rootes
Greg Bowman
Gwyn Lewis
Hadil Balzan
Hamish Russell
Hanna Randall
Hannah Dougherty
Hannah Ellul-Knight
Hannah Freeman
Hannah Mayblin
Hannah Procter
Hannah Vidmark
Hannah Jane
     Lownsbrough
Hans Lazda
Harriet Wade
Haydon Spenceley
Heather Tipon

Hebe George
Helen Berry
Helen Brady
Helen Brooker
Helen Collins
Helen Coombes
Helen Moor
Helen Wilson
Henrike Laehnemann
Henry Patino
Holly Down
Howard Robinson
Hugh Gilmore
Hugh Schoonover
Hugo Ferraz Gomes
Hyoung-Won Park
Ian Barnett
Ian C. Fraser
Ian Hagues
Ian McMillan
Ian Mond
Ian Randall
Iciar Murphy
Ida Grochowska
Ifer Moore
Ilana Doran
Ilona Abb
Irene Mansfield
Irina Tzanova
Isabella Livorni
Isabella Weibrecht
Isobel Dixon
Isobel Foxford
Jacinta Perez Gavilan
     Torres
Jack Brown
Jack Hargreaves
Jack Shinder
Jacob Blizard
Jacob Swan Hyam
Jacqueline Haskell
Jacqueline Lademann
Jacqueline Ting Lin
Jacqueline Vint
Jacqui Jackson
Jake Nicholls
James Attlee
James Beck

James Crossley
James Cubbon
James Dahm
James Lehmann
James Lesniak
James Portlock
James Russell
James Scudamore
James Ward
Jamie Cox
Jamie Mollart
Jamie Veitch
Jamie Walsh
Jane Anderton
Jane Dolman
Jane Fairweather
Jane Roberts
Jane Woollard
Janne Støen
Jannik Lyhne
Jasmine Gideon
Jasmine Haniff
Jayne Watson
JC Sutcliffe
Jeannie Lambert
Jeff Collins
Jeff Questad
Jeff Van Campen
Jeffrey Danielson
Jeffrey Davies
Jen Calleja
Jenifer Logie
Jennifer Arnold
Jennifer Bernstein
Jennifer Harvey
Jennifer Humbert
Jennifer Robare
Jennifer Watts
Jennifer Wiegele
Jennifer Obrien
Jenny Huth
Jenny Newton
Jeremy Koenig
Jess Howard-Armitage
Jesse Coleman
Jessica Kibler
Jessica Laine
Jessica Martin

Jessica Queree
Jethro Soutar
Jo Goodall
Jo Harding
Jo Woolf
Joanna Luloff
Joanne Alder
Joanne Osborn
Joanne Smith
Joao Pedro Bragatti
    Winckler
JoDee Brandon
Jodie Adams
Joe Bratccher
Joel Swerdlow
Joelle Young
Johanna Eliasson
Johannes Menzel
Johannes Georg Zipp
John Bennett
John Berube
John Bogg
John Conway
John Down
John Gent
John Higginson
John Hodgson
John Kelly
John Mckee
John Royley
John Shaw
John Steigerwald
John Winkelman
John Wyatt
Jon Riches
Jon Talbot
Jonathan Blaney
Jonathan Fiedler
Jonathan Huston
Jonathan Ruppin
Jonathan Watkiss
Jonny Kiehlmann
Jorge Cino
Jorid Martinsen
Joseph Hiller
Joseph Schreiber
Josh Calvo
Josh Sumner

Joshua Davis
Joshua McNamara
Joy Paul
Judith Austin
Judith Gruet-Kaye
Judy Lee-Fenton
Judy Tomlinson
Julia Harkey D'Angelo
Julia Rochester
Julia Sutton-Mattocks
Julie Greenwalt
Julie Hutchinson
Julie Winter
Juliet and Nick Davies
Juliet Swann
Justin Ahlbach
Justine Sherwood
K Elkes
Kaarina Hollo
Karen Waloschek
Kasper Haakansson
Kasper Hartmann
Kat Burdon
Kate Attwooll
Kate Beswick
Kate Gardner
Kate Shires
Katharina Liehr
Katharine Freeman
Katherine Mackinnon
Katharine Robbins
Katherine Sotejeff-Wilson
Kathryn Dawson
Kathryn Edwards
Kathryn Oliver
Kathryn Williams
Katie Brown
Katie Lewin
Katie Wolstencroft
Katie Grant
Katie Smart
Katrina Thomas
Keith Walker
Kenneth Blythe
Kenneth Michaels
Kent McKernan
Kerry Parke
Kieran Rollin

Kieron James
Kim McGowan
Kirsten Hey
Kirsten Ward
Kirsty Doole
KL Ee
Klara Rešetič
Kris Ann Trimis
Kristin Djuve
Kristina Rudinskas
Krystine Phelps
Lana Selby
Lander Hawes
Lara Vergnaud
Laura Blasena
Laura Lea
Laura Lonsdale
Laura Smith
Laura Williams
Lauren Carroll
Lauren Schluneger
Laurence Laluyaux
Laurie Sheck &
        Jim Peck
Leanne Radojkovich
Lee Harbour
Leeanne Parker
Lesli Green
Leslie Baillie
Lewis Green
Lidia Winnicka
Liliana Lobato
Lillie Rosen
Lily Hersov
Lindsay Attree
Lindsay Brammer
Lindsey Stuart
Lindsey Ford
Line Langebek Knudsen
Linette Arthurton Bruno
Lisa Agostini
Lisa Fransson
Lisa Leahigh
Lisa Simpson
Liz Clifford
Liz Ketch
Liz Wilding
Lola Boorman

Lori Frecker
Lorna Bleach
Lottie Smith
Louise Evans
Louise Greebverg
Louise Smith
Louise Whittaker
Luc Daley
Luc Verstraete
Lucia Rotheray
Lucile Lesage
Lucy Beevor
Lucy Moffatt
Luke Healey
Luke Loftiss
Lydia Trethewey
Lyn Curthoys
Lynn Martin
Lynn Fung
M Manfre
Mads Pihl Rasmussen
Maeve Lambe
Maggie Humm
Maggie Livesey
Maggie Redway
Mahan L Ellison &
        K Ashley Dickson
Malgorzata Rokicka
Marcel Schlamowitz
Margaret Briggs
Margaret Jull Costa
Maria Ahnhem Farrar
Maria Lomunno
Maria Losada
Maria Pia Tissot
Mariana Bode
Marie Bagley
Marie Cloutier
Marie Donnelly
Marike Dokter
Marina Altoé
Marina Castledine
Marina Jones
Mario Cianci
Mario Sifuentez
Marjorie Schulman
Mark Dawson
Mark Harris

Mark Huband
Mark Sargent
Mark Sheets
Mark Sztyber
Mark Waters
Marlene Adkins
Martha Nicholson
Martha Stevns
Martin Brown
Martin Jones
Martin Price
Mary Brockson
Mary Heiss
Mary Morton
Mary Nash
Mary O'Donnell
Mary Wang
Mary Ellen Nagle
Mathieu Trudeau
Matt Davies
Matt Greene
Matt Jones
Matt O'Connor
Matthew Adamson
Matthew Armstrong
Matthew Banash
Matthew Black
Matthew Cullinan
Matthew Eatough
Matthew Francis
Matthew Gill
Matthew Hiscock
Matthew Lowe
Matthew Rhymer
Matthew Scott
Matthew Warshauer
Matthew Woodman
Matty Ross
Maurice Mengel
Max Cairnduff
Max Garrone
Max Longman
Meaghan Delahunt
Meg Lovelock
Megan Oxholm
Megan Wittling
Melanie Tebb
Melissa Beck

Melissa Quignon-Finch
Melynda Nuss
Meredith Jones
Meryl Wingfield
Michael Aguilar
Michael Bichko
Michael Carver
Michael Gavin
Michael Kuhn
Michael Moran
Michael Roess
Michael Schneiderman
Michael Shayer
Michael Ward
Michael James Eastwood
Michelle Lotherington
Milla Rautio
Miranda Gold
Miriam McBride
Moira Sweeney
Molly Foster
Moray Teale
Morgan Lyons
Moshe Prigan
MP Boardman
Muireann Maguire
Myles Nolan
N Tsolak
Nan Craig
Nancy Jacobson
Nancy Oakes
Naomi Kruger
Natalie Charles
Natalie & Richard
Nathalie Atkinson
Nathan Rowley
Nathan Weida
Neferti Tadiar
Neil George
Nicholas Brown
Nick Chapman
Nick Flegel
Nick James
Nick Nelson &
    Rachel Eley
Nick Rombes
Nick Sidwell
Nick Twemlow

Nicola Hart
Nicola Meyer
Nicola Mira
Nicola Sandiford
Nicola Todd
Nicole Matteini
Nigel Fishburn
Niki Davison
Nina Alexandersen
Nina de la Mer
Niven Kumar
Odilia Corneth
Olga Zilberbourg
Olivia Payne
Olivia Turner
Pamela Ritchie
Pamela Tao
Pat Bevins
Patricia Appleyard
Patricia Aronsson
Patrick McGuinness
Paul Cray
Paul Daintry
Paul Jones
Paul Munday
Paul Myatt
Paul Scott
Paul Segal
Paula Edwards
Paula Ely
Pauline Westerbarkey
Pavlos Stavropoulos
Paz Berlese
Peggy Wood
Penelope Hewett Brown
Penny Simpson
Peter McBain
Peter McCambridge
Peter Rowland
Peter Vilbig
Peter Wells
Petra Stapp
Philip Lewis
Philip Lom
Philip Nulty
Philip Scott
Philip Warren
Philipp Jarke

Phoebe Harrison
Phyllis Reeve
Pia Figge
Piet Van Bockstal
Pippa Tolfts
Polly Morris
PRAH Foundation
Rachael de Moravia
Rachael Williams
Rachel Andrews
Rachel Carter
Rachel Darnley-Smith
Rachel Goodall
Rachel Van Riel
Rachel Watkins
Ralph Cowling
Rea Cris
Rebecca Braun
Rebecca Carter
Rebecca Gaskell
Rebecca Moss
Rebecca Rosenthal
Rhiannon Armstrong
Rich Sutherland
Richard Ashcroft
Richard Bauer
Richard Carter
Richard Dew
Richard Gwyn
Richard Mansell
Richard Priest
Richard Shea
Richard Soundy
Richard Santos
Richard Steward
Rishi Dastidar
Rita O'Brien
Robert Gillett
Robert Hamilton
Robert Hannah
Robert Wolff
Robin Taylor
Roger Newton
Roger Ramsden
Rory Williamson
Rosalind May
Rosalind Ramsay
Rosanna Foster

Rosie Pinhorn
Ross Trenzinger
Rowan Sullivan
Roxanne O'Del Ablett
Royston Tester
Roz Simpson
Ruby Kane
Rupert Ziziros
Ruth Morgan
Ruth Porter
Ryan Farrell
Sabine Griffiths
Sally Baker
Sally Foreman
Sally Warner
Sally Whitehill
Sam Gordon
Sam Reese
Sam Stern
Samantha Cox
Samuel Crosby
Sara Sherwood
Sara Quiroz
Sarah Arboleda
Sarah Booker
Sarah Davies-Bennion
Sarah Lucas
Sarah Pybus
Sarah Wert
Sarah Roff
Sarah Ryan
Scott Chiddister
Scott Astrada
Sean Birnie
Sean McGivern
Sez Kiss
Shane Horgan
Shannon Knapp
Sharon Dogar
Sharon Mccammon
Shaun Whiteside
Shauna Gilligan
Sheridan Marshall
Sheryl Jermyn
Shira Lob
Sian Hannah
Simon Pitney
Simon Robertson

Simonette Foletti
Siriol Hugh-Jones
SK Grout
Sonia McLintock
Sophia Wickham
Soren Murhart
ST Dabbagh
Stacy Rodgers
Stefanie Schrank
Stefano Mula
Stephan Eggum
Stephanie Lacava
Stephanie Smee
Stephen Eisenhammer
Stephen Pearsall
Steve Dearden
Steven & Gitte Evans
Steven Willborn
Stu Sherman
Stuart Wilkinson
Sue Craven
Sunny Payson
Susan Howard
Susan Winter
Susie Roberson
Susie Sell
Suzanne Kirkham
Suzy Hounslow
Sylvie Zannier-Betts
Tamara Larsen
Tania Hershman
Tanya Royer
Tara Roman
Tasmin Maitland
Teresa Werner
The Mighty Douche
    Softball Team
Therese Oulton
Thom Keep
Thomas Bell
Thomas Mitchell
Thomas Sharrad
Thomas van den Bout
Tiffany Lehr
Tim Kelly
Tim Scott
Tim Theroux
Timothy Pilbrow

Tina Andrews
Tina Rotherham-
    Winqvist
Toby Halsey
Toby Hyam
Toby Ryan
Tom Darby
Tom Doyle
Tom Franklin
Tom Gray
Tom Mooney
Tom Stafford
Tom Whatmore
Tony Bastow
Tory Jeffay
Tracey Martin
Tracy Heuring
Tracy Northup
Trevor Wald
Val Challen
Valerie O'Riordan
Valerie Sirr
Vanessa Dodd
Vanessa Heggie
Vanessa Nolan
Vanessa Rush
Vanessa
Veronica Barnsley
Vicky van der Luit
Victor Meadowcroft
Victoria Goodbody
Victoria Huggins
Victoria Larroque
Victoria Maitland
Victoria Steeves
Vijay Pattisapu
Vikki O'Neill
Walter Fircowycz
Walter Smedley
Wendy Langridge
Wendy Olson
William Dennehy
William Franklin
William Mackenzie
William Schwartz
Yasmin Alam
Zachary Hope
Zoë Brasier

CURRENT & UPCOMING BOOKS

DEB OLIN UNFERTH is the author of six books, most recently *Barn 8*, which is her UK debut. She has received fellowships from the Guggenheim Foundation and Creative Capital, has won three Pushcart Prizes, and was a finalist for the National Book Critics Circle Award. An associate professor at the University of Texas in Austin, she also teaches creative writing at a prison in southern Texas.